THE NIGHT WANDERER

A GRAPHIC NOVEL

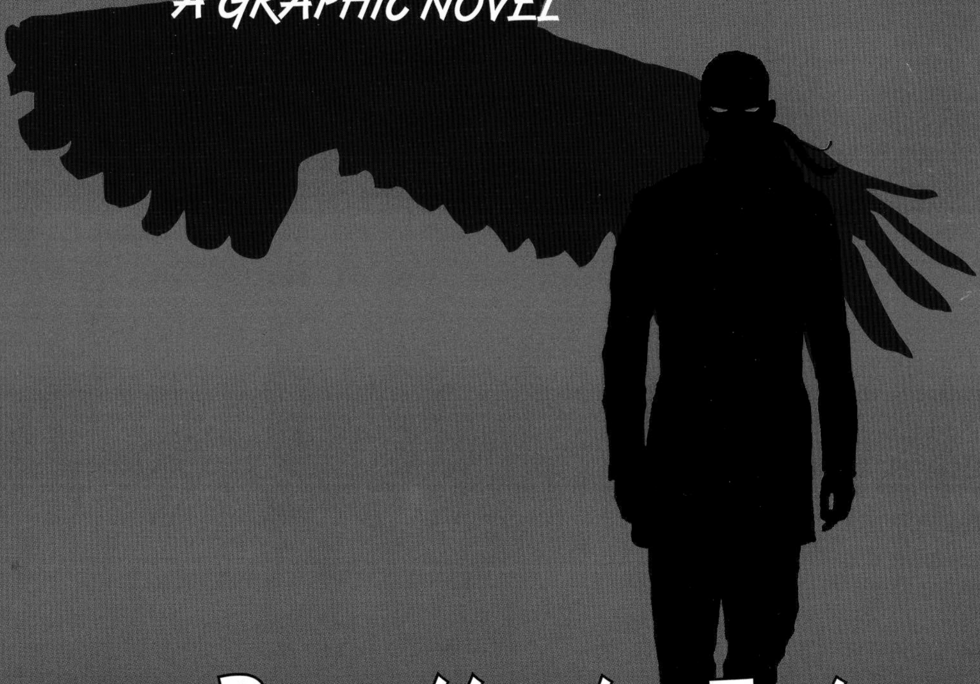

Drew Hayden Taylor
Art by Michael Wyatt
Graphic adaptation by Alison Kooistra

annick press
toronto + berkeley

Third printing, January 2020

Graphic novel adaptation by Alison Kooistra
Based on the novel *The Night Wanderer: A Native Gothic Novel*, © 2007 Drew Hayden Taylor
Cover art by Michael Wyatt
Cover design by Sheryl Shapiro
Proofread by Tanya Trafford

Annick Press Ltd.

We acknowledge the support of the Canada Council for the Arts and the Ontario Arts Council, and the participation of the Government of Canada/la participation du gouvernement du Canada for our publishing activities.

Canada

ONTARIO ARTS COUNCIL
CONSEIL DES ARTS DE L'ONTARIO
an Ontario government agency
un organisme du gouvernement de l'Ontario

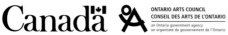

Cataloging in Publication
Taylor, Drew Hayden, 1962-
The night wanderer : a graphic novel / by Drew Hayden Taylor; art by Michael Wyatt ; graphic adaptation by Alison Kooistra.

Adaptation of the novel: The night wanderer.
Issued also in electronic formats.
ISBN 978-1-55451-573-8 (bound).—ISBN 978-1-55451-572-1 (pbk.)

1. Graphic novels. I. Wyatt, Mike, 1966- II. Kooistra, Alison, 1979- III. Taylor, Drew Hayden, 1962- . Night wanderer. IV. Title.

PN6733.T39N54 2013 j741.5'971 C2013-901752-6

Printed and bound in China.

Published in the U.S.A. by Annick Press (U.S.) Ltd.
Distributed in Canada by University of Toronto Press.
Distributed in the U.S.A. by Publishers Group West.

Visit us at: **www.annickpress.com**
Visit Drew Hayden Taylor at: **www.drewhaydentaylor.com**
Visit Michael Wyatt at: **mgwyatt.blogspot.ca**

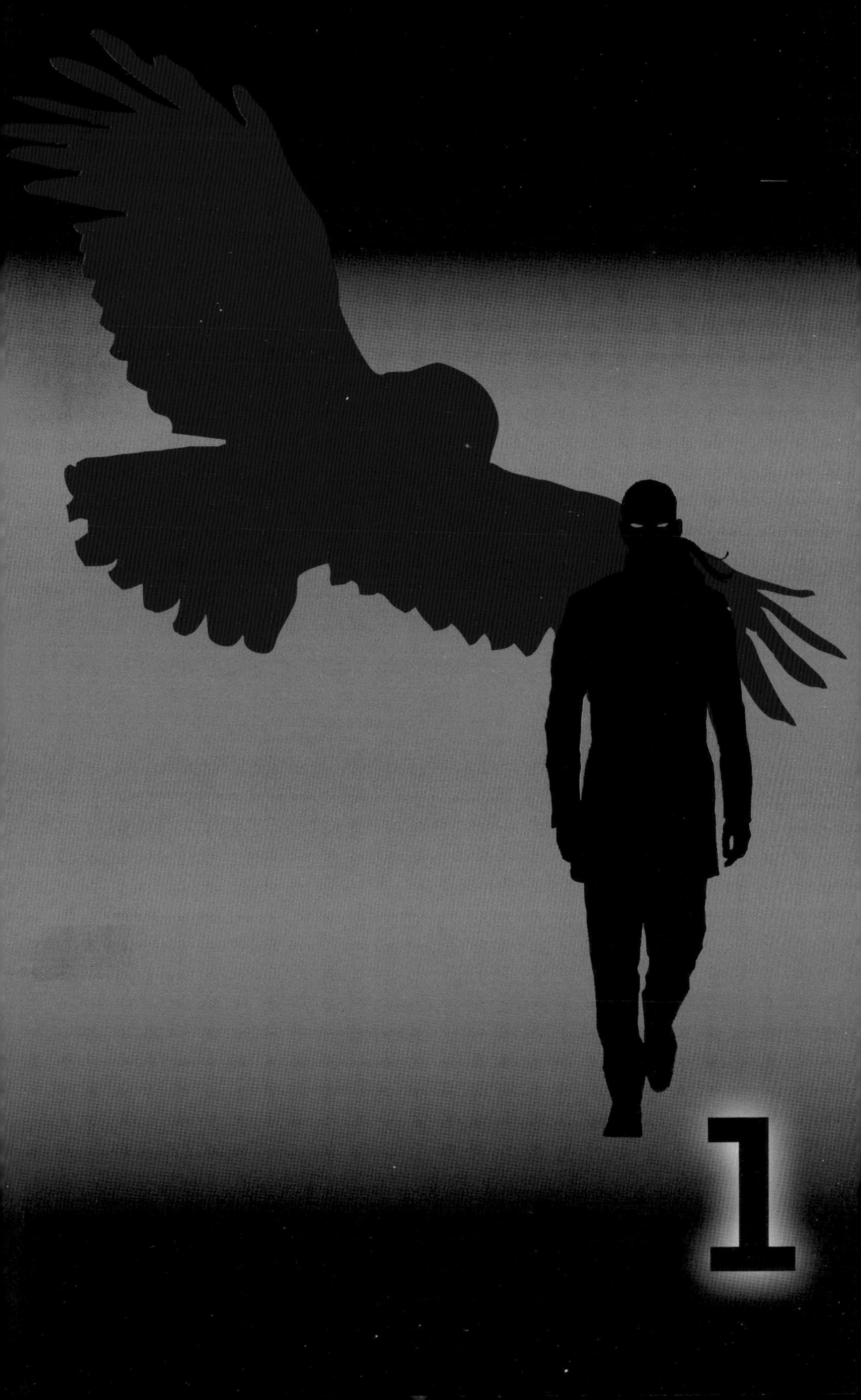
1

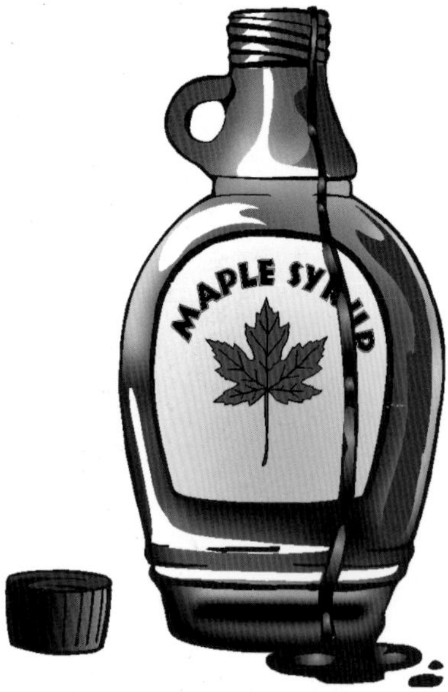
MAPLE SY

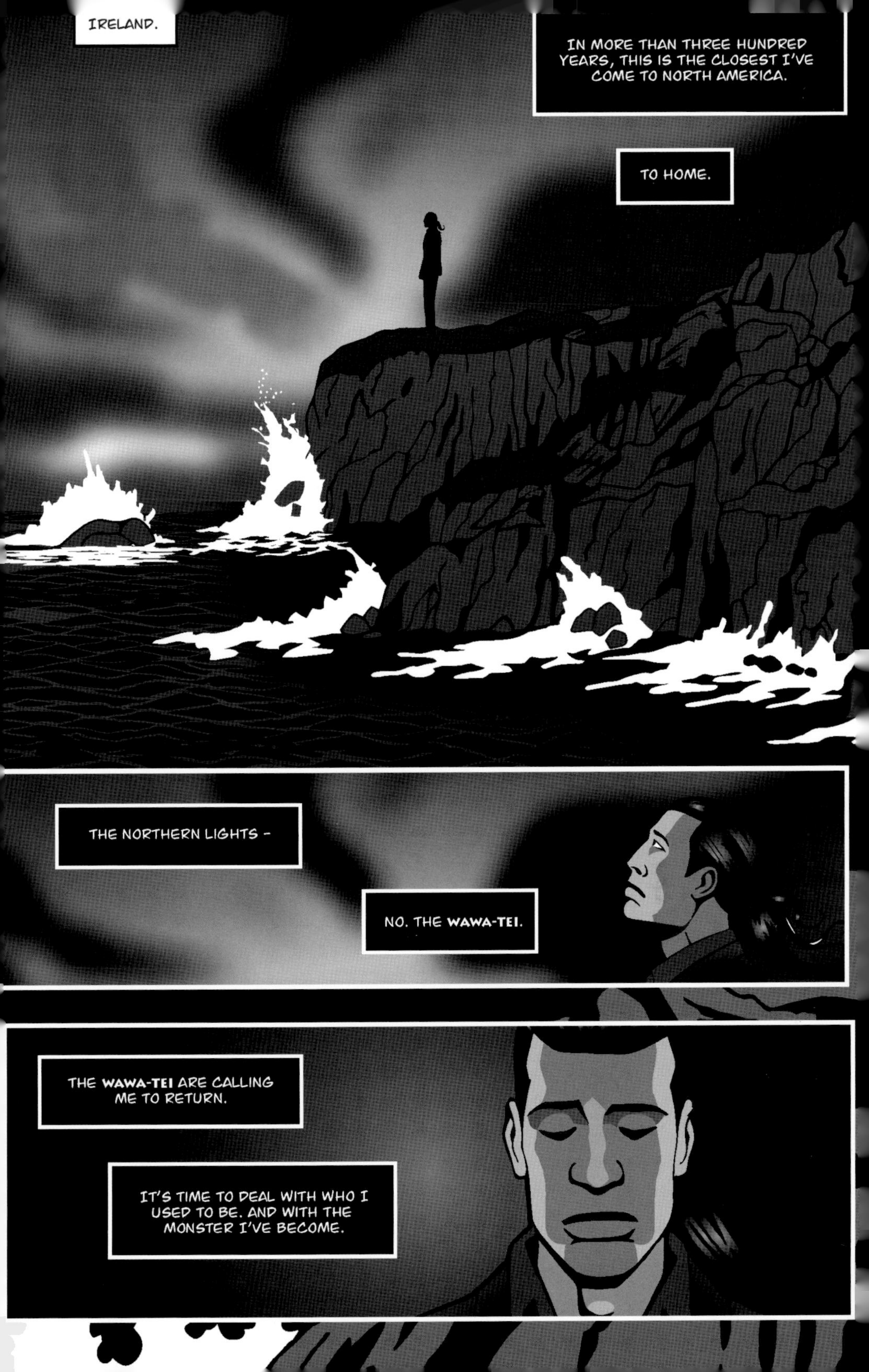
IRELAND.
IN MORE THAN THREE HUNDRED YEARS, THIS IS THE CLOSEST I'VE COME TO NORTH AMERICA.
TO HOME.
THE NORTHERN LIGHTS –
NO. THE **WAWA-TEI**.
THE **WAWA-TEI** ARE CALLING ME TO RETURN.
IT'S TIME TO DEAL WITH WHO I USED TO BE. AND WITH THE MONSTER I'VE BECOME.

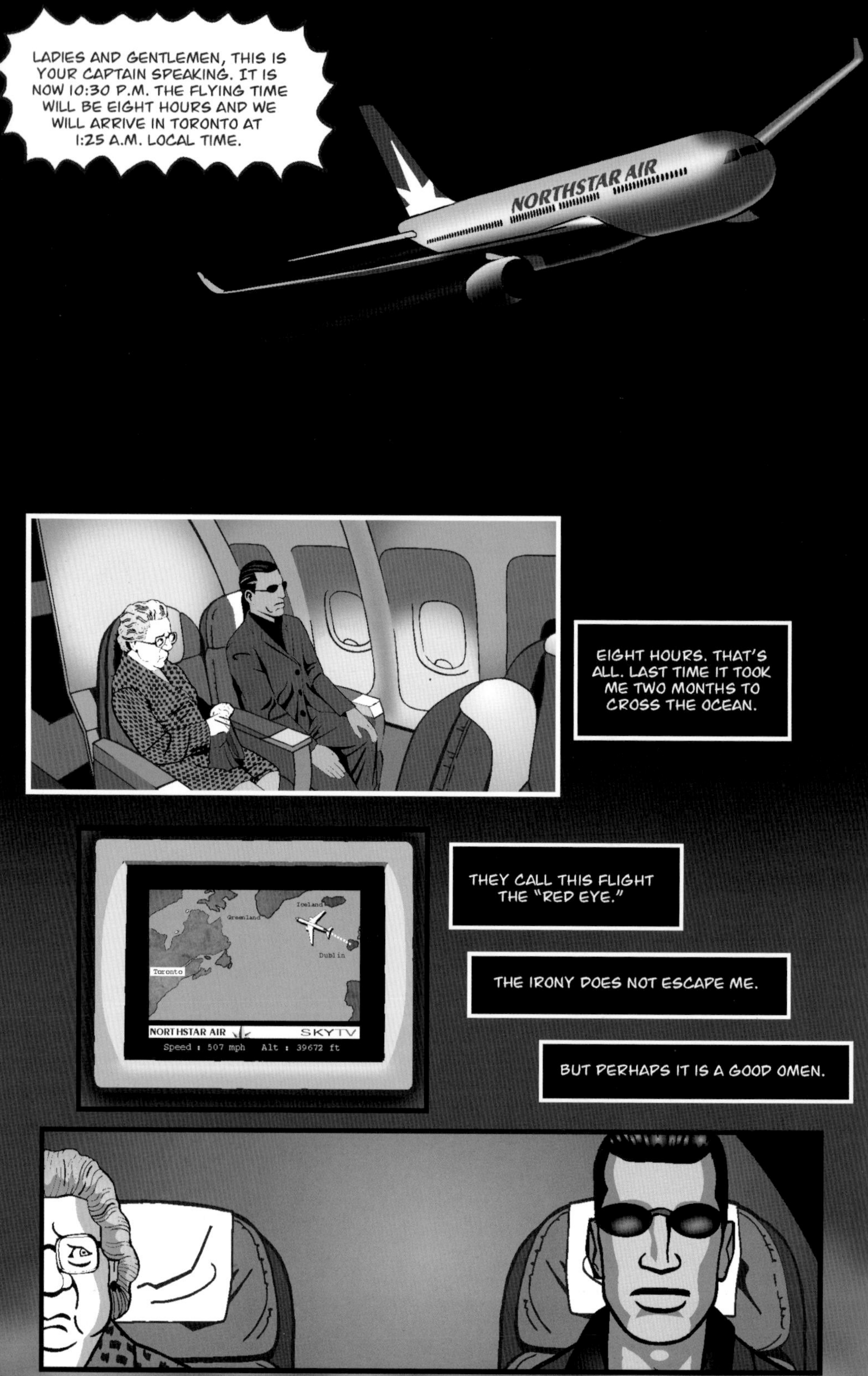
LADIES AND GENTLEMEN, THIS IS YOUR CAPTAIN SPEAKING. IT IS NOW 10:30 P.M. THE FLYING TIME WILL BE EIGHT HOURS AND WE WILL ARRIVE IN TORONTO AT 1:25 A.M. LOCAL TIME.
NORTHSTAR AIR
EIGHT HOURS. THAT'S ALL. LAST TIME IT TOOK ME TWO MONTHS TO CROSS THE OCEAN.
Iceland
Greenland
Dublin
Toronto
NORTHSTAR AIR
SKYTV
Speed : 507 mph Alt : 39672 ft
THEY CALL THIS FLIGHT THE "RED EYE."
THE IRONY DOES NOT ESCAPE ME.
BUT PERHAPS IT IS A GOOD OMEN.

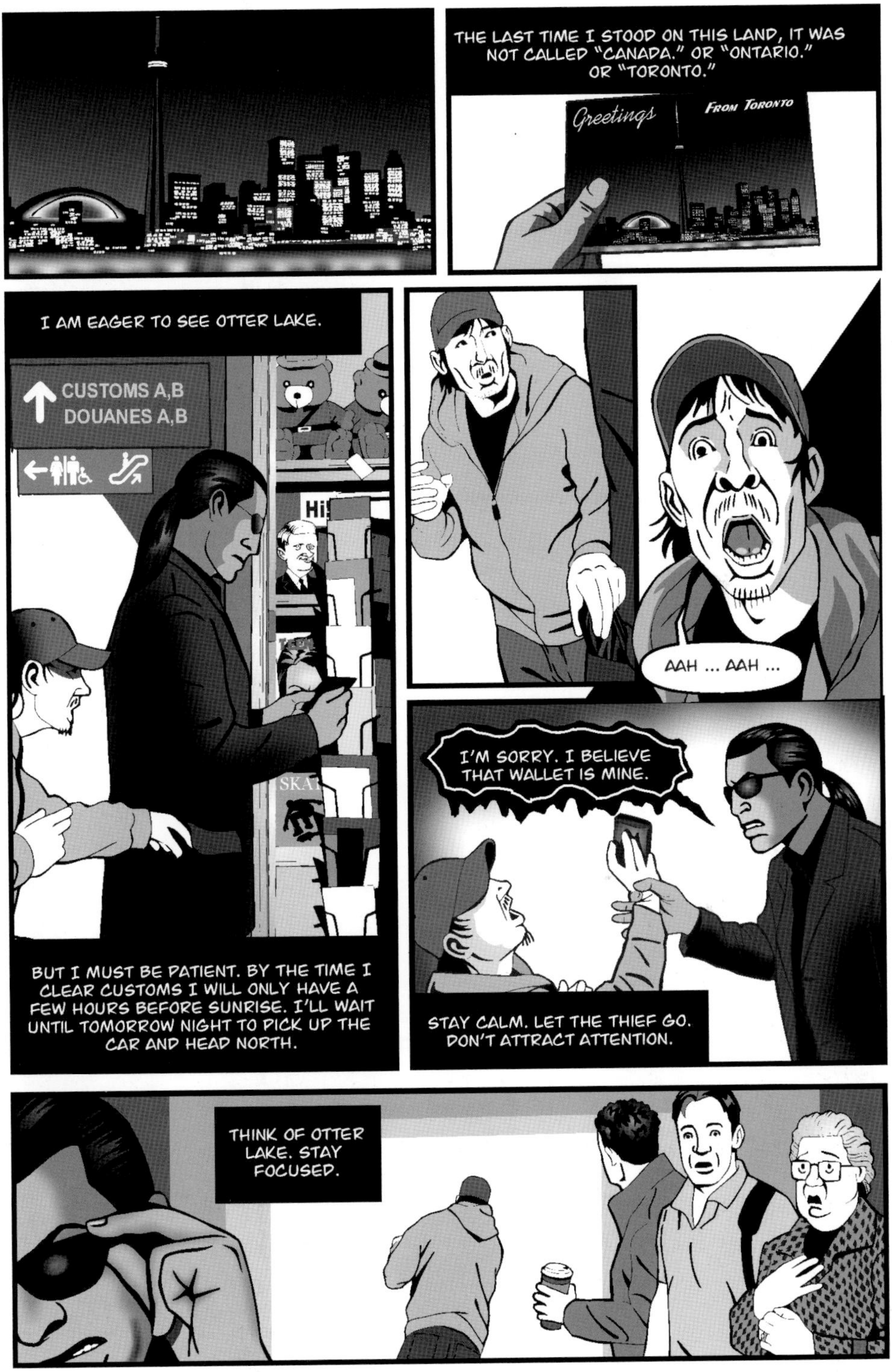

THE LAST TIME I STOOD ON THIS LAND, IT WAS NOT CALLED "CANADA." OR "ONTARIO." OR "TORONTO."
Greetings
FROM TORONTO
I AM EAGER TO SEE OTTER LAKE.
CUSTOMS A,B
DOUANES A,B
BUT I MUST BE PATIENT. BY THE TIME I CLEAR CUSTOMS I WILL ONLY HAVE A FEW HOURS BEFORE SUNRISE. I'LL WAIT UNTIL TOMORROW NIGHT TO PICK UP THE CAR AND HEAD NORTH.
AAH ... AAH ...
I'M SORRY. I BELIEVE THAT WALLET IS MINE.
STAY CALM. LET THE THIEF GO. DON'T ATTRACT ATTENTION.
THINK OF OTTER LAKE. STAY FOCUSED.

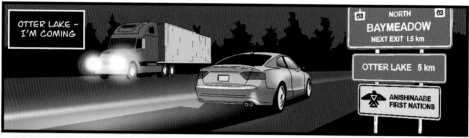

OTTER LAKE – I'M COMING

NORTH
63 BAYMEADOW 63
NEXT EXIT 1.5 km

OTTER LAKE 5 km

ANISHINAABE
FIRST NATIONS

BUT DAA—AADD!

TIFFANY, WE NEED THE MONEY. SINCE YOUR MOTHER LEFT, I'M NOT MAKING ENOUGH TO SUPPORT US. SO WE'RE TAKING IN A BOARDER.

SO AUTOMATICALLY HE GETS MY ROOM? THE HELL WITH TIFFANY, JUST LIKE ALWAYS.

LISTEN! I'M THE FATHER. YOU'RE THE DAUGHTER. DO AS I SAY FOR ONCE! GO PUT YOUR STUFF IN THE BASEMENT.

THIS BLOWS!

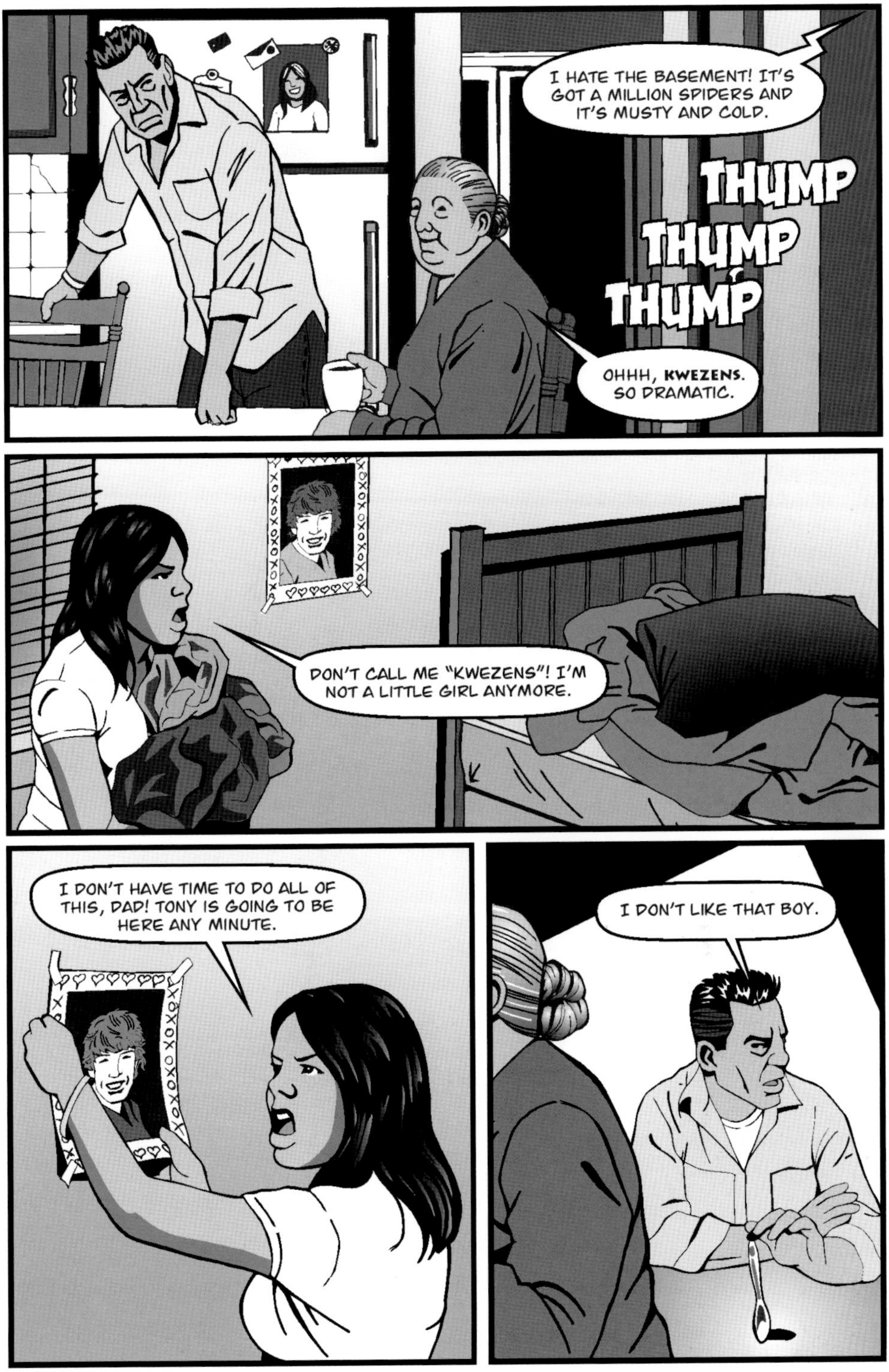
I HATE THE BASEMENT! IT'S GOT A MILLION SPIDERS AND IT'S MUSTY AND COLD.
THUMP
THUMP
THUMP
OHHH, KWEZENS. SO DRAMATIC.
DON'T CALL ME "KWEZENS"! I'M NOT A LITTLE GIRL ANYMORE.
I DON'T HAVE TIME TO DO ALL OF THIS, DAD! TONY IS GOING TO BE HERE ANY MINUTE.
I DON'T LIKE THAT BOY.

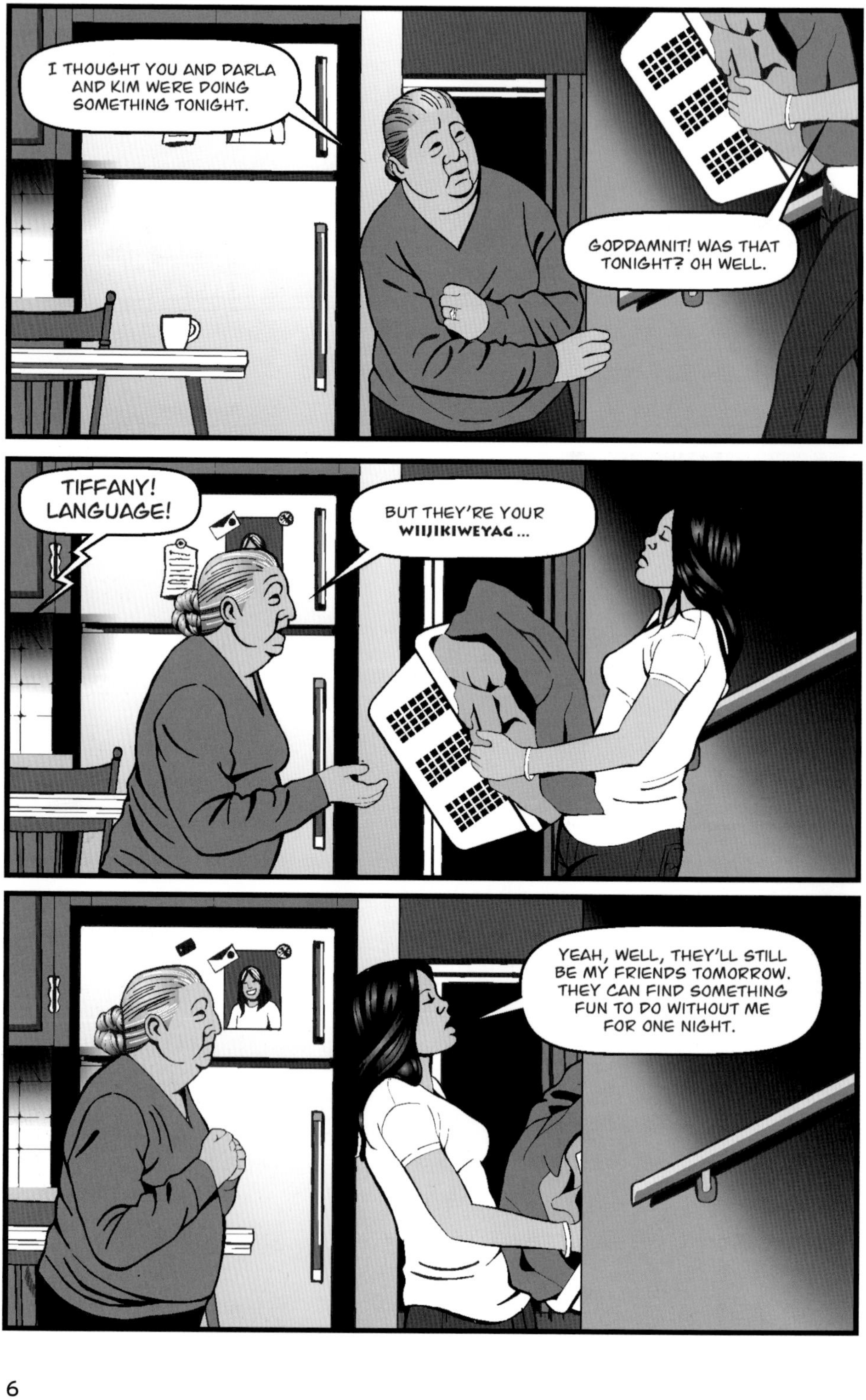
I THOUGHT YOU AND DARLA AND KIM WERE DOING SOMETHING TONIGHT.
GODDAMNIT! WAS THAT TONIGHT? OH WELL.
TIFFANY! LANGUAGE!
BUT THEY'RE YOUR **WIIJIKIWEYAG**...
YEAH, WELL, THEY'LL STILL BE MY FRIENDS TOMORROW. THEY CAN FIND SOMETHING FUN TO DO WITHOUT ME FOR ONE NIGHT.

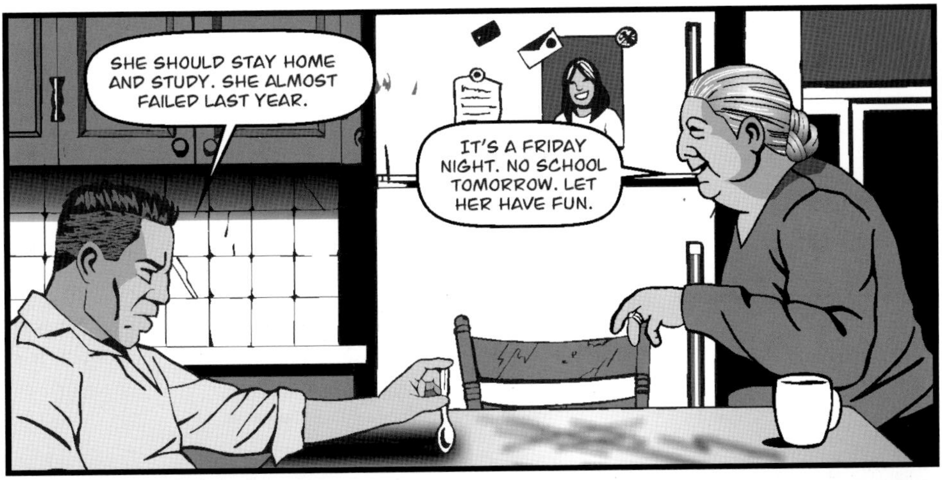
SHE SHOULD STAY HOME AND STUDY. SHE ALMOST FAILED LAST YEAR.
IT'S A FRIDAY NIGHT. NO SCHOOL TOMORROW. LET HER HAVE FUN.

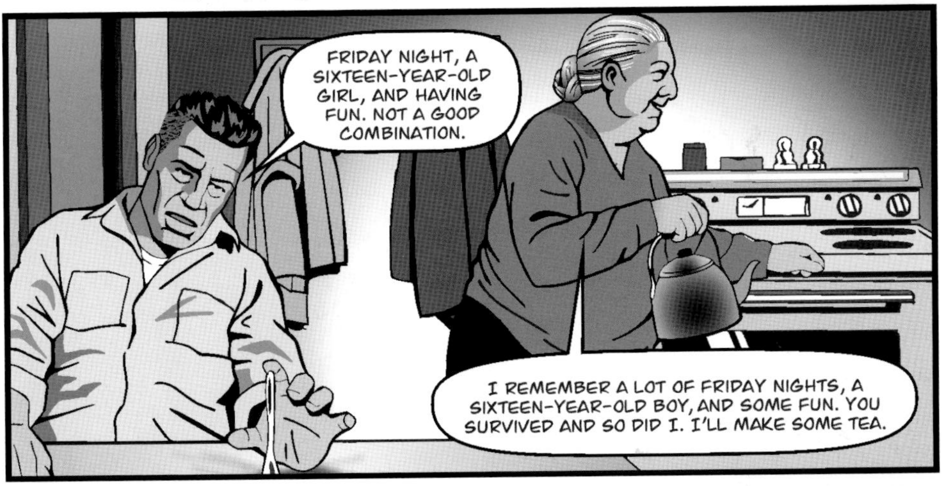
FRIDAY NIGHT, A SIXTEEN-YEAR-OLD GIRL, AND HAVING FUN. NOT A GOOD COMBINATION.
I REMEMBER A LOT OF FRIDAY NIGHTS, A SIXTEEN-YEAR-OLD BOY, AND SOME FUN. YOU SURVIVED AND SO DID I. I'LL MAKE SOME TEA.

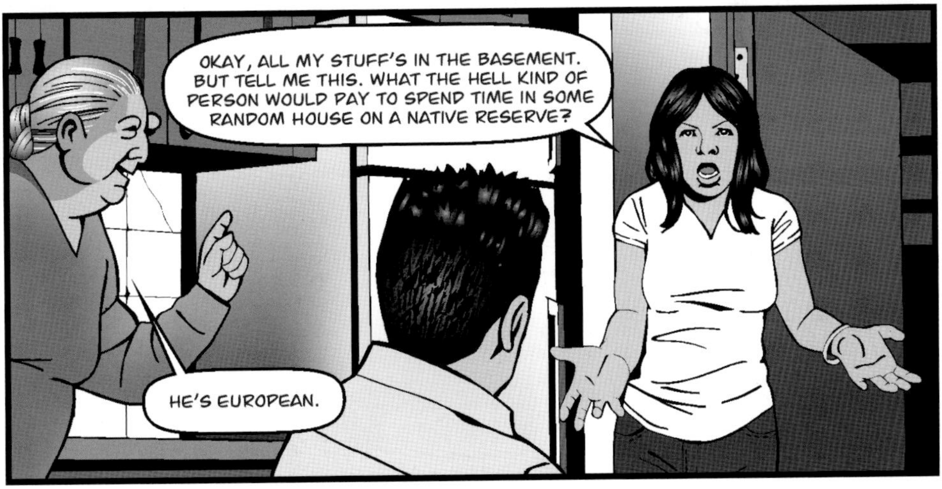
OKAY, ALL MY STUFF'S IN THE BASEMENT. BUT TELL ME THIS. WHAT THE HELL KIND OF PERSON WOULD PAY TO SPEND TIME IN SOME RANDOM HOUSE ON A NATIVE RESERVE?
HE'S EUROPEAN.

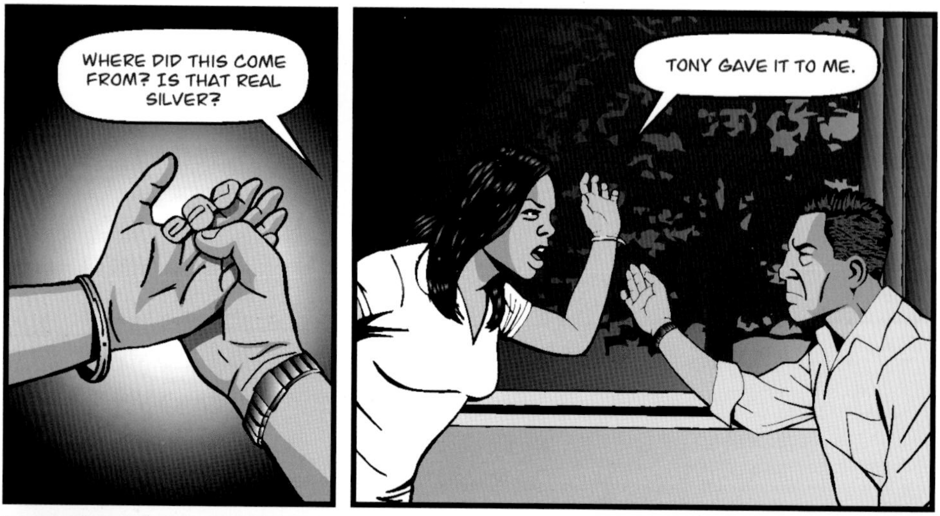
WHERE DID THIS COME FROM? IS THAT REAL SILVER?
TONY GAVE IT TO ME.

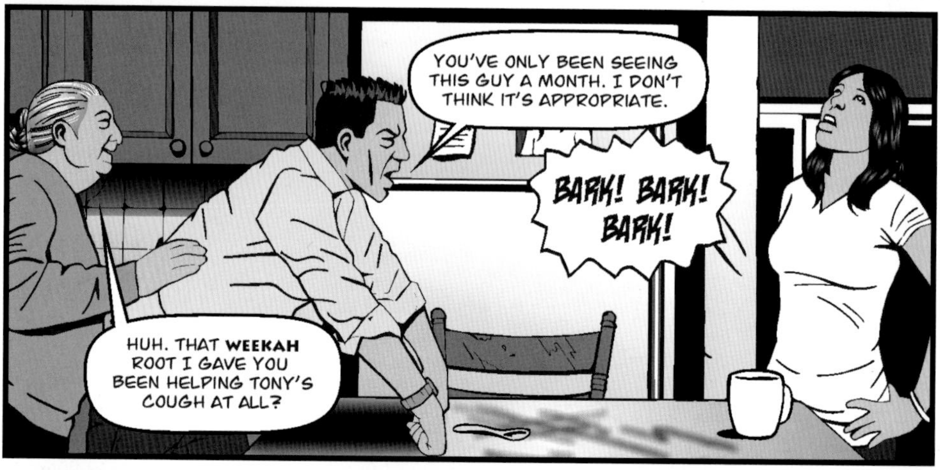
YOU'VE ONLY BEEN SEEING THIS GUY A MONTH. I DON'T THINK IT'S APPROPRIATE.
BARK! BARK! BARK!
HUH. THAT **WEEKAH** ROOT I GAVE YOU BEEN HELPING TONY'S COUGH AT ALL?

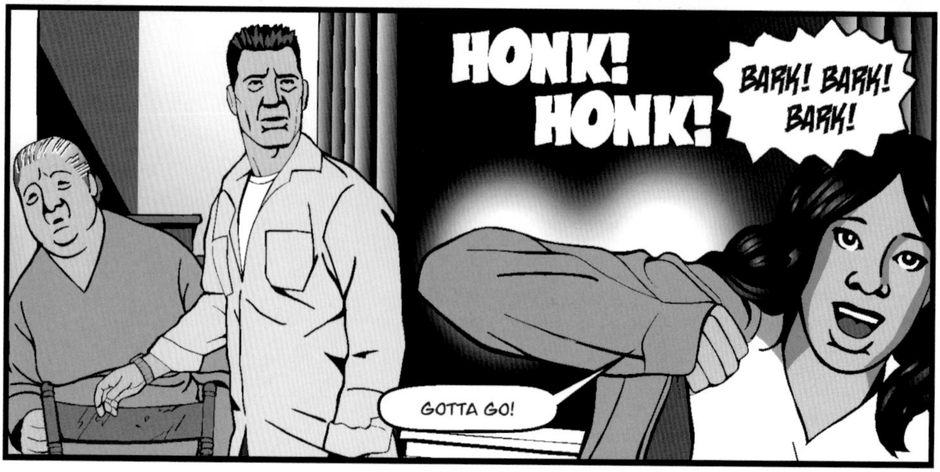
HONK! HONK!
BARK! BARK! BARK!
GOTTA GO!

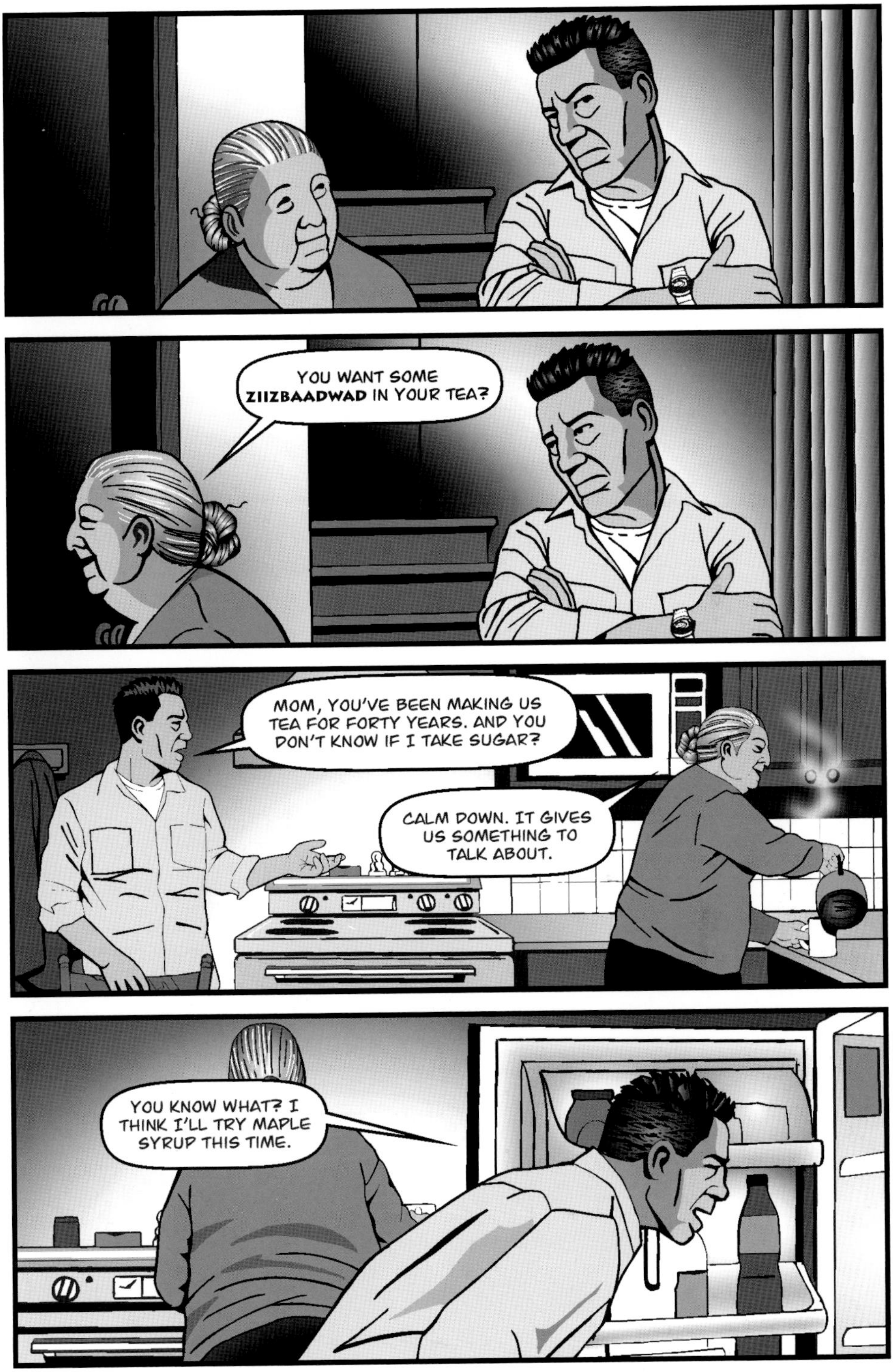
YOU WANT SOME ZIIZBAADWAD IN YOUR TEA?
MOM, YOU'VE BEEN MAKING US TEA FOR FORTY YEARS. AND YOU DON'T KNOW IF I TAKE SUGAR?
CALM DOWN. IT GIVES US SOMETHING TO TALK ABOUT.
YOU KNOW WHAT? I THINK I'LL TRY MAPLE SYRUP THIS TIME.

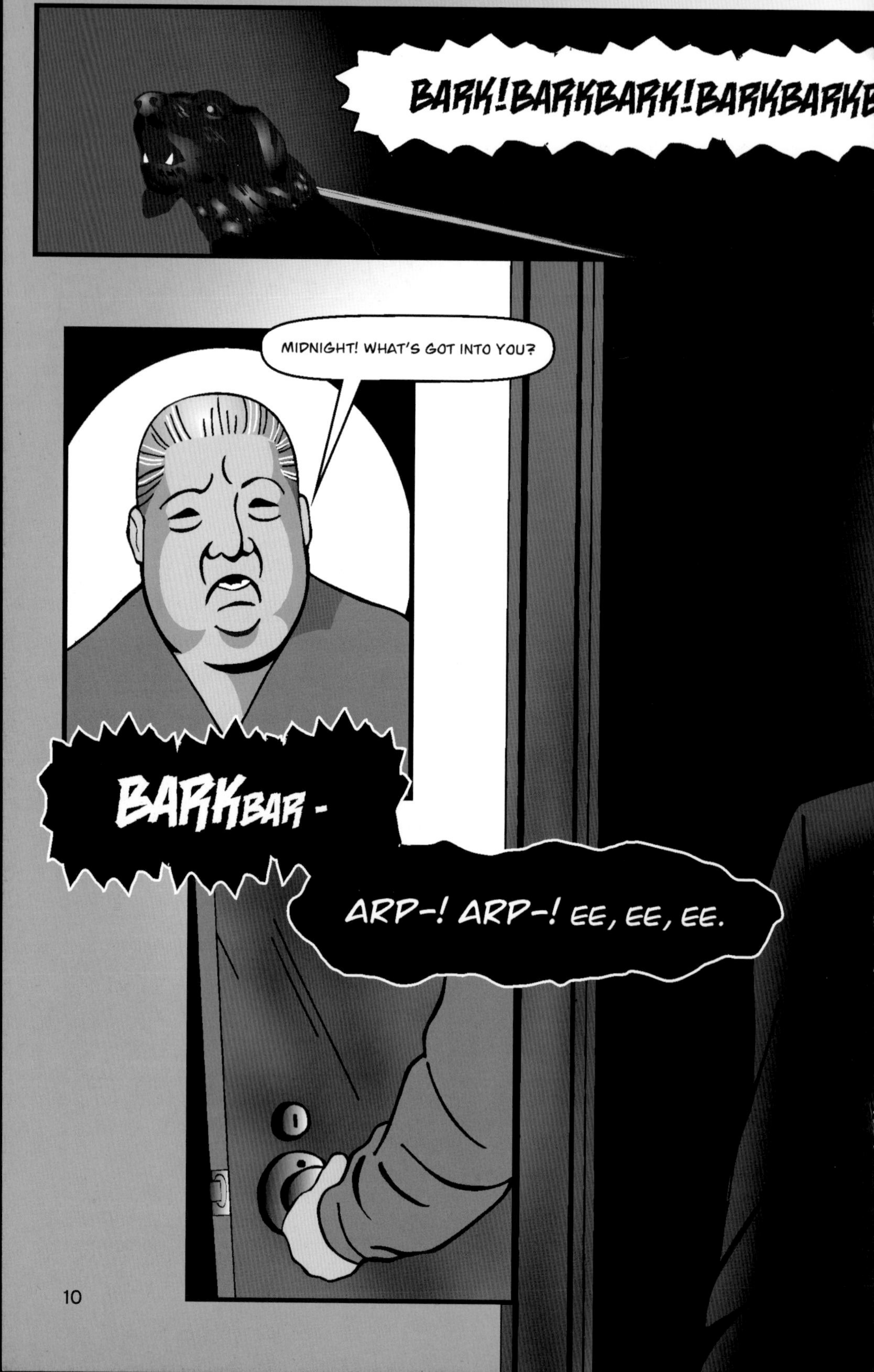
BARK!BARKBARK!BARKBARKB
MIDNIGHT! WHAT'S GOT INTO YOU?
BARKBAR-
ARP-! ARP-! EE, EE, EE.

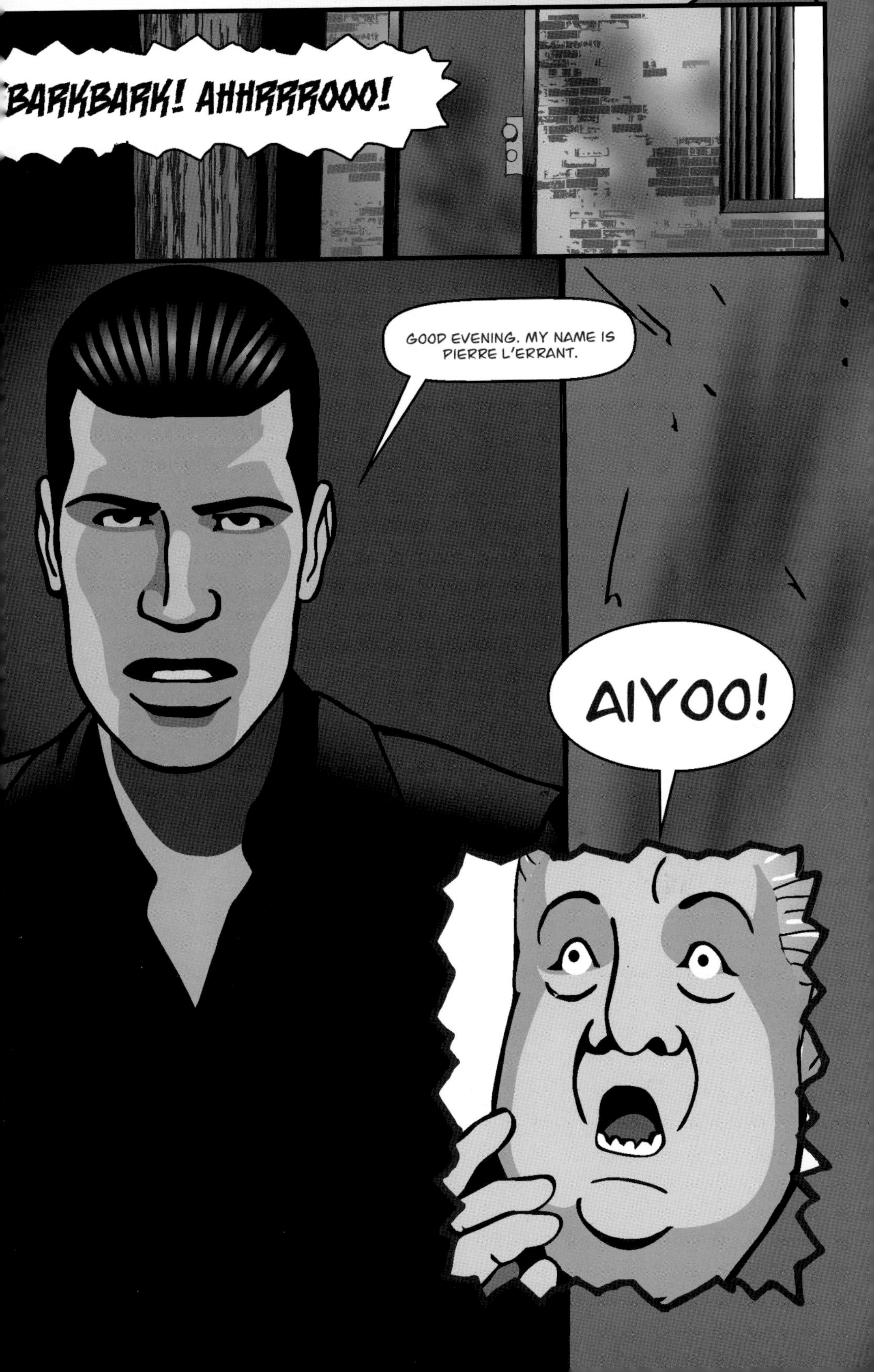
BARKBARK! AHHRRROOO!
GOOD EVENING. MY NAME IS PIERRE L'ERRANT.
AIYOO!

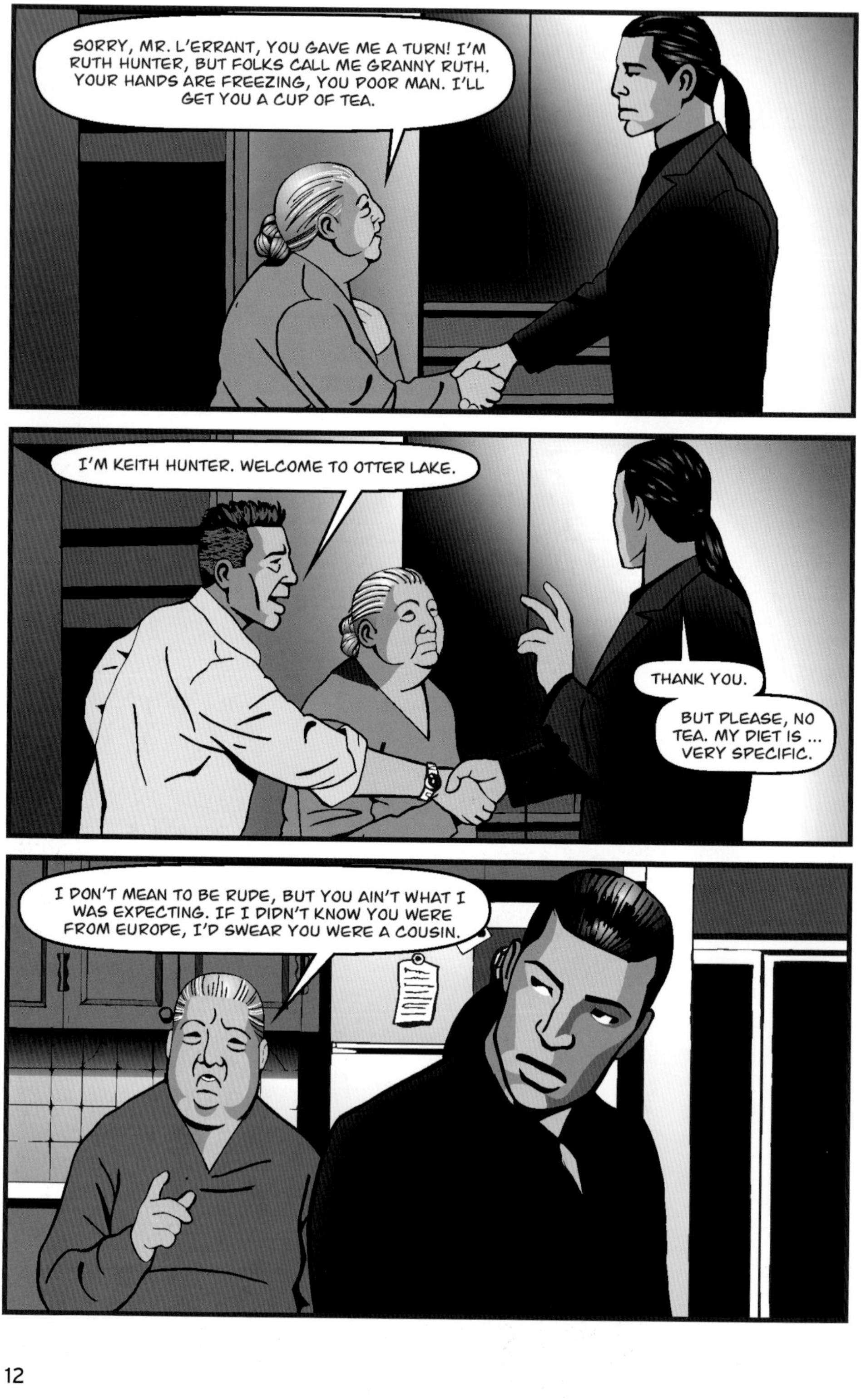
SORRY, MR. L'ERRANT, YOU GAVE ME A TURN! I'M RUTH HUNTER, BUT FOLKS CALL ME GRANNY RUTH. YOUR HANDS ARE FREEZING, YOU POOR MAN. I'LL GET YOU A CUP OF TEA.
I'M KEITH HUNTER. WELCOME TO OTTER LAKE.
THANK YOU.
BUT PLEASE, NO TEA. MY DIET IS ... VERY SPECIFIC.
I DON'T MEAN TO BE RUDE, BUT YOU AIN'T WHAT I WAS EXPECTING. IF I DIDN'T KNOW YOU WERE FROM EUROPE, I'D SWEAR YOU WERE A COUSIN.

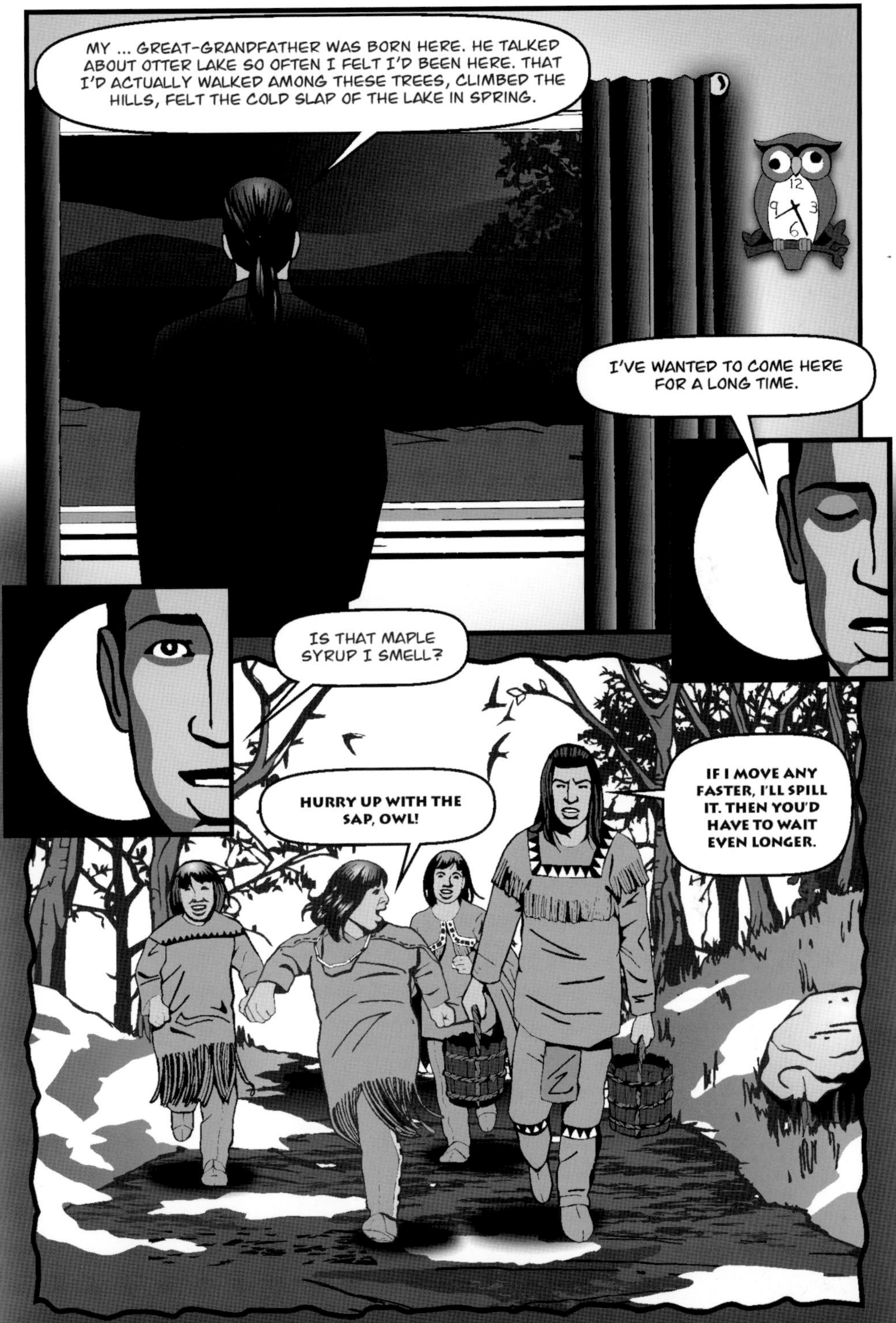
MY ... GREAT-GRANDFATHER WAS BORN HERE. HE TALKED ABOUT OTTER LAKE SO OFTEN I FELT I'D BEEN HERE. THAT I'D ACTUALLY WALKED AMONG THESE TREES, CLIMBED THE HILLS, FELT THE COLD SLAP OF THE LAKE IN SPRING.
12 3 6 9
I'VE WANTED TO COME HERE FOR A LONG TIME.
IS THAT MAPLE SYRUP I SMELL?
HURRY UP WITH THE SAP, OWL!
IF I MOVE ANY FASTER, I'LL SPILL IT. THEN YOU'D HAVE TO WAIT EVEN LONGER.

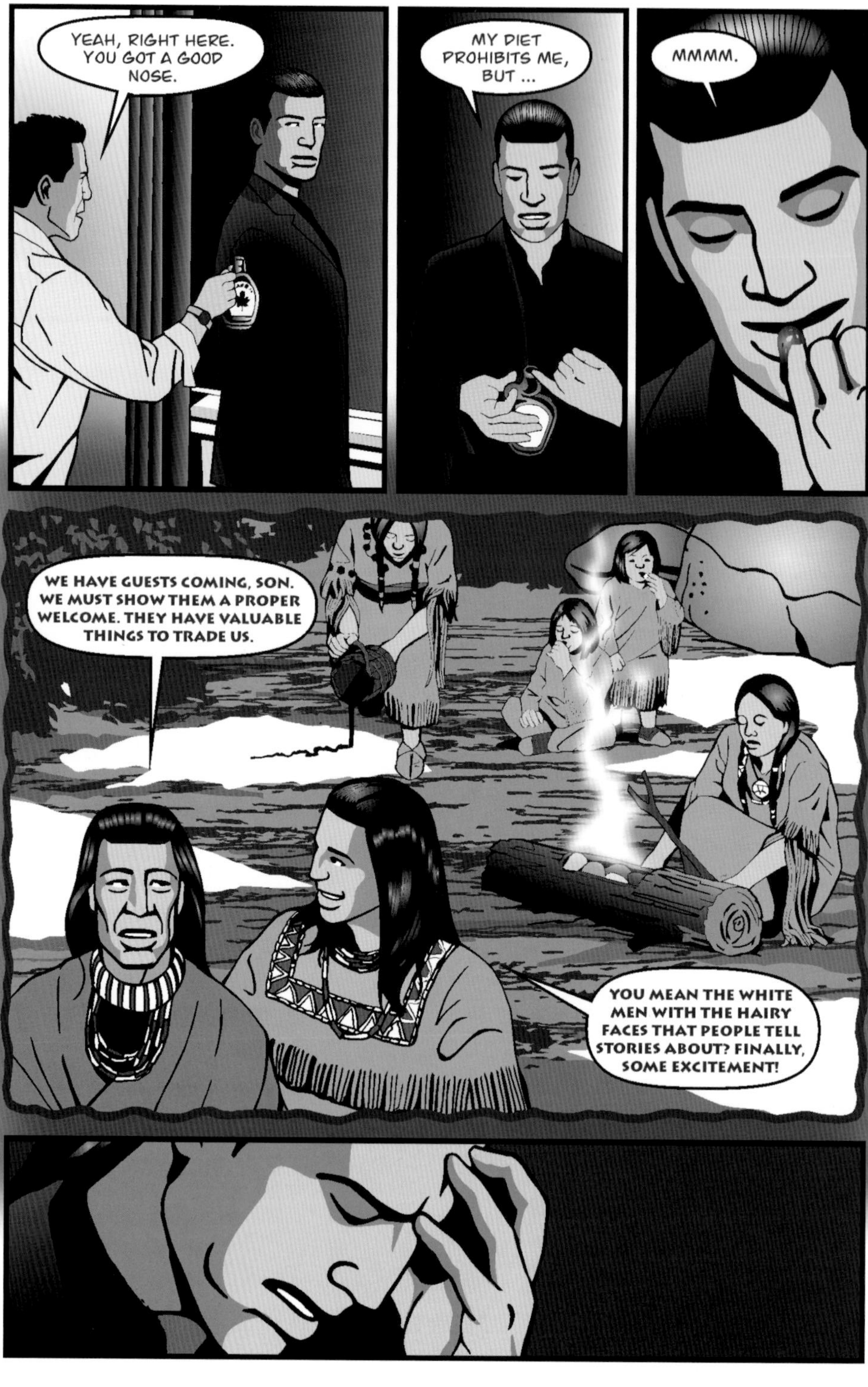
YEAH, RIGHT HERE. YOU GOT A GOOD NOSE.
MY DIET PROHIBITS ME, BUT ...
MMMM.
WE HAVE GUESTS COMING, SON. WE MUST SHOW THEM A PROPER WELCOME. THEY HAVE VALUABLE THINGS TO TRADE US.
YOU MEAN THE WHITE MEN WITH THE HAIRY FACES THAT PEOPLE TELL STORIES ABOUT? FINALLY, SOME EXCITEMENT!

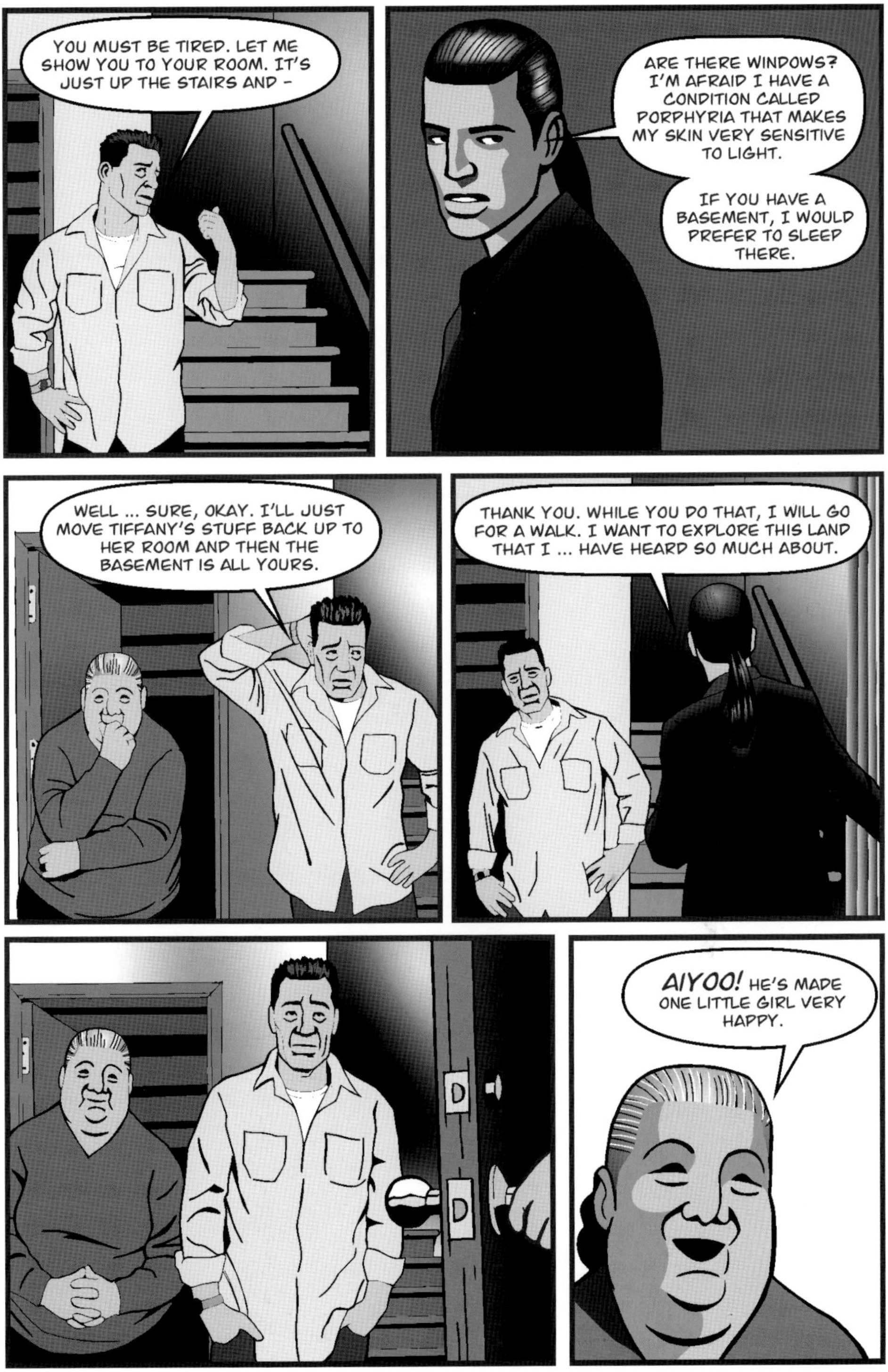
YOU MUST BE TIRED. LET ME SHOW YOU TO YOUR ROOM. IT'S JUST UP THE STAIRS AND –
ARE THERE WINDOWS? I'M AFRAID I HAVE A CONDITION CALLED PORPHYRIA THAT MAKES MY SKIN VERY SENSITIVE TO LIGHT.
IF YOU HAVE A BASEMENT, I WOULD PREFER TO SLEEP THERE.
WELL ... SURE, OKAY. I'LL JUST MOVE TIFFANY'S STUFF BACK UP TO HER ROOM AND THEN THE BASEMENT IS ALL YOURS.
THANK YOU. WHILE YOU DO THAT, I WILL GO FOR A WALK. I WANT TO EXPLORE THIS LAND THAT I ... HAVE HEARD SO MUCH ABOUT.
D
D
AIYOO! HE'S MADE ONE LITTLE GIRL VERY HAPPY.

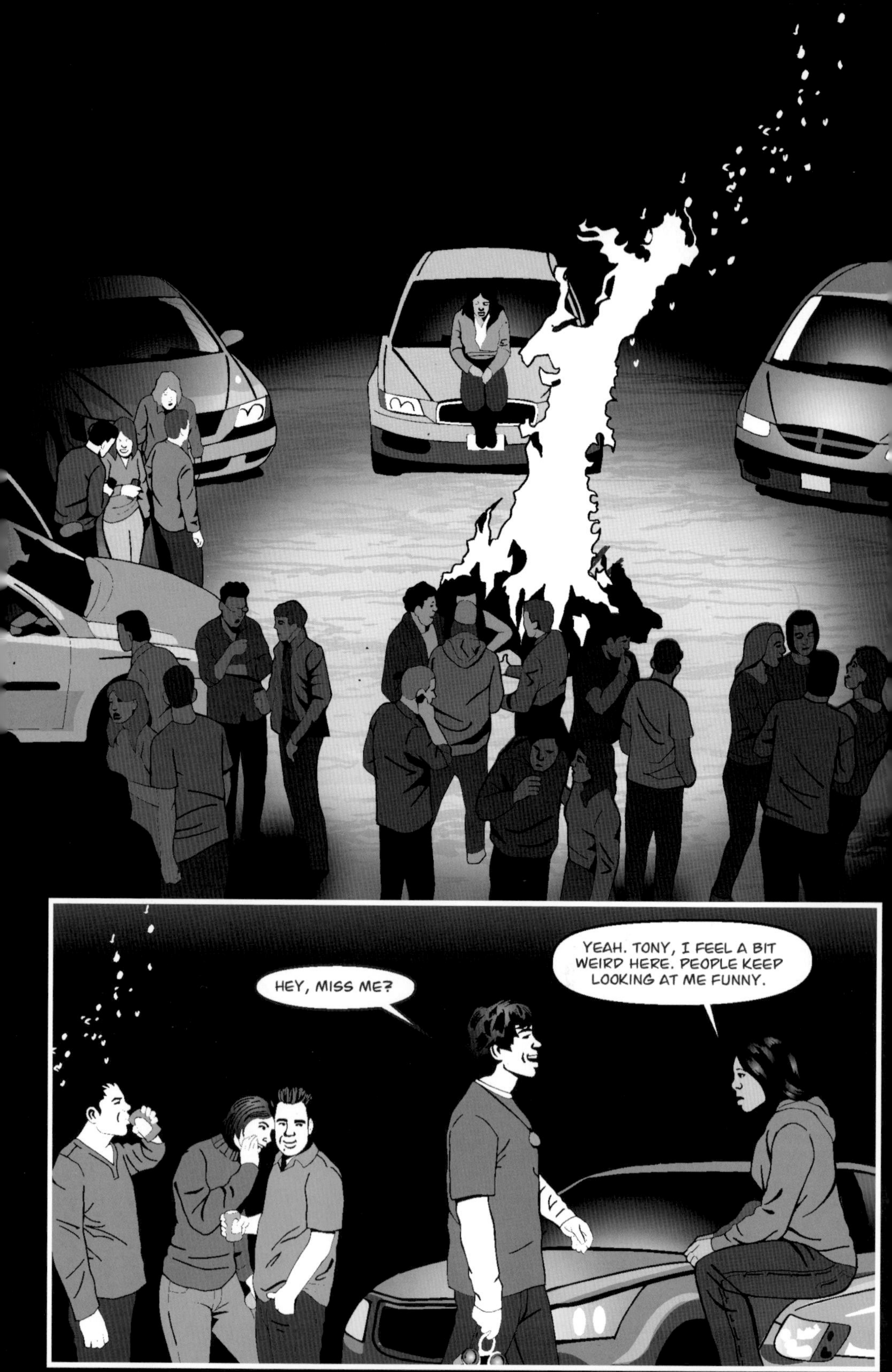
HEY, MISS ME?
YEAH. TONY, I FEEL A BIT WEIRD HERE. PEOPLE KEEP LOOKING AT ME FUNNY.

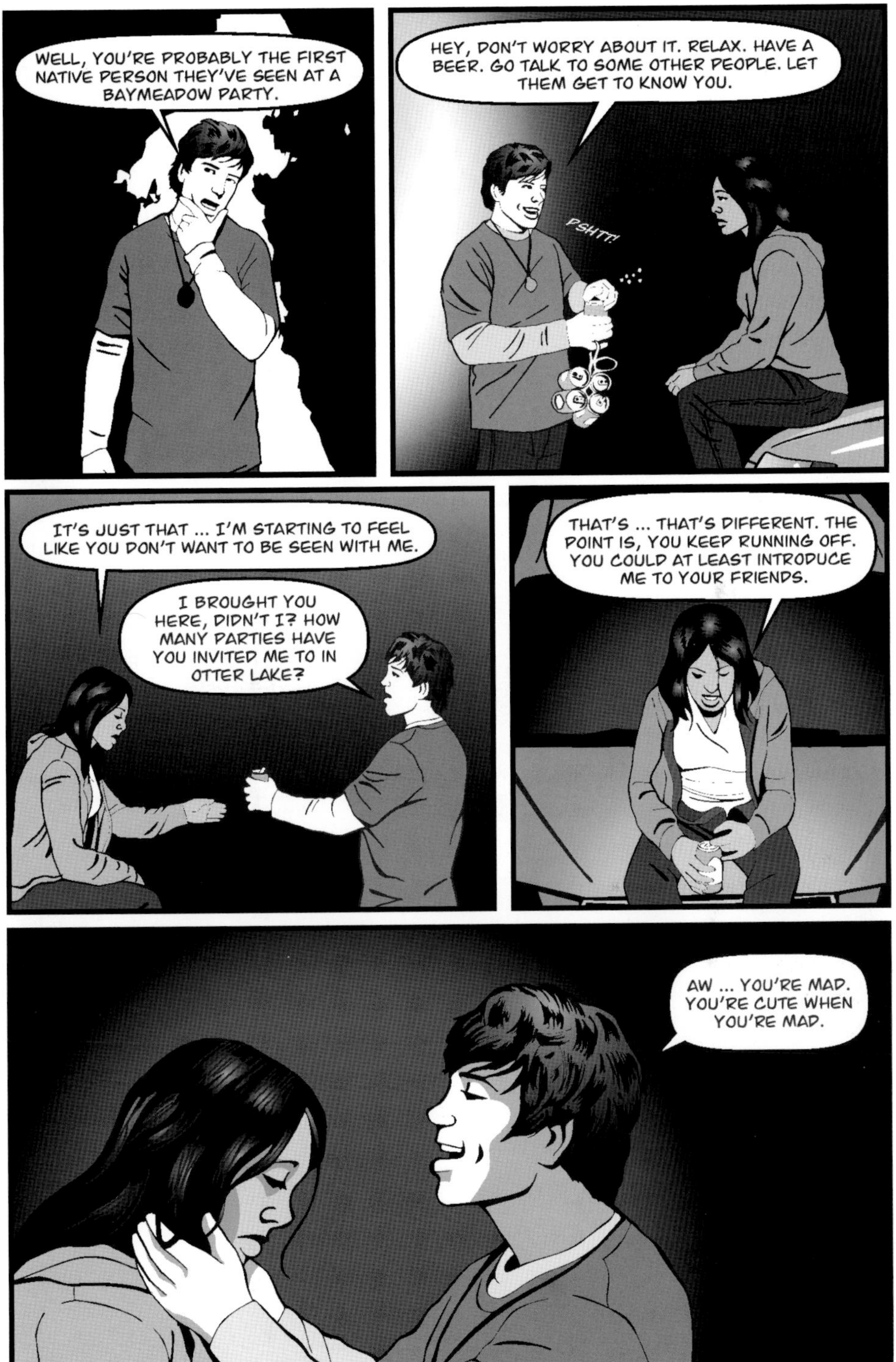
WELL, YOU'RE PROBABLY THE FIRST NATIVE PERSON THEY'VE SEEN AT A BAYMEADOW PARTY.
HEY, DON'T WORRY ABOUT IT. RELAX. HAVE A BEER. GO TALK TO SOME OTHER PEOPLE. LET THEM GET TO KNOW YOU.
PSHTT!
IT'S JUST THAT ... I'M STARTING TO FEEL LIKE YOU DON'T WANT TO BE SEEN WITH ME.
I BROUGHT YOU HERE, DIDN'T I? HOW MANY PARTIES HAVE YOU INVITED ME TO IN OTTER LAKE?
THAT'S ... THAT'S DIFFERENT. THE POINT IS, YOU KEEP RUNNING OFF. YOU COULD AT LEAST INTRODUCE ME TO YOUR FRIENDS.
AW ... YOU'RE MAD. YOU'RE CUTE WHEN YOU'RE MAD.

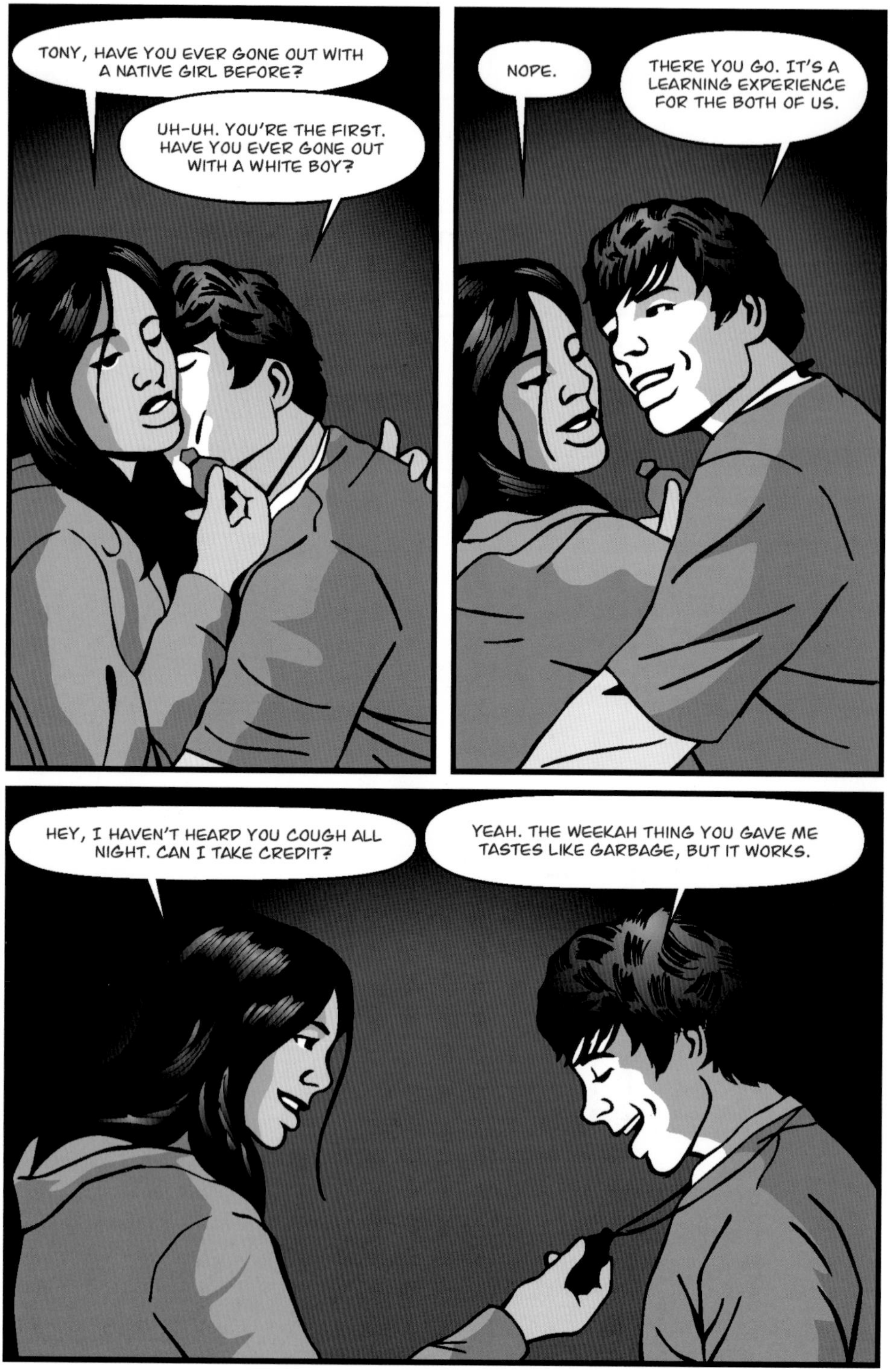
TONY, HAVE YOU EVER GONE OUT WITH A NATIVE GIRL BEFORE?
UH-UH. YOU'RE THE FIRST. HAVE YOU EVER GONE OUT WITH A WHITE BOY?
NOPE.
THERE YOU GO. IT'S A LEARNING EXPERIENCE FOR THE BOTH OF US.
HEY, I HAVEN'T HEARD YOU COUGH ALL NIGHT. CAN I TAKE CREDIT?
YEAH. THE WEEKAH THING YOU GAVE ME TASTES LIKE GARBAGE, BUT IT WORKS.

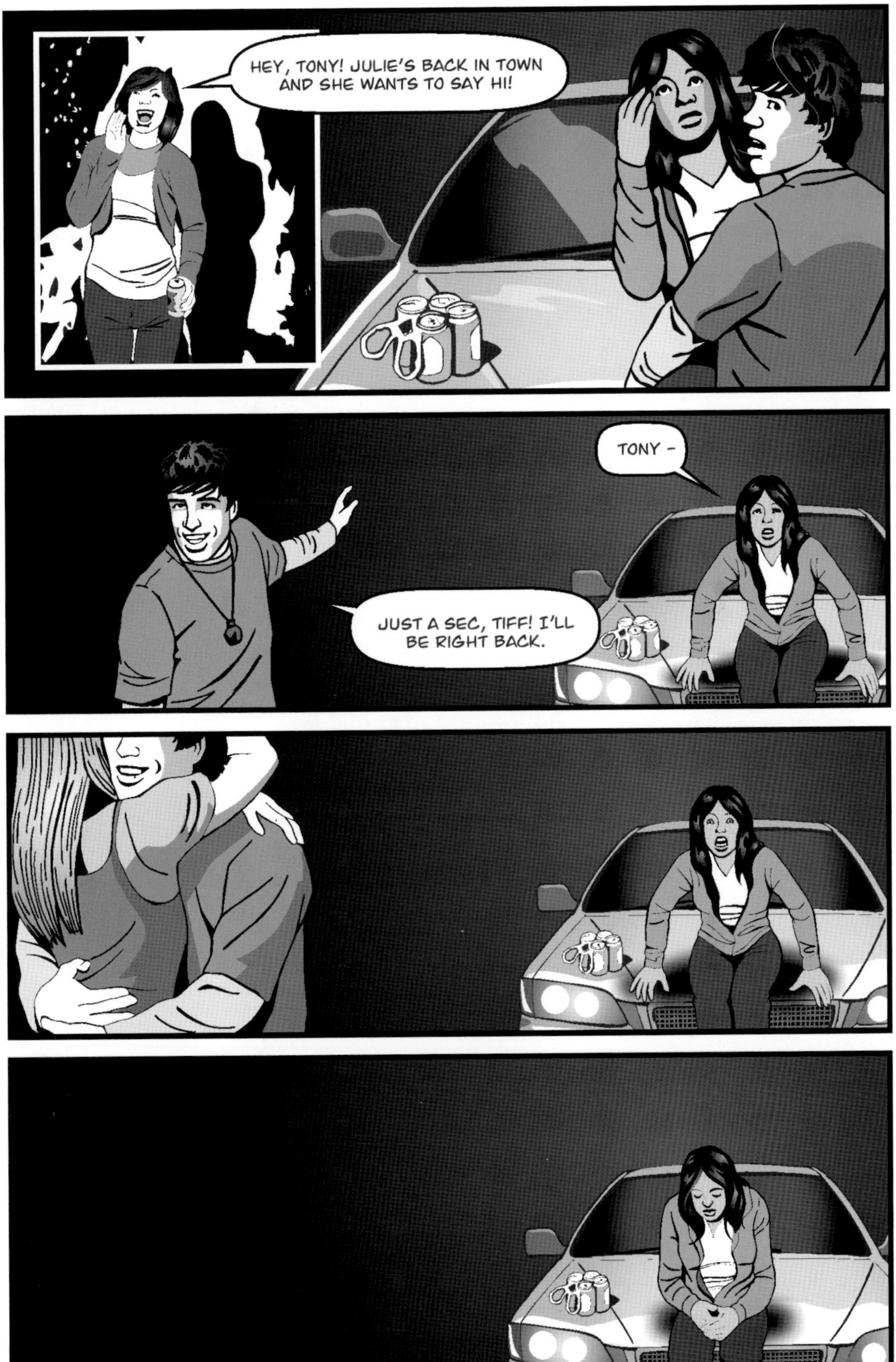
HEY, TONY! JULIE'S BACK IN TOWN AND SHE WANTS TO SAY HI!
TONY -
JUST A SEC, TIFF! I'LL BE RIGHT BACK.

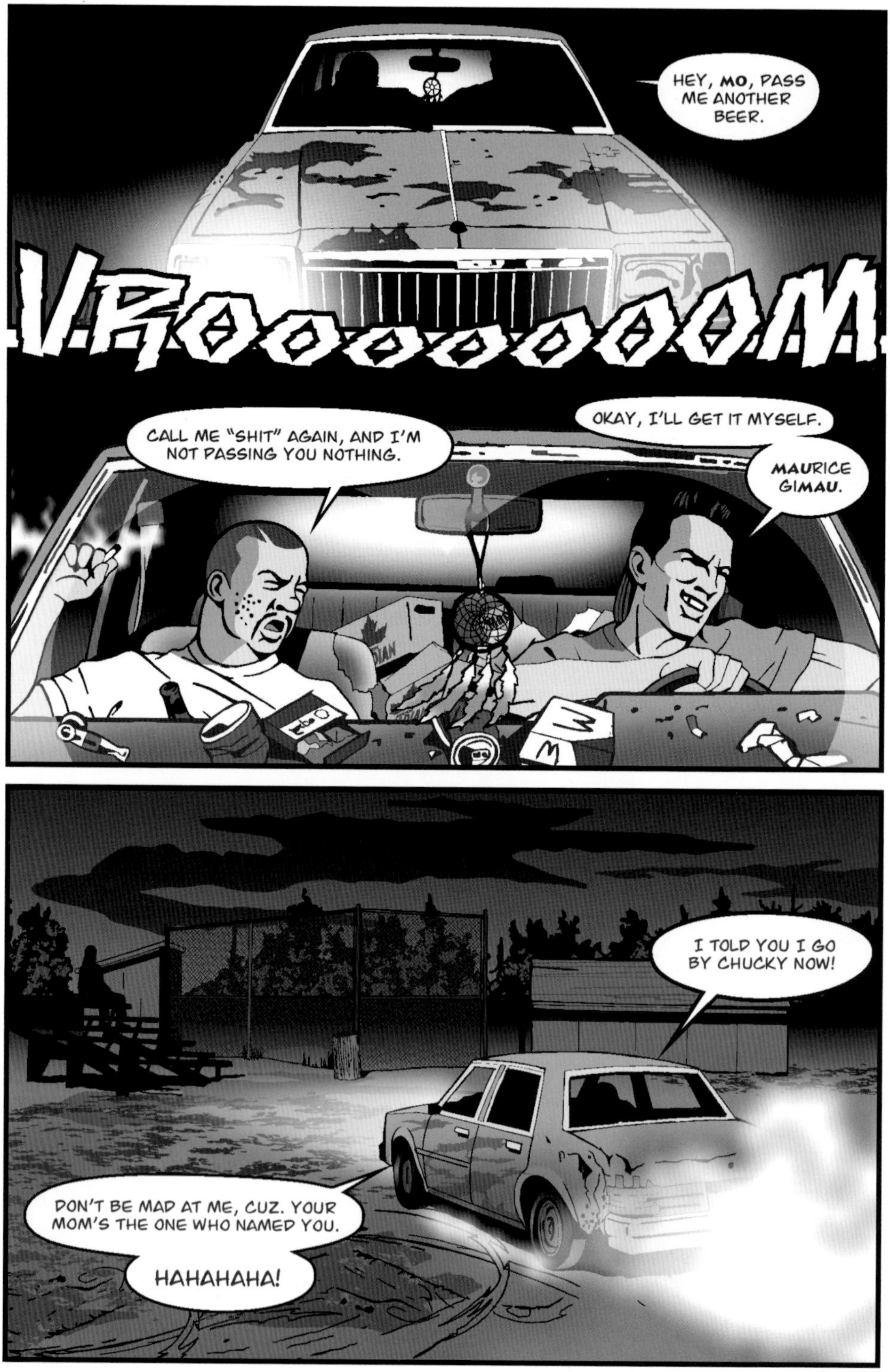
HEY, MO, PASS ME ANOTHER BEER.
VROOOOOOOOM
CALL ME "SHIT" AGAIN, AND I'M NOT PASSING YOU NOTHING.
OKAY, I'LL GET IT MYSELF.
MAURICE GIMAU.
I TOLD YOU I GO BY CHUCKY NOW!
DON'T BE MAD AT ME, CUZ. YOUR MOM'S THE ONE WHO NAMED YOU.
HAHAHAHA!

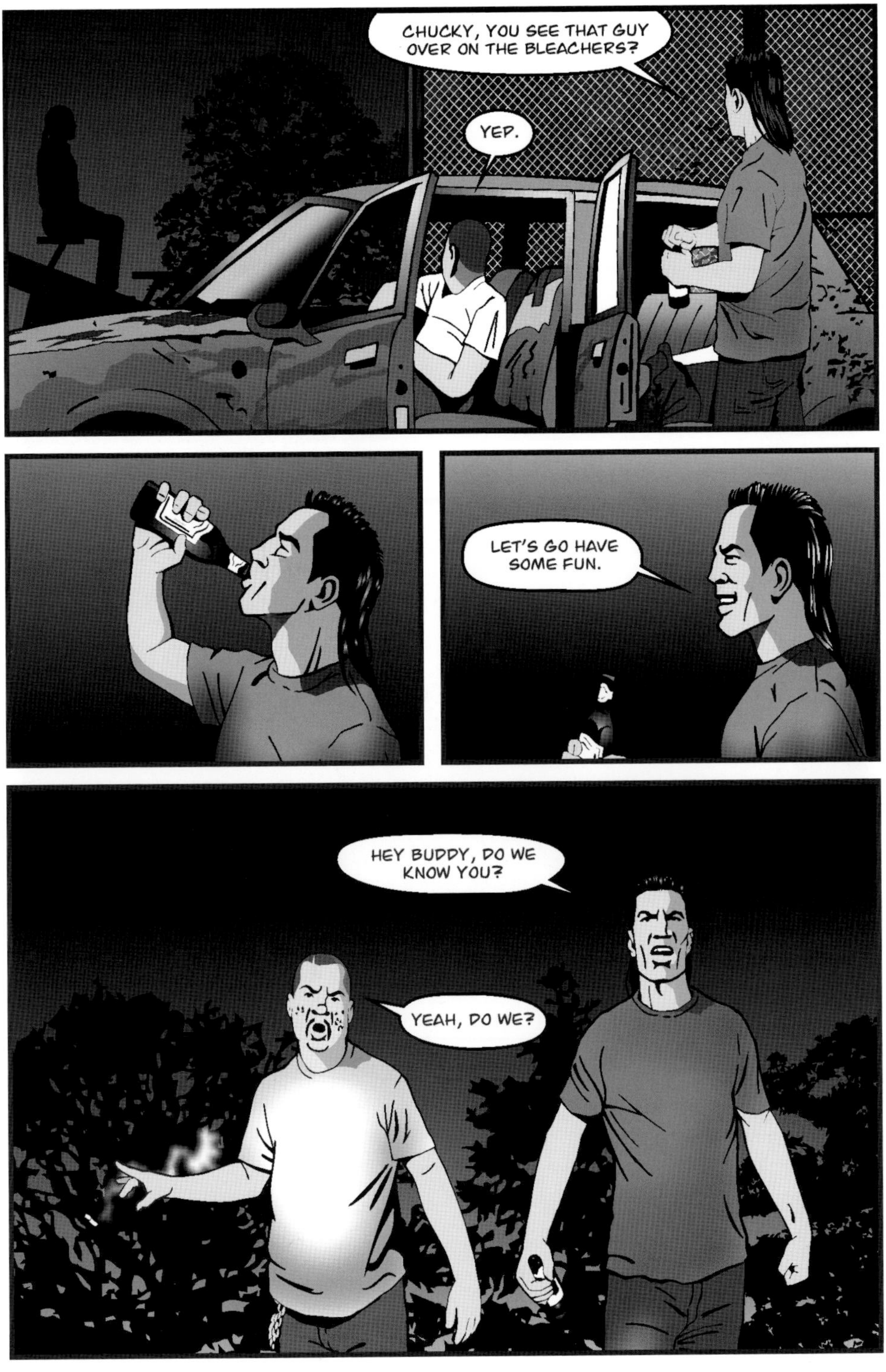
CHUCKY, YOU SEE THAT GUY OVER ON THE BLEACHERS?
YEP.
LET'S GO HAVE SOME FUN.
HEY BUDDY, DO WE KNOW YOU?
YEAH, DO WE?

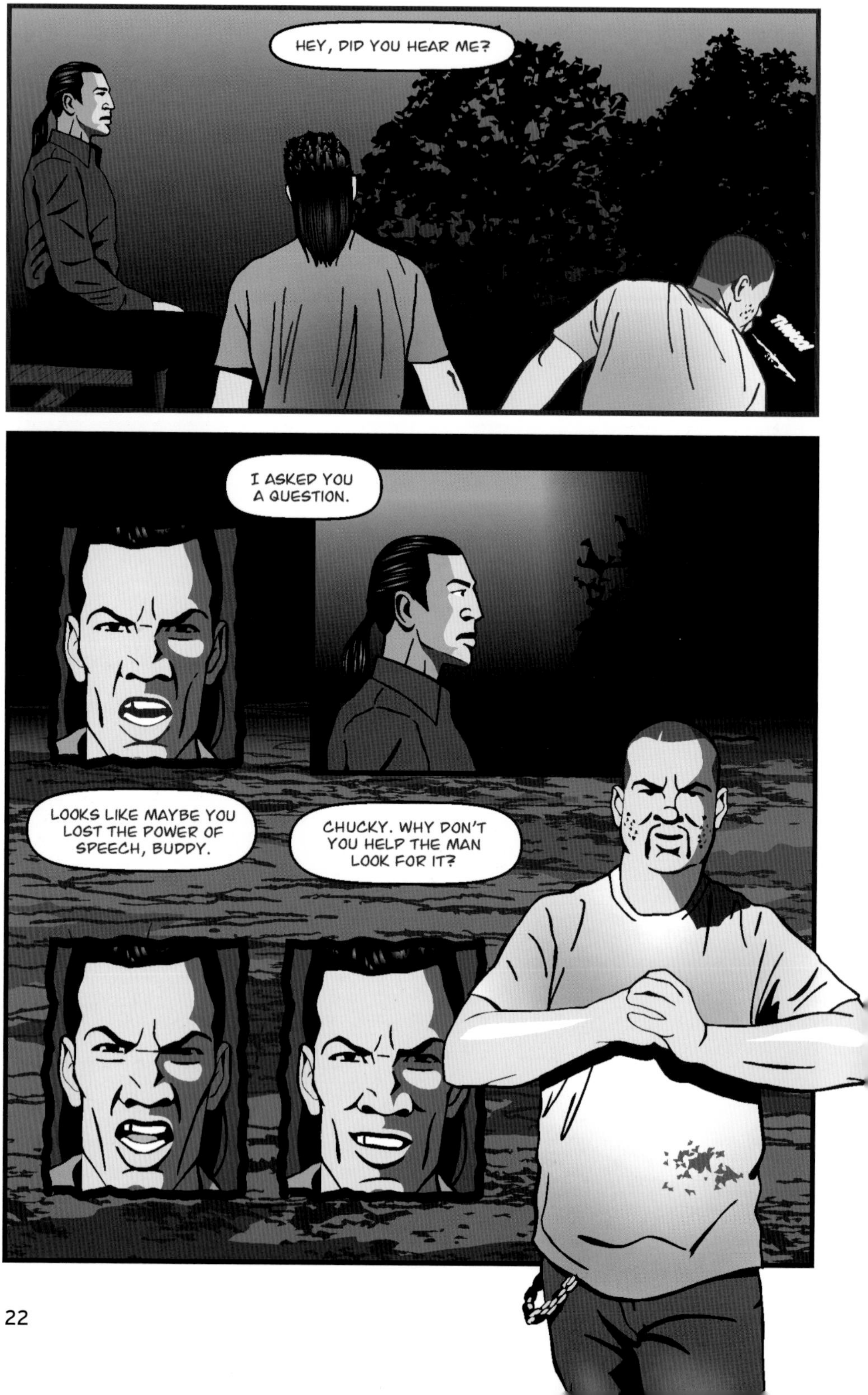
HEY, DID YOU HEAR ME?
I ASKED YOU A QUESTION.
LOOKS LIKE MAYBE YOU LOST THE POWER OF SPEECH, BUDDY.
CHUCKY. WHY DON'T YOU HELP THE MAN LOOK FOR IT?

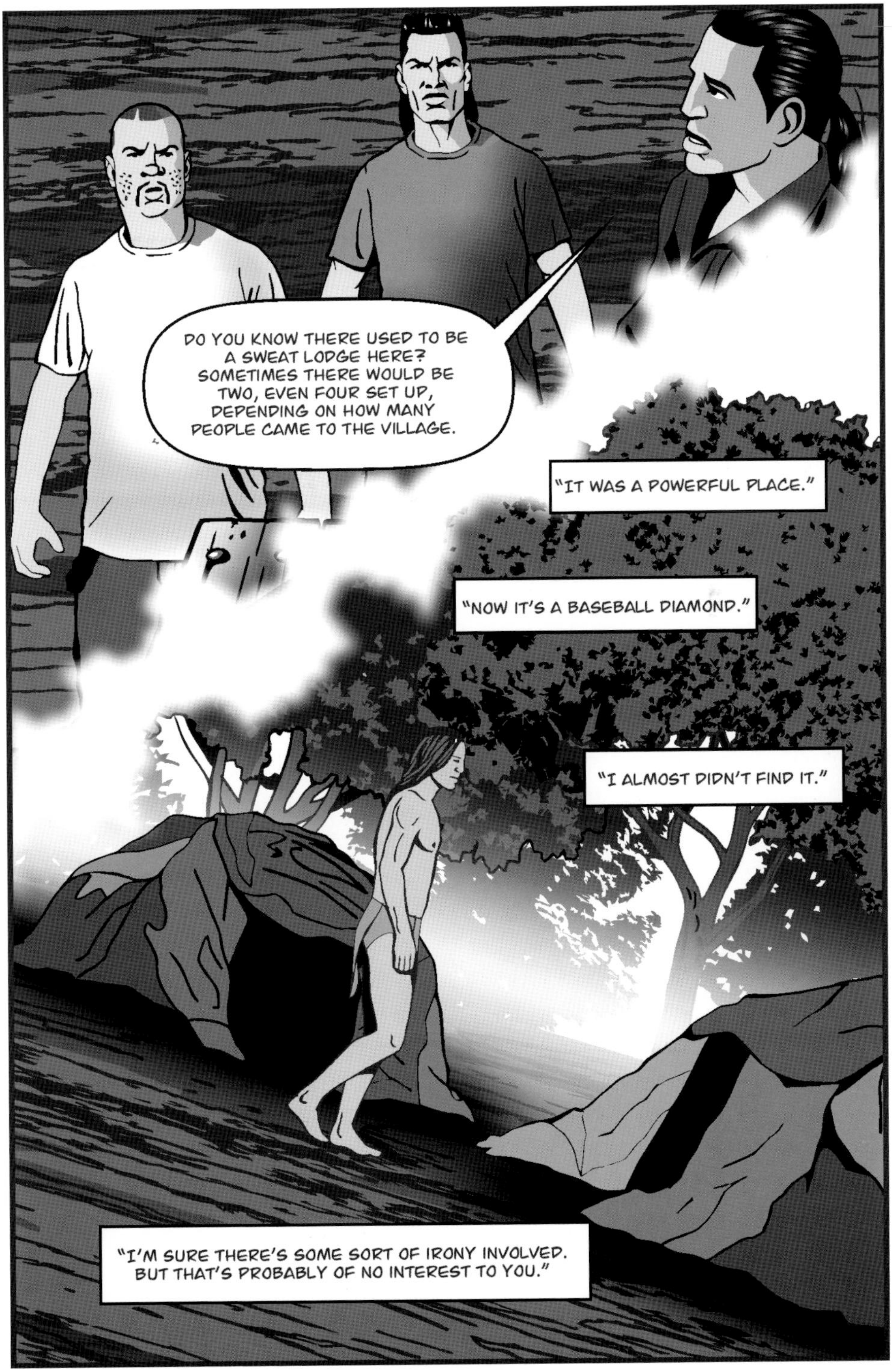
DO YOU KNOW THERE USED TO BE A SWEAT LODGE HERE? SOMETIMES THERE WOULD BE TWO, EVEN FOUR SET UP, DEPENDING ON HOW MANY PEOPLE CAME TO THE VILLAGE.
"IT WAS A POWERFUL PLACE."
"NOW IT'S A BASEBALL DIAMOND."
"I ALMOST DIDN'T FIND IT."
"I'M SURE THERE'S SOME SORT OF IRONY INVOLVED. BUT THAT'S PROBABLY OF NO INTEREST TO YOU."

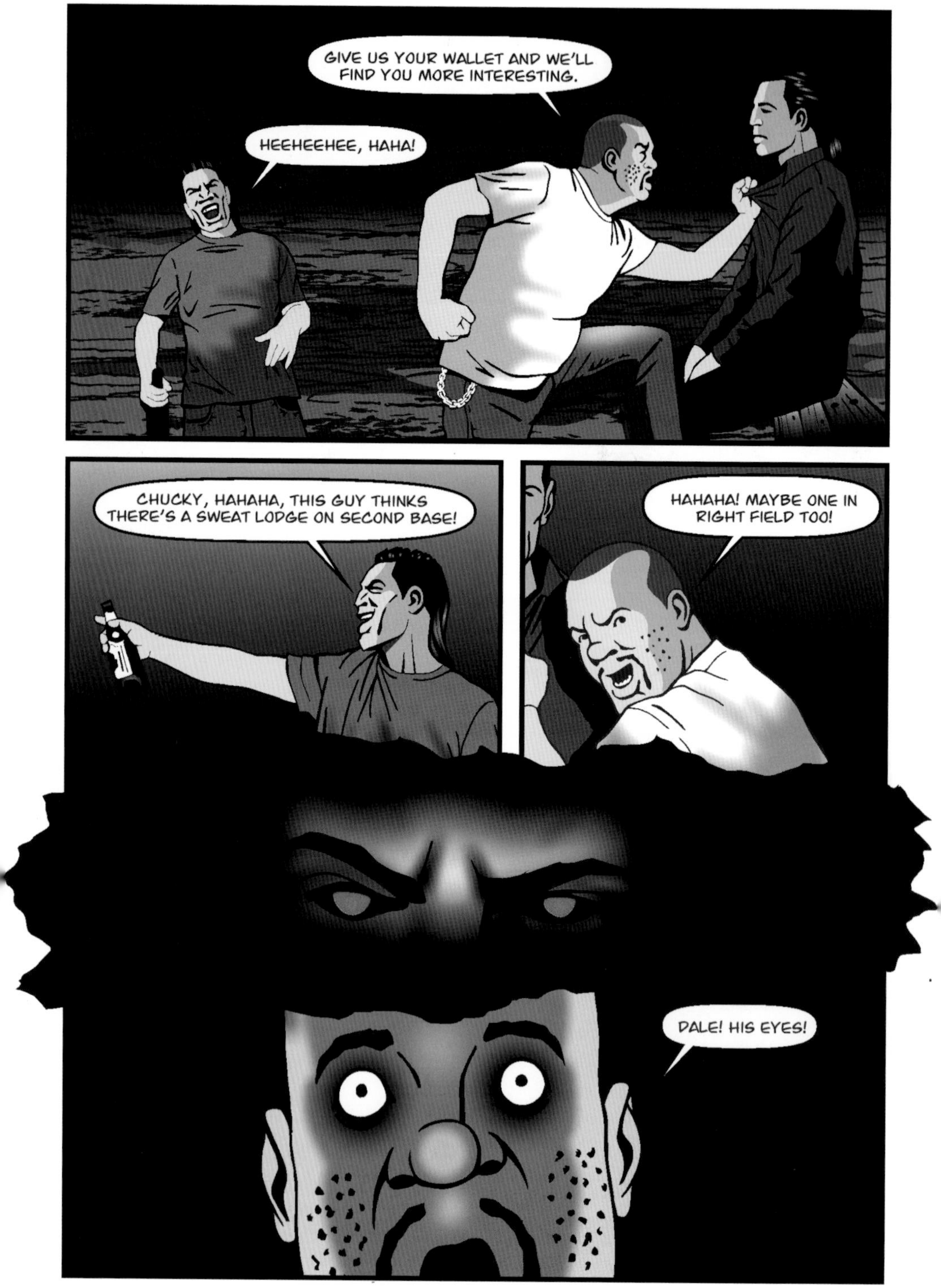
HEEHEEHEE, HAHA!
GIVE US YOUR WALLET AND WE'LL FIND YOU MORE INTERESTING.
CHUCKY, HAHAHA, THIS GUY THINKS THERE'S A SWEAT LODGE ON SECOND BASE!
HAHAHA! MAYBE ONE IN RIGHT FIELD TOO!
DALE! HIS EYES!

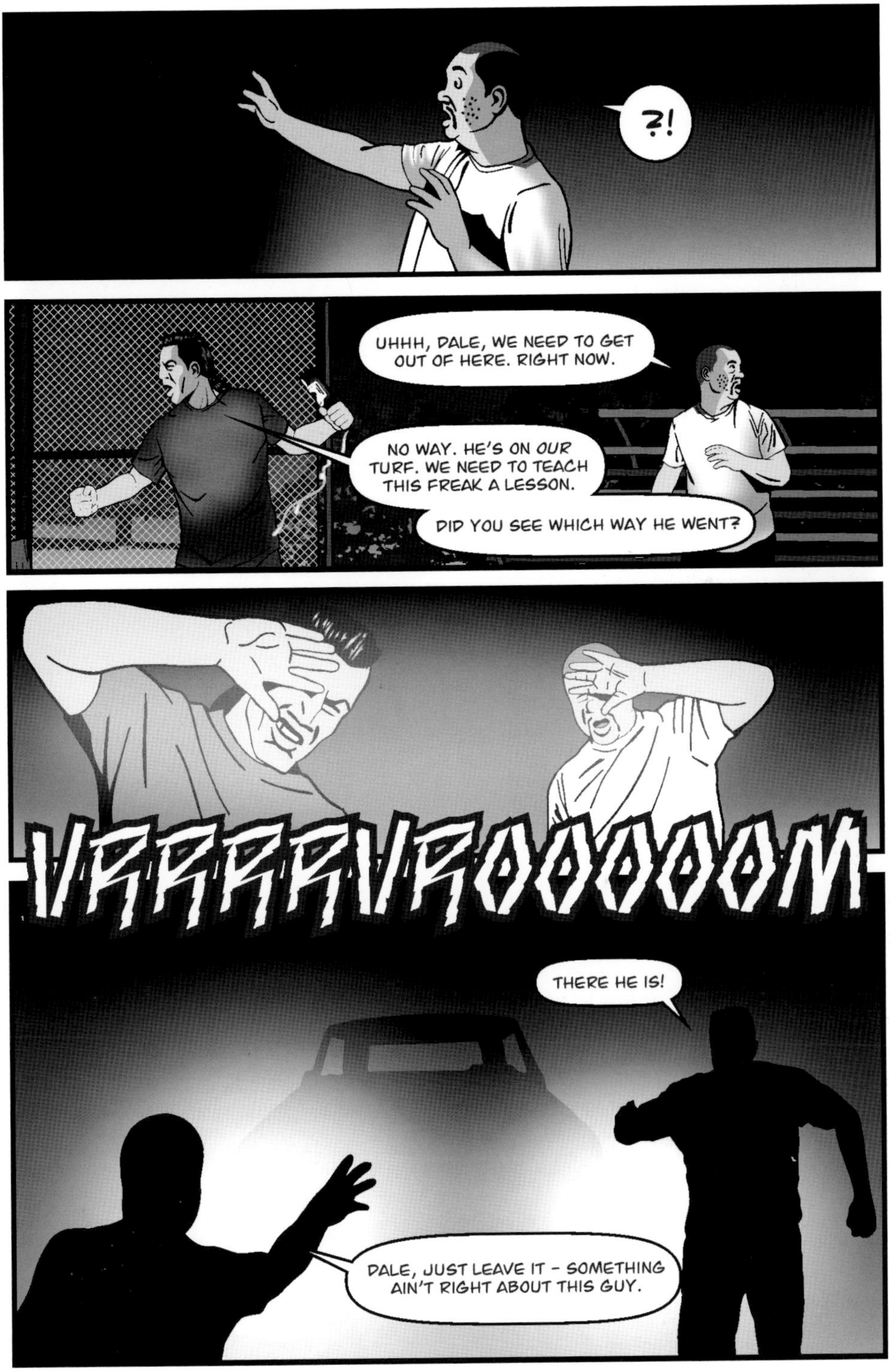
?!
UHHH, DALE, WE NEED TO GET OUT OF HERE. RIGHT NOW.
NO WAY. HE'S ON OUR TURF. WE NEED TO TEACH THIS FREAK A LESSON.
DID YOU SEE WHICH WAY HE WENT?
VRRRRVROOOOOM
THERE HE IS!
DALE, JUST LEAVE IT – SOMETHING AIN'T RIGHT ABOUT THIS GUY.

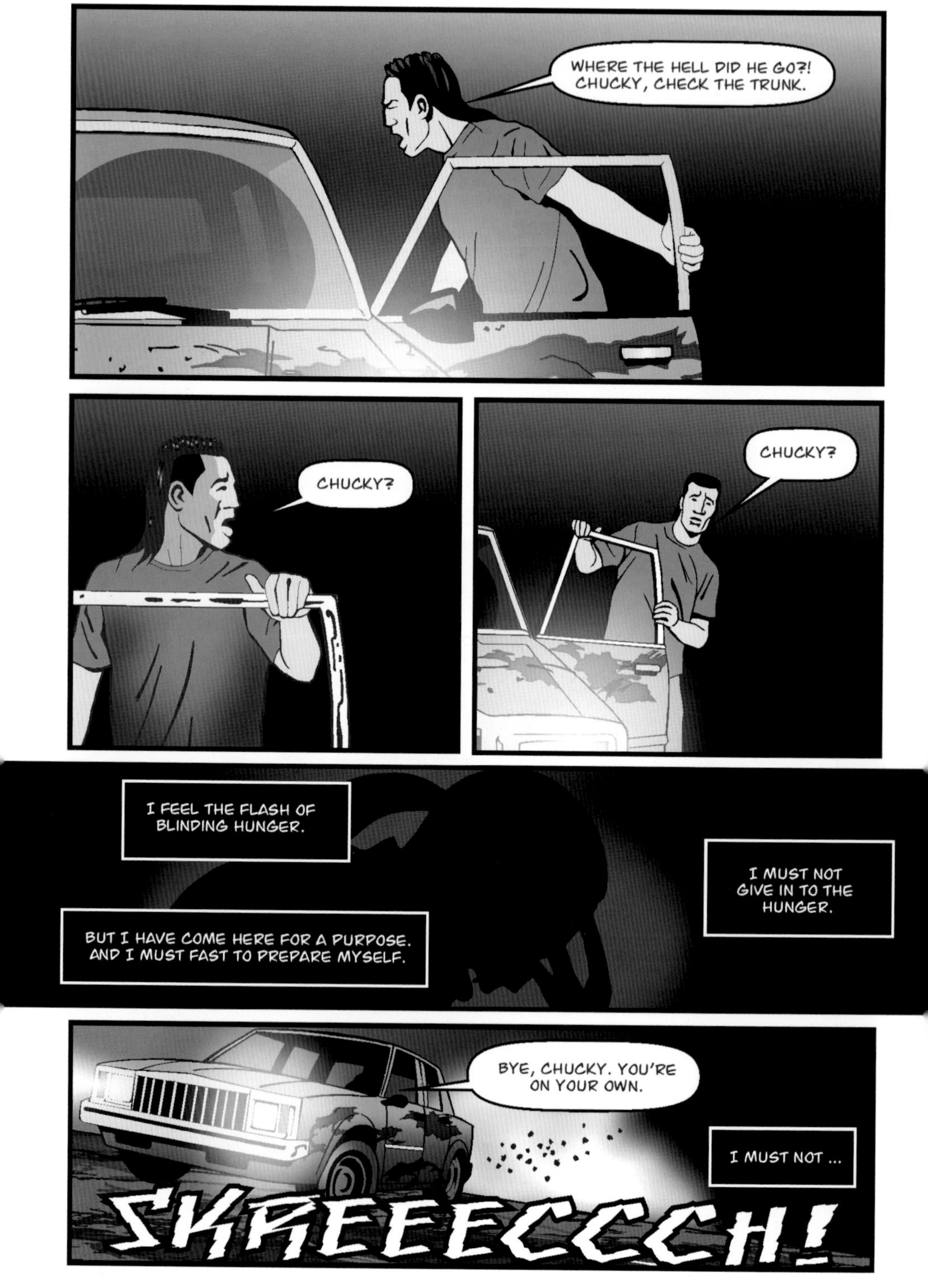
WHERE THE HELL DID HE GO?! CHUCKY, CHECK THE TRUNK.
CHUCKY?
CHUCKY?
I FEEL THE FLASH OF BLINDING HUNGER.
BUT I HAVE COME HERE FOR A PURPOSE. AND I MUST FAST TO PREPARE MYSELF.
I MUST NOT GIVE IN TO THE HUNGER.
BYE, CHUCKY. YOU'RE ON YOUR OWN.
I MUST NOT ...
SKREEECCCH!

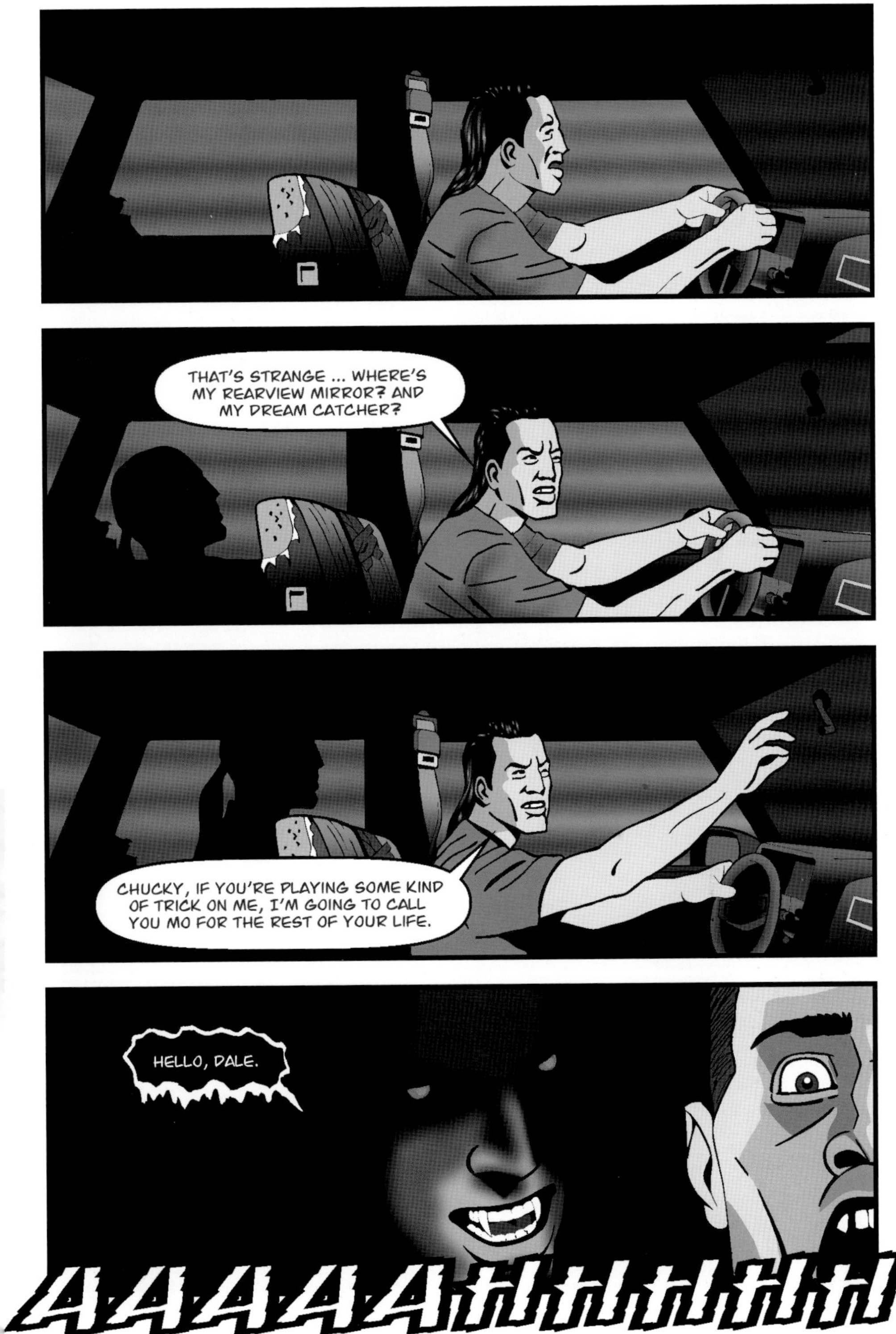
THAT'S STRANGE ... WHERE'S MY REARVIEW MIRROR? AND MY DREAM CATCHER?
CHUCKY, IF YOU'RE PLAYING SOME KIND OF TRICK ON ME, I'M GOING TO CALL YOU MO FOR THE REST OF YOUR LIFE.
HELLO, DALE.
AAAAAHHHHHH

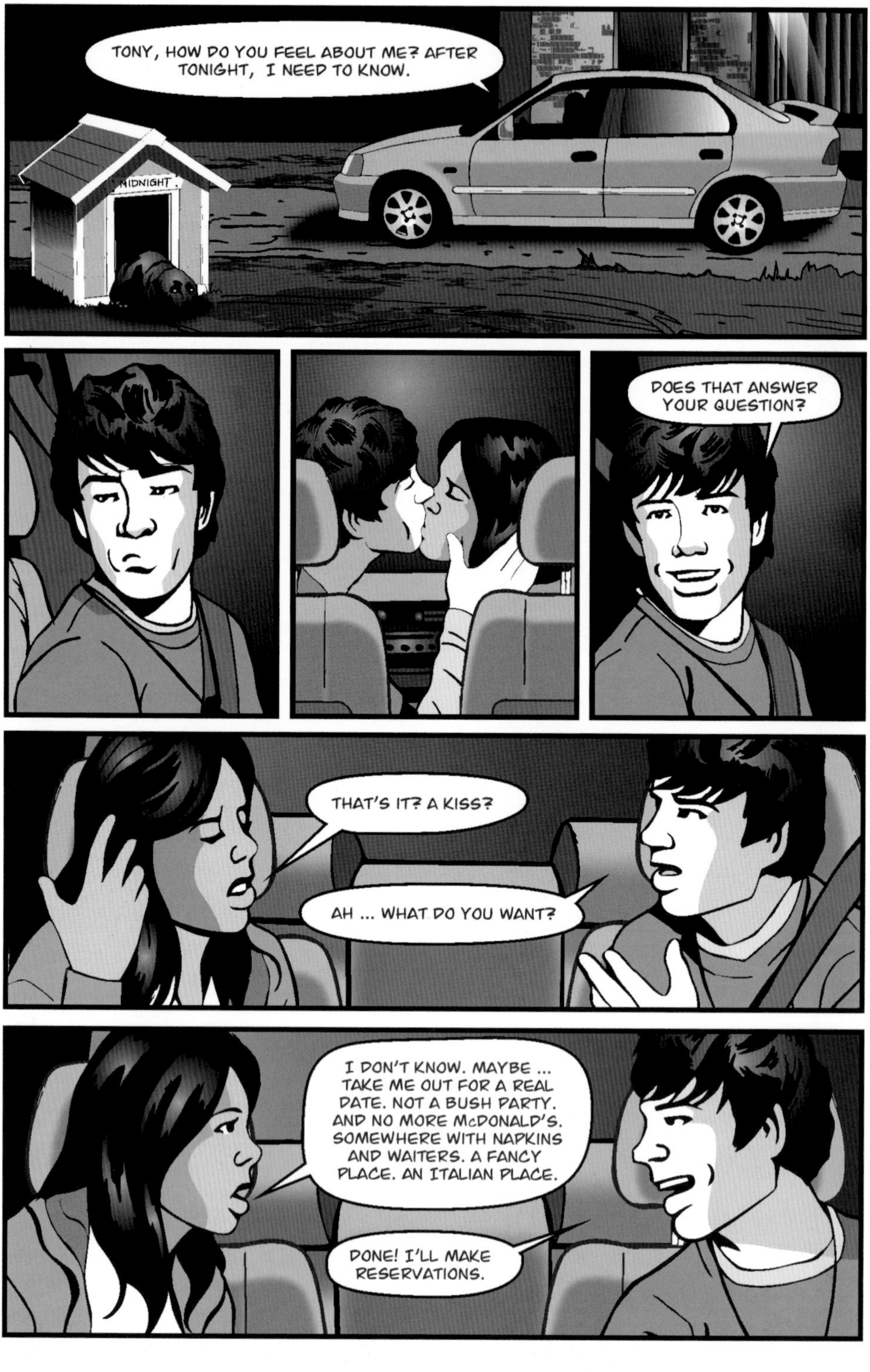
TONY, HOW DO YOU FEEL ABOUT ME? AFTER TONIGHT, I NEED TO KNOW.
MIDNIGHT
DOES THAT ANSWER YOUR QUESTION?
THAT'S IT? A KISS?
AH ... WHAT DO YOU WANT?
I DON'T KNOW. MAYBE ... TAKE ME OUT FOR A REAL DATE. NOT A BUSH PARTY. AND NO MORE McDONALD'S. SOMEWHERE WITH NAPKINS AND WAITERS. A FANCY PLACE. AN ITALIAN PLACE.
DONE! I'LL MAKE RESERVATIONS.

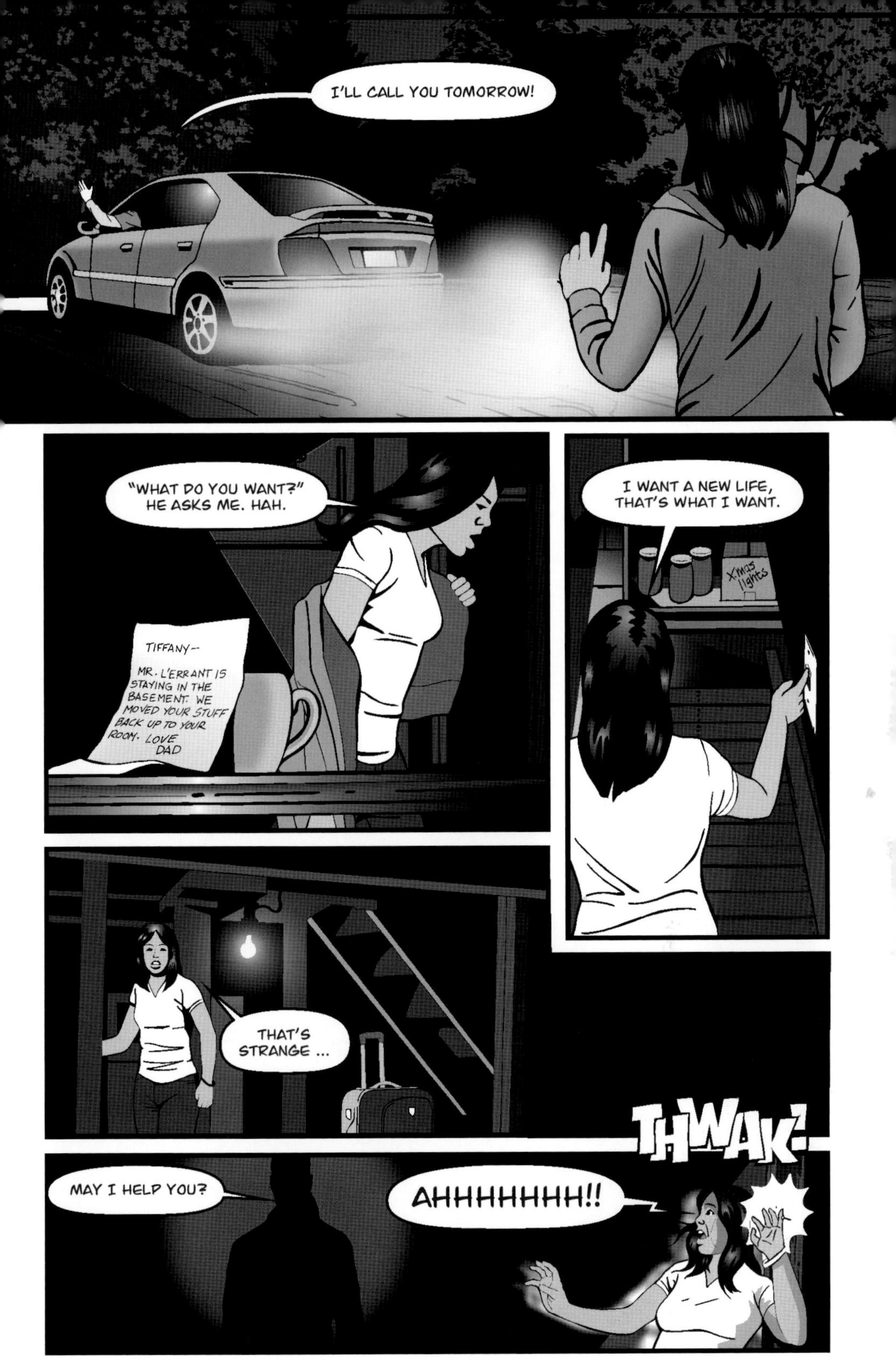

I'LL CALL YOU TOMORROW!
"WHAT DO YOU WANT?" HE ASKS ME. HAH.
TIFFANY--
MR. L'ERRANT IS STAYING IN THE BASEMENT. WE MOVED YOUR STUFF BACK UP TO YOUR ROOM. LOVE DAD
I WANT A NEW LIFE, THAT'S WHAT I WANT.
X-mas lights
THAT'S STRANGE ...
THWAK!
MAY I HELP YOU?
AHHHHHHHH!!

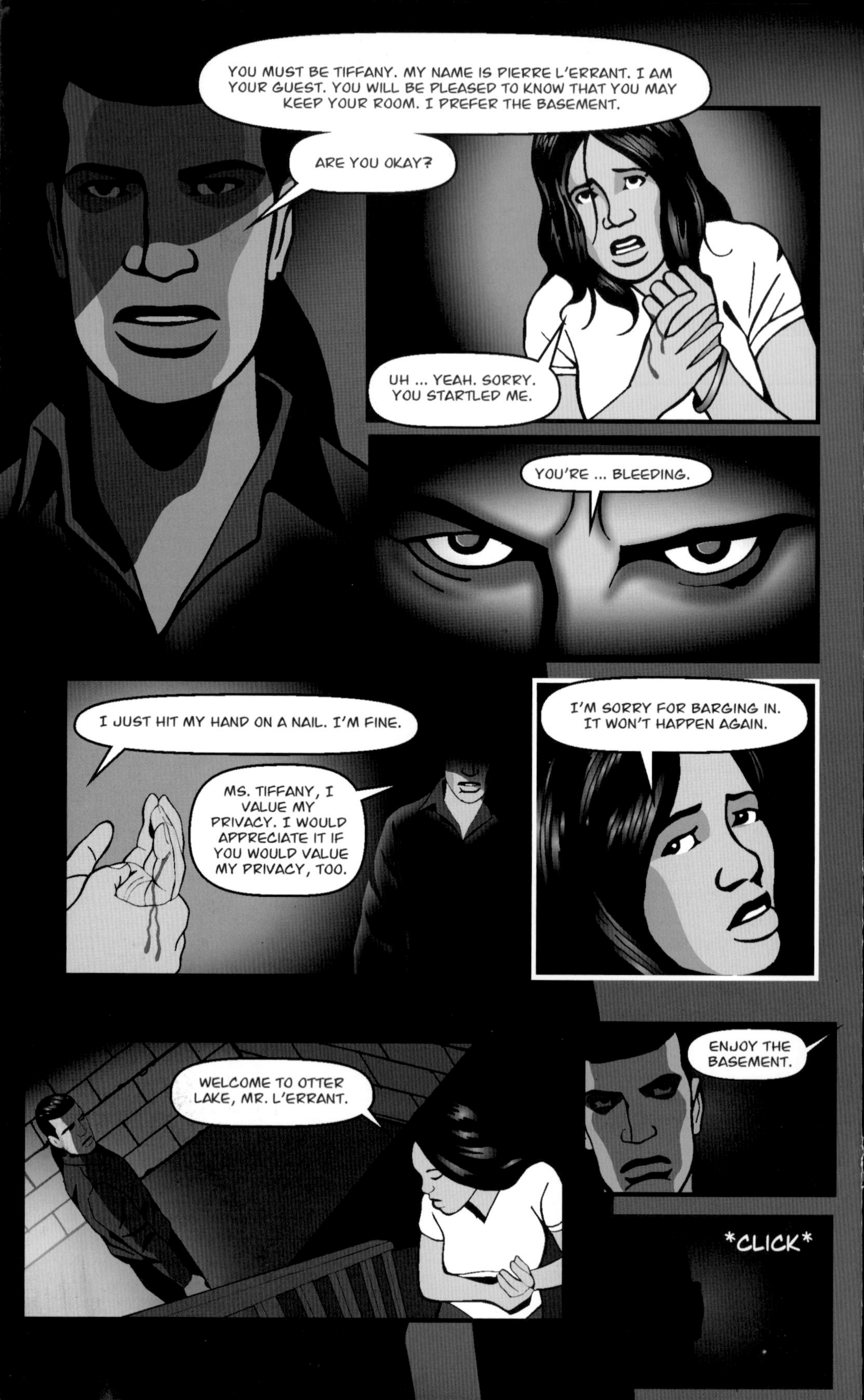
YOU MUST BE TIFFANY. MY NAME IS PIERRE L'ERRANT. I AM YOUR GUEST. YOU WILL BE PLEASED TO KNOW THAT YOU MAY KEEP YOUR ROOM. I PREFER THE BASEMENT.
ARE YOU OKAY?
UH ... YEAH. SORRY. YOU STARTLED ME.
YOU'RE ... BLEEDING.
I JUST HIT MY HAND ON A NAIL. I'M FINE.
MS. TIFFANY, I VALUE MY PRIVACY. I WOULD APPRECIATE IT IF YOU WOULD VALUE MY PRIVACY, TOO.
I'M SORRY FOR BARGING IN. IT WON'T HAPPEN AGAIN.
WELCOME TO OTTER LAKE, MR. L'ERRANT.
ENJOY THE BASEMENT.
CLICK

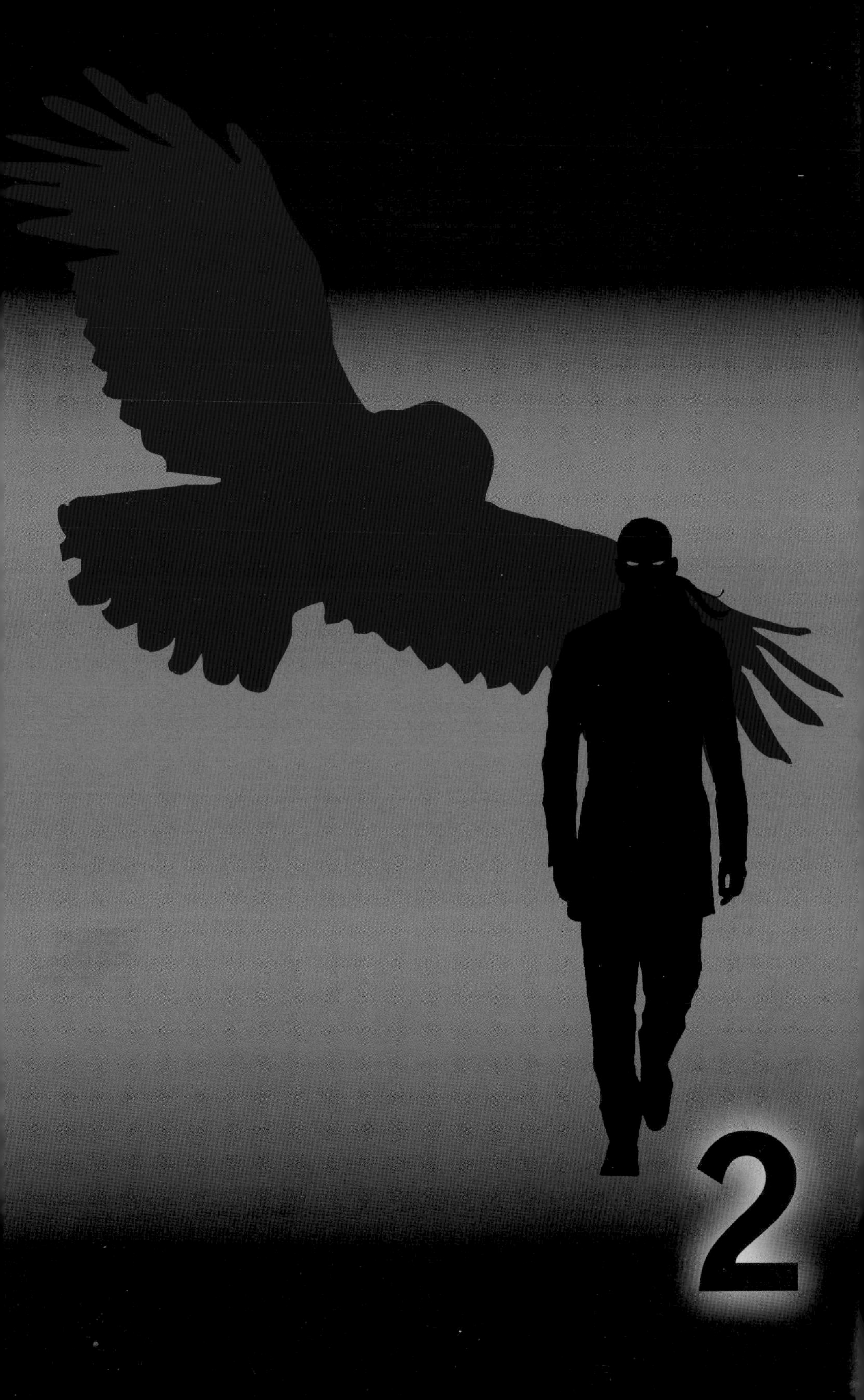
2

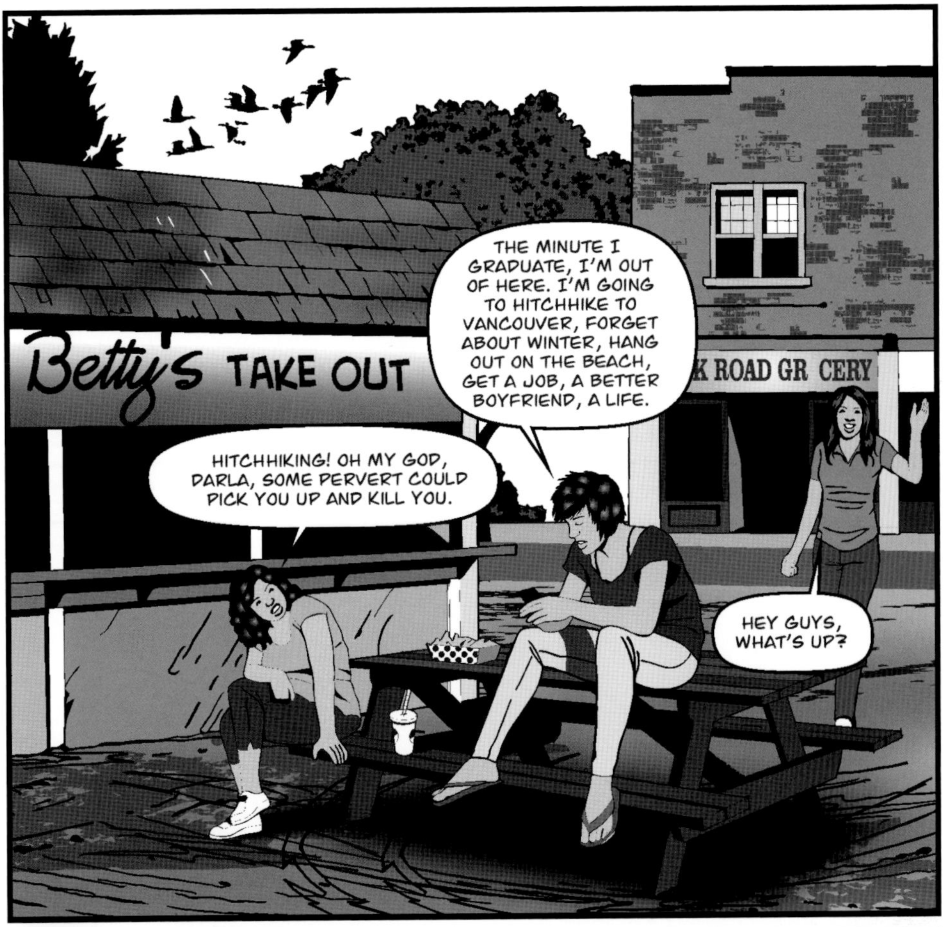
Betty's TAKE OUT
K ROAD GR CERY
THE MINUTE I GRADUATE, I'M OUT OF HERE. I'M GOING TO HITCHHIKE TO VANCOUVER, FORGET ABOUT WINTER, HANG OUT ON THE BEACH, GET A JOB, A BETTER BOYFRIEND, A LIFE.
HITCHHIKING! OH MY GOD, DARLA, SOME PERVERT COULD PICK YOU UP AND KILL YOU.
HEY GUYS, WHAT'S UP?

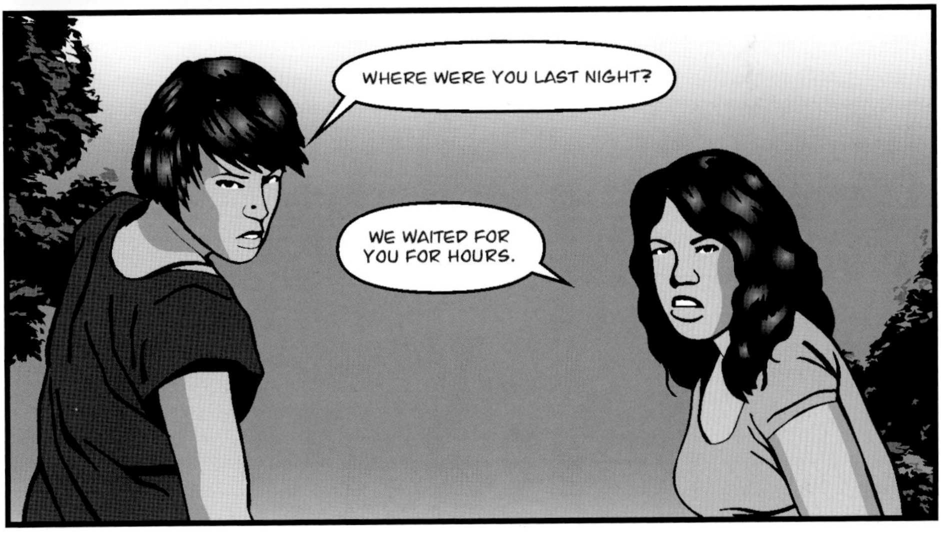
WHERE WERE YOU LAST NIGHT?
WE WAITED FOR YOU FOR HOURS.

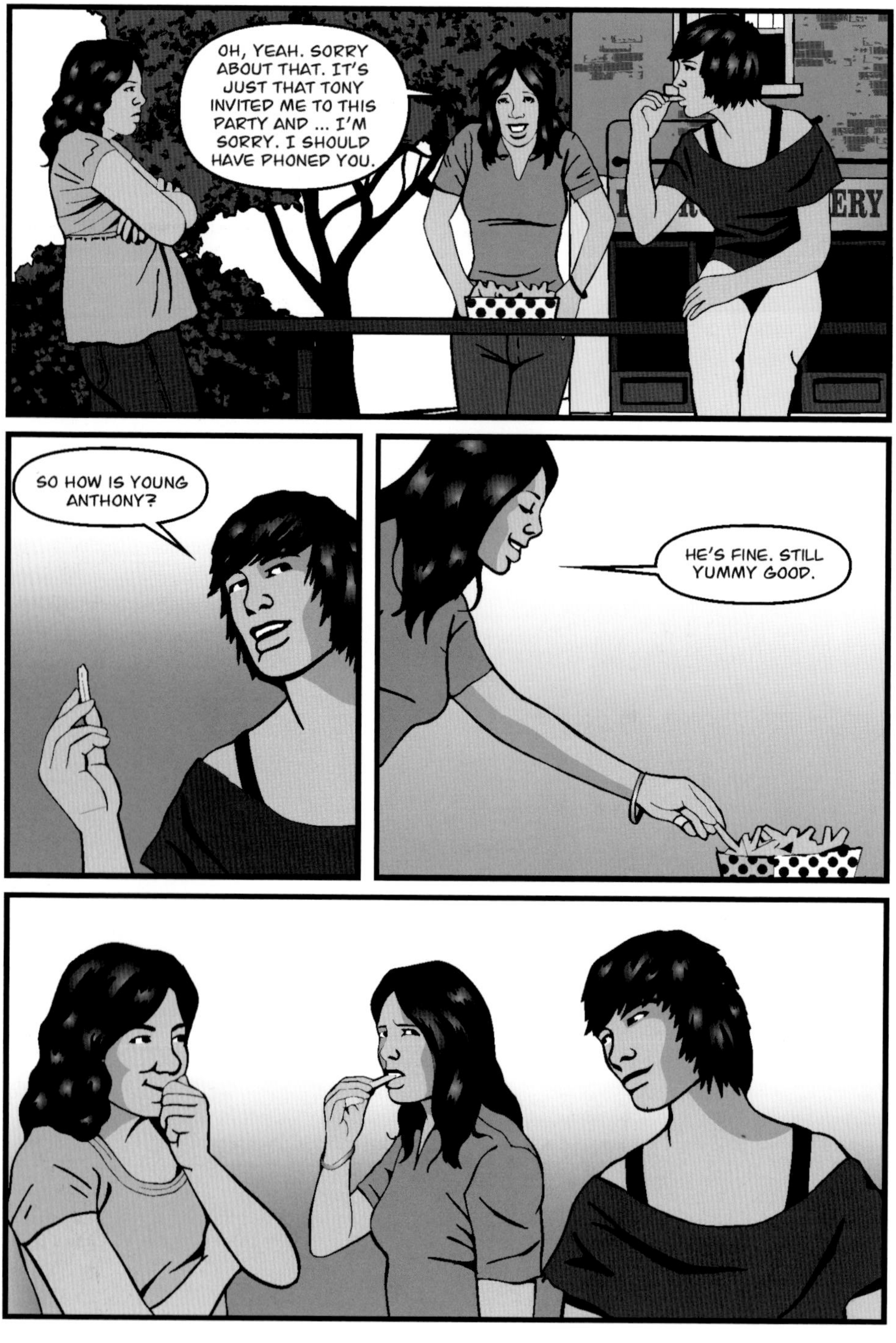
OH, YEAH. SORRY ABOUT THAT. IT'S JUST THAT TONY INVITED ME TO THIS PARTY AND ... I'M SORRY. I SHOULD HAVE PHONED YOU.
SO HOW IS YOUNG ANTHONY?
HE'S FINE. STILL YUMMY GOOD.

WAS JULIE BANES AT THE PARTY TOO?

YEAH. WHY?

WE HEARD SHE'S GOT A BRACELET JUST LIKE YOURS. ONLY HERS IS SOLID GOLD.

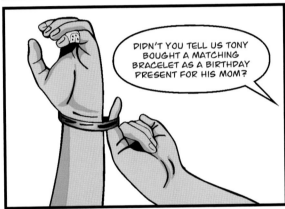

DIDN'T YOU TELL US TONY BOUGHT A MATCHING BRACELET AS A BIRTHDAY PRESENT FOR HIS MOM?

YOU HAVE TO ADMIT THAT'S PRETTY WEIRD.

I HEARD TONY AND JULIE USED TO DATE WHEN THEY WERE IN GRADE EIGHT, BUT HER DAD MADE THEM BREAK UP BECAUSE THEY WERE TOO YOUNG.

I HAVE TO GO.

BIG SURPRISE. SHE'S DITCHING US AGAIN.

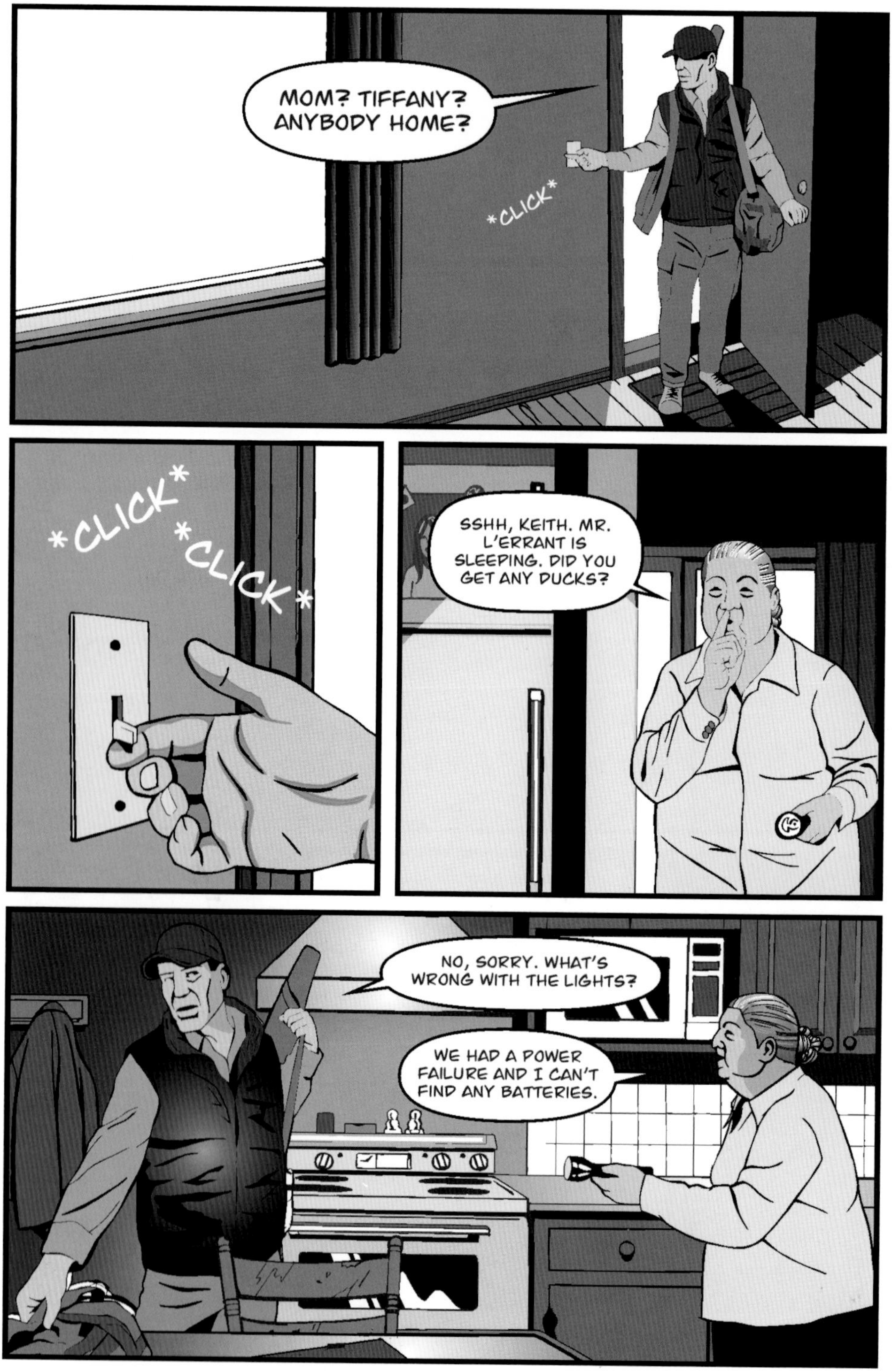
MOM? TIFFANY? ANYBODY HOME?
CLICK
CLICK
CLICK
SSHH, KEITH. MR. L'ERRANT IS SLEEPING. DID YOU GET ANY DUCKS?
NO, SORRY. WHAT'S WRONG WITH THE LIGHTS?
WE HAD A POWER FAILURE AND I CAN'T FIND ANY BATTERIES.

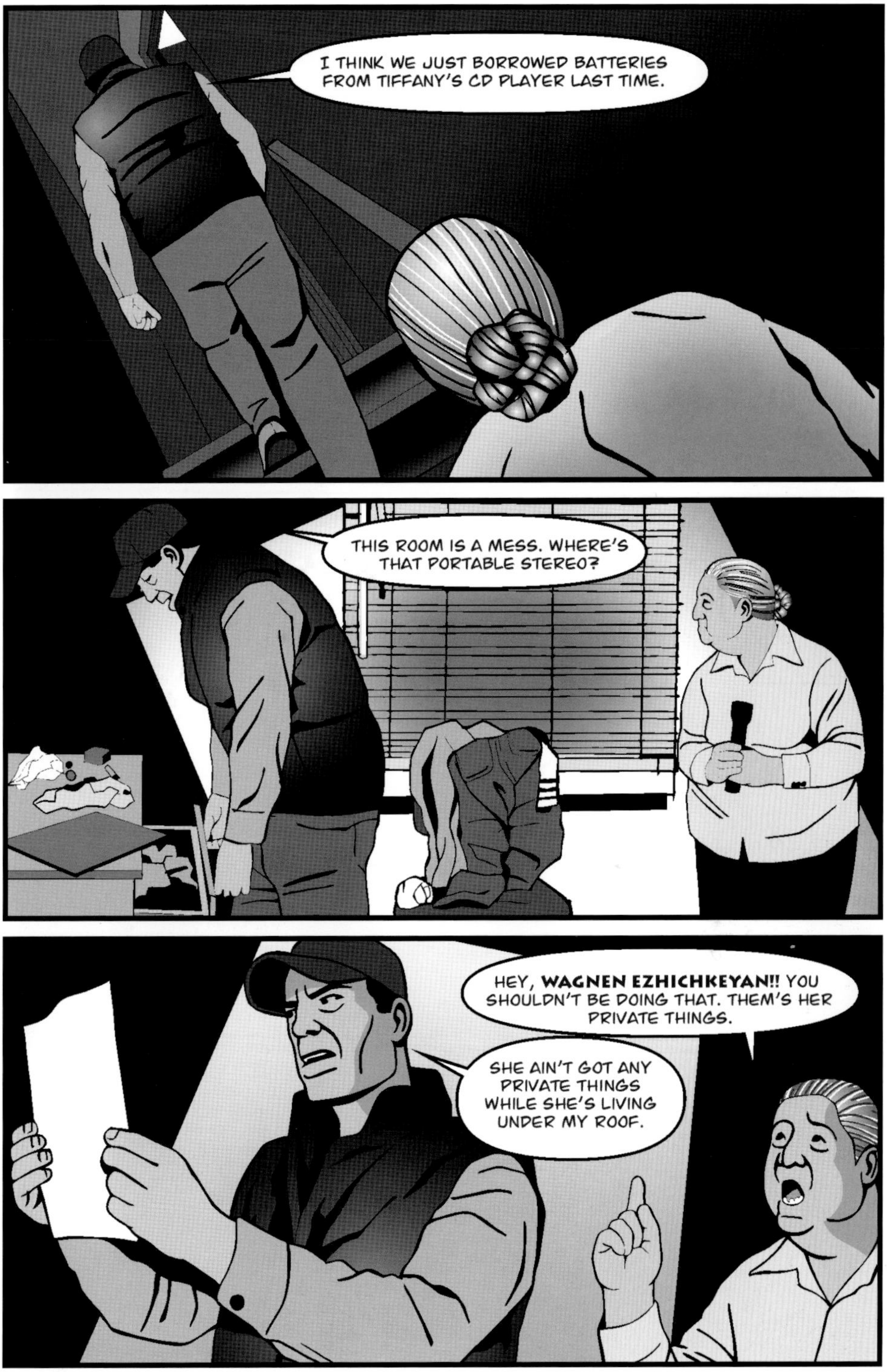
I THINK WE JUST BORROWED BATTERIES FROM TIFFANY'S CD PLAYER LAST TIME.
THIS ROOM IS A MESS. WHERE'S THAT PORTABLE STEREO?
HEY, **WAGNEN EZHICHKEYAN!!** YOU SHOULDN'T BE DOING THAT. THEM'S HER PRIVATE THINGS.
SHE AIN'T GOT ANY PRIVATE THINGS WHILE SHE'S LIVING UNDER MY ROOF.

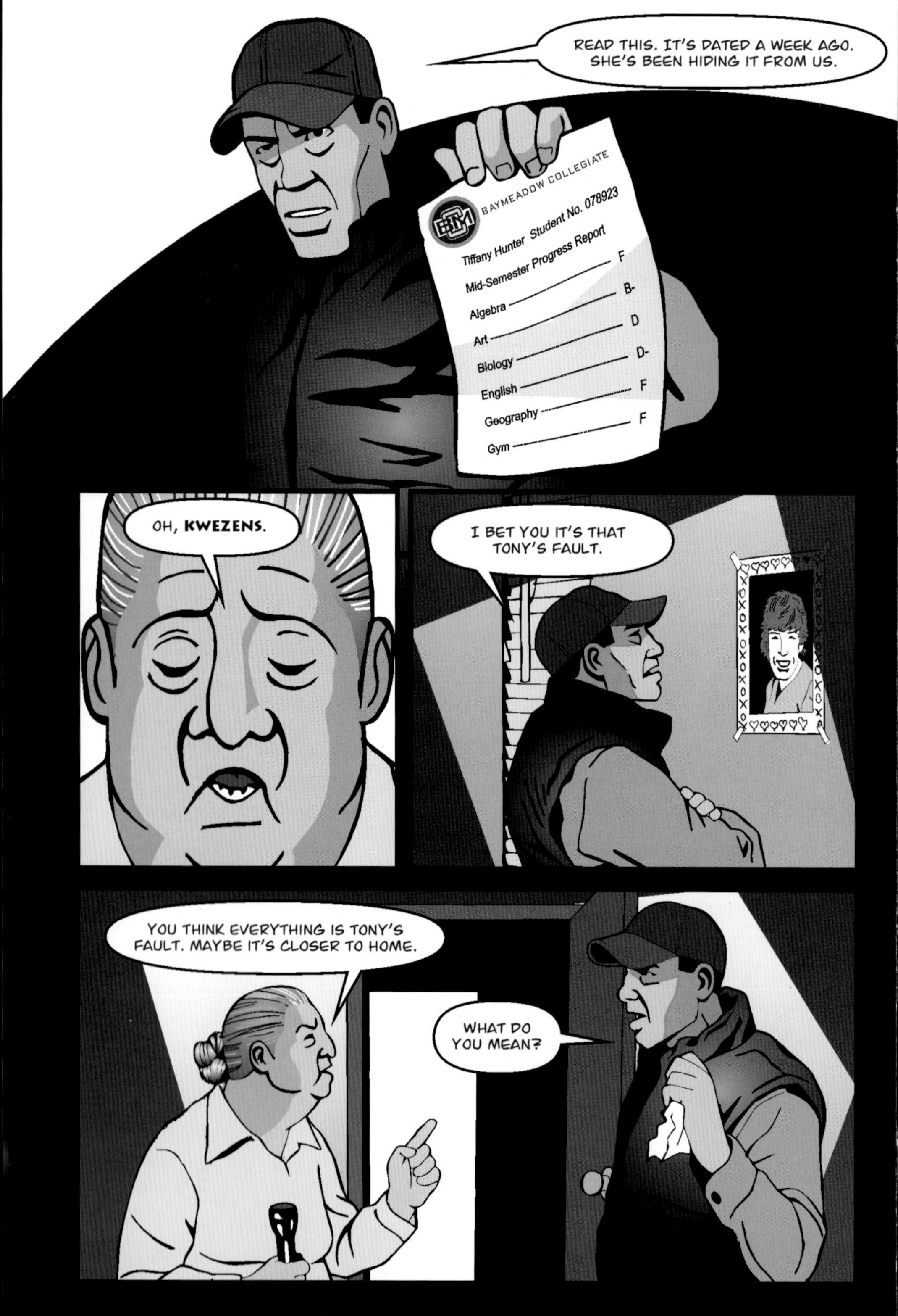
READ THIS. IT'S DATED A WEEK AGO. SHE'S BEEN HIDING IT FROM US.
BAYMEADOW COLLEGIATE
Tiffany Hunter Student No. 078923
Mid-Semester Progress Report
Algebra F
Art B-
Biology D
English D-
Geography F
Gym F
OH, KWEZENS.
I BET YOU IT'S THAT TONY'S FAULT.
YOU THINK EVERYTHING IS TONY'S FAULT. MAYBE IT'S CLOSER TO HOME.
WHAT DO YOU MEAN?

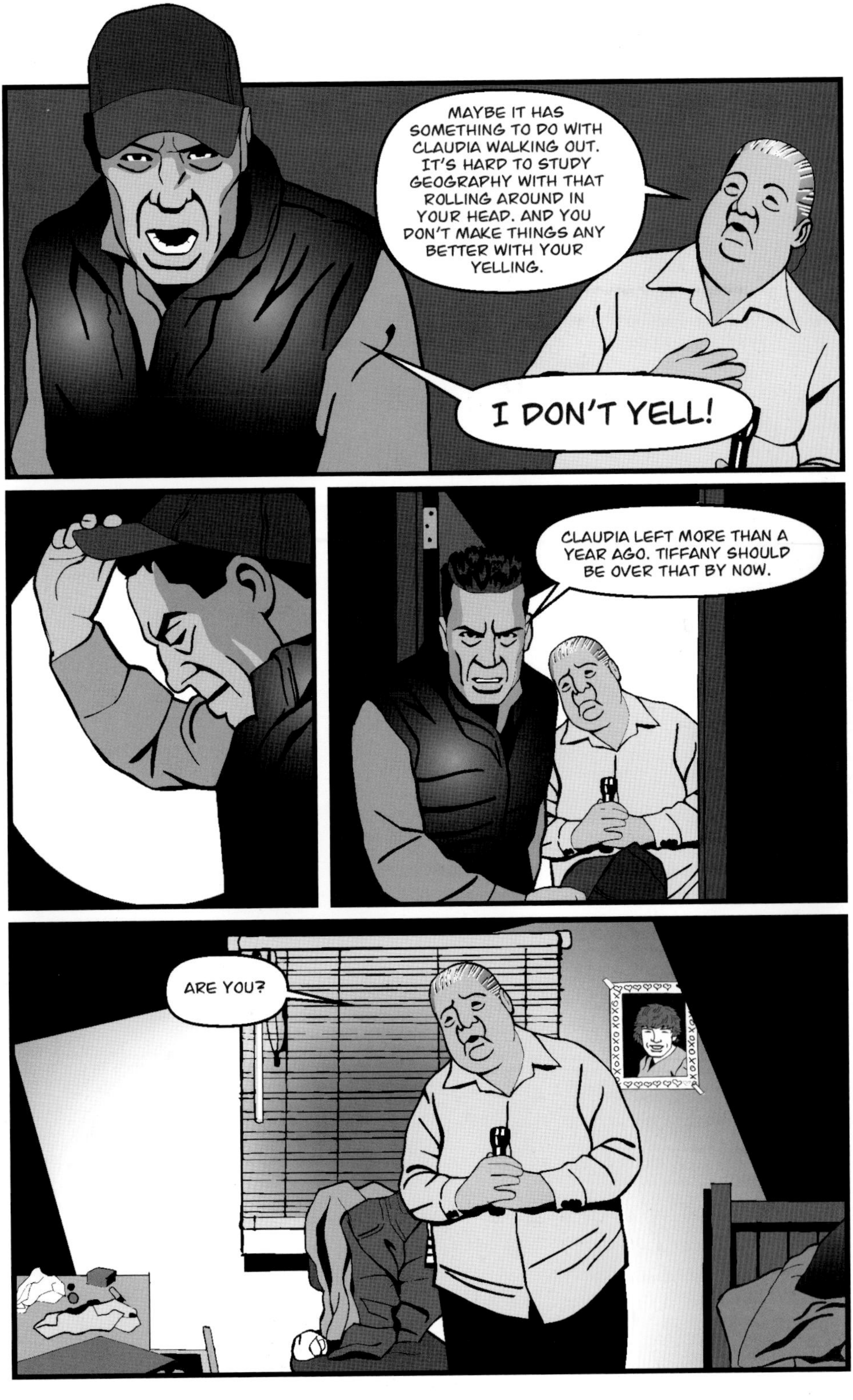
MAYBE IT HAS SOMETHING TO DO WITH CLAUDIA WALKING OUT. IT'S HARD TO STUDY GEOGRAPHY WITH THAT ROLLING AROUND IN YOUR HEAD. AND YOU DON'T MAKE THINGS ANY BETTER WITH YOUR YELLING.
I DON'T YELL!
CLAUDIA LEFT MORE THAN A YEAR AGO. TIFFANY SHOULD BE OVER THAT BY NOW.
ARE YOU?

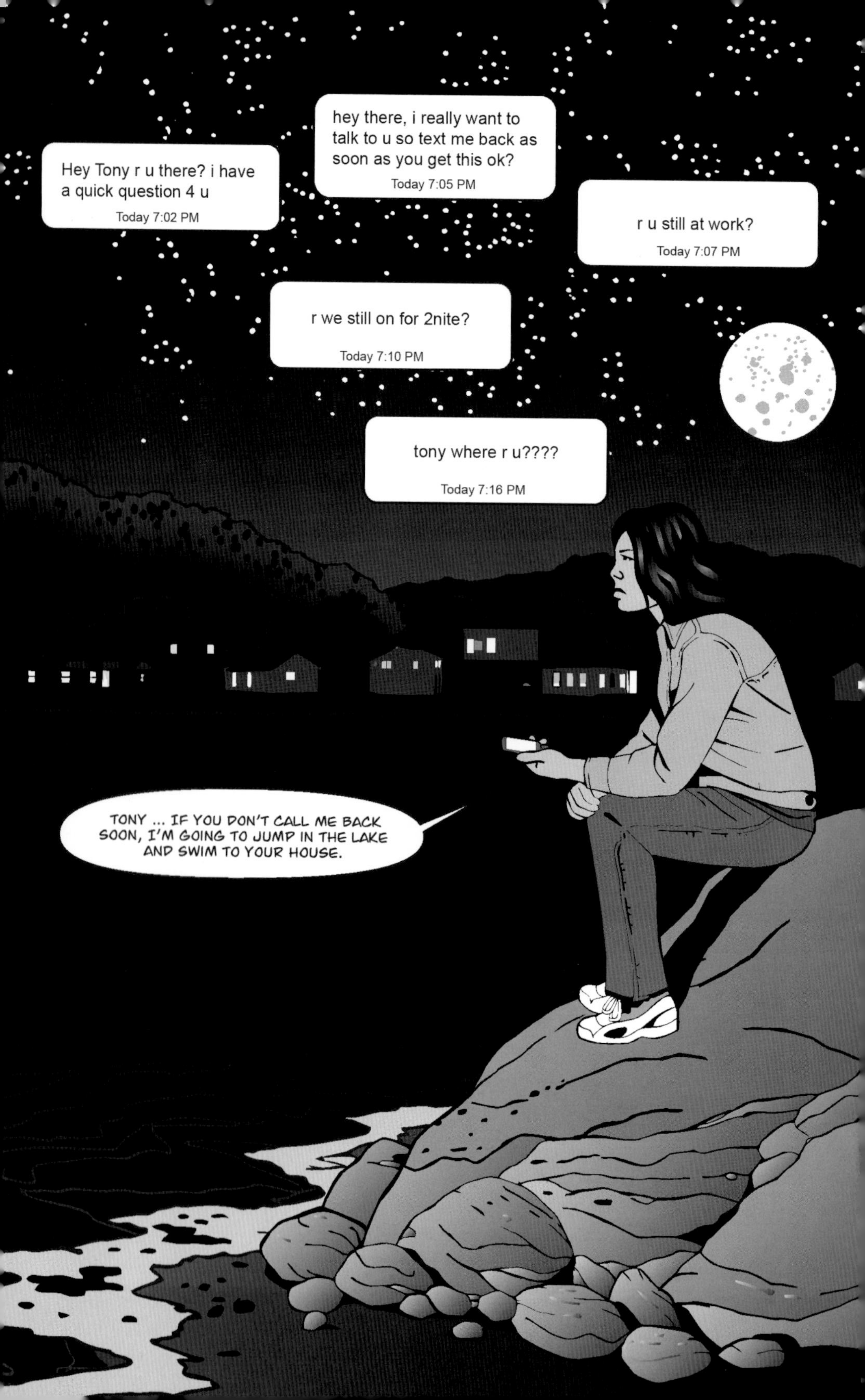
Hey Tony r u there? i have a quick question 4 u
Today 7:02 PM
hey there, i really want to talk to u so text me back as soon as you get this ok?
Today 7:05 PM
r u still at work?
Today 7:07 PM
r we still on for 2nite?
Today 7:10 PM
tony where r u????
Today 7:16 PM
TONY ... IF YOU DON'T CALL ME BACK SOON, I'M GOING TO JUMP IN THE LAKE AND SWIM TO YOUR HOUSE.

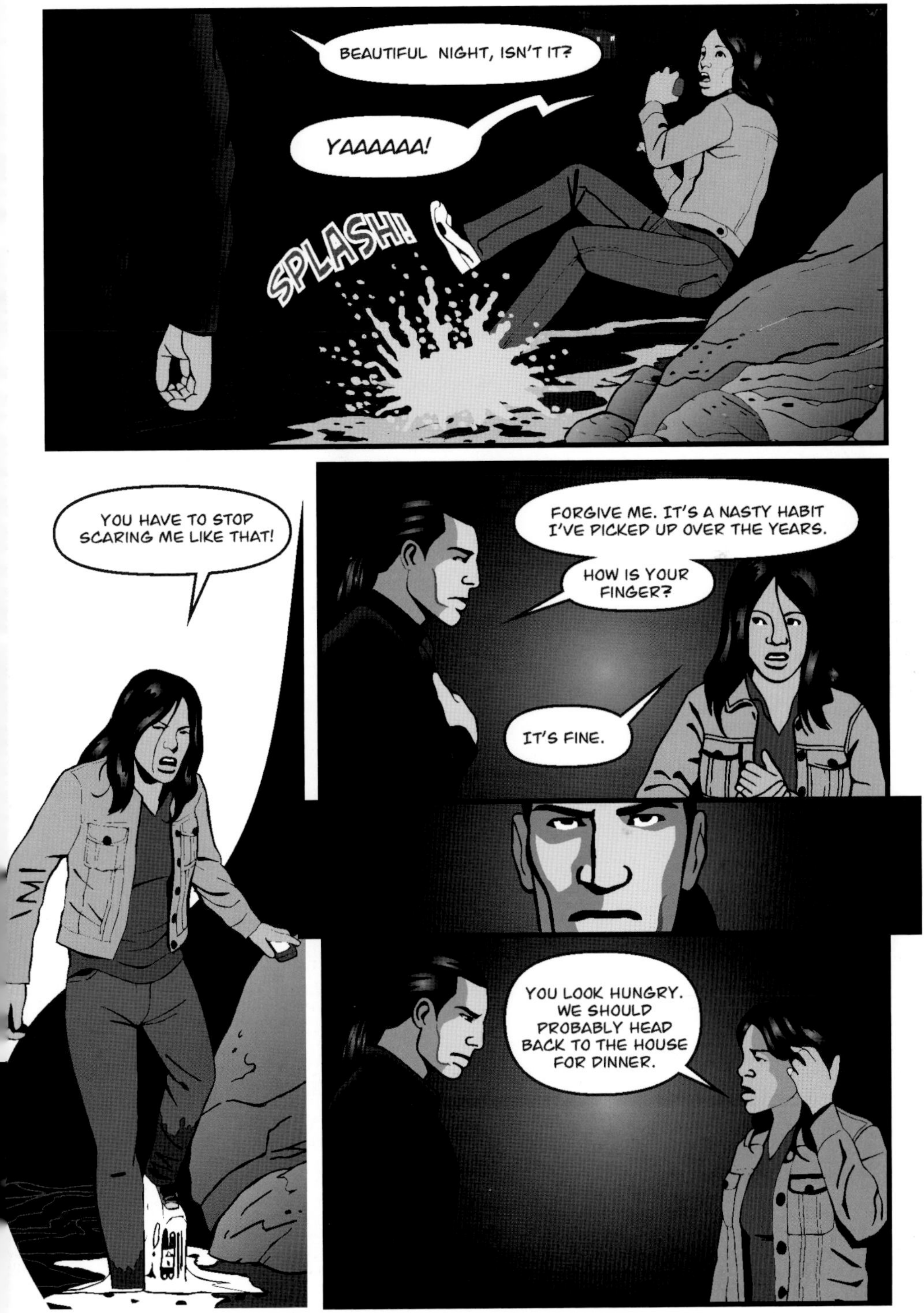
BEAUTIFUL NIGHT, ISN'T IT?
YAAAAAA!
SPLASH!
YOU HAVE TO STOP SCARING ME LIKE THAT!
FORGIVE ME. IT'S A NASTY HABIT I'VE PICKED UP OVER THE YEARS.
HOW IS YOUR FINGER?
IT'S FINE.
YOU LOOK HUNGRY. WE SHOULD PROBABLY HEAD BACK TO THE HOUSE FOR DINNER.

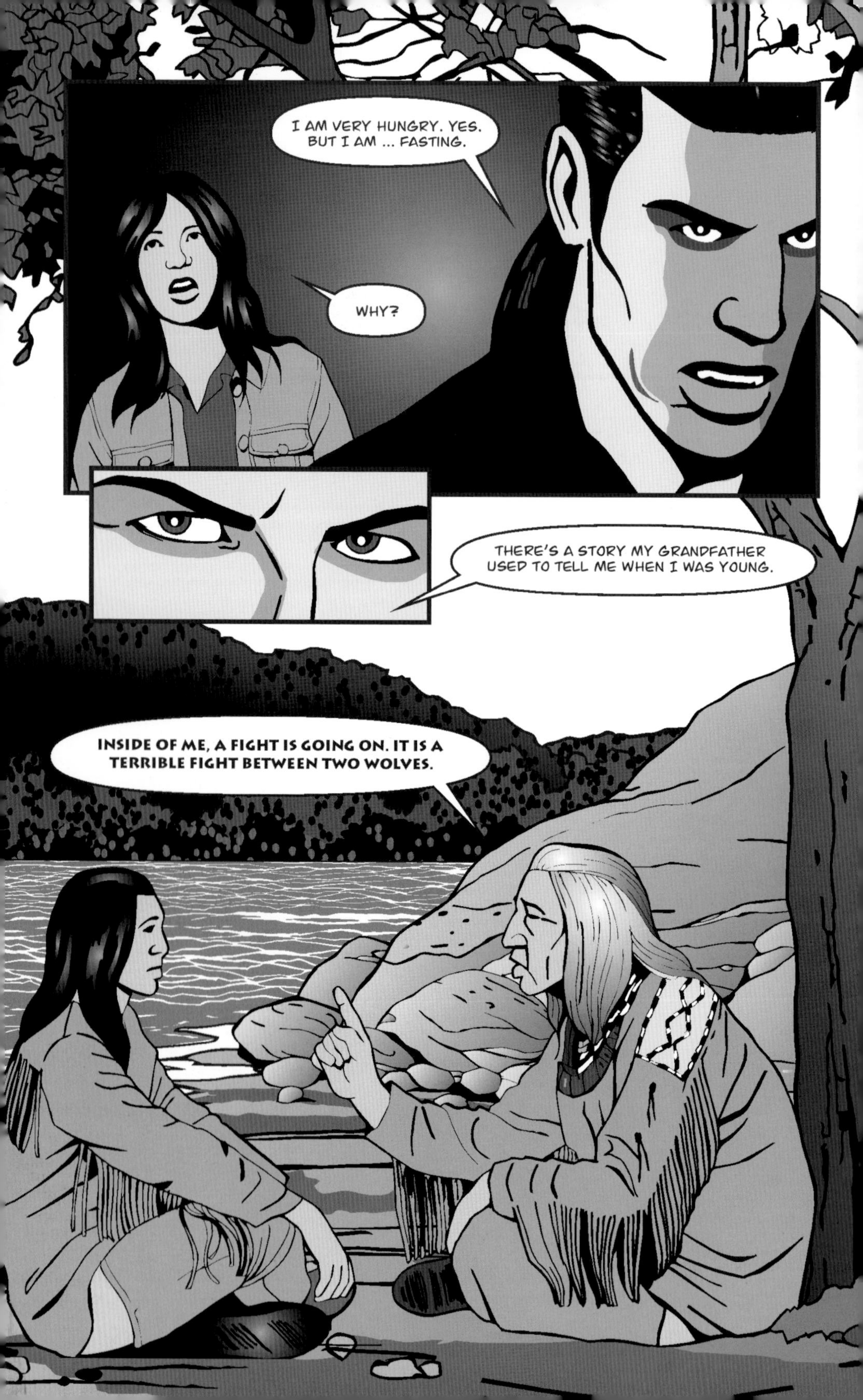
I AM VERY HUNGRY. YES. BUT I AM ... FASTING.
WHY?
THERE'S A STORY MY GRANDFATHER USED TO TELL ME WHEN I WAS YOUNG.
INSIDE OF ME, A FIGHT IS GOING ON. IT IS A TERRIBLE FIGHT BETWEEN TWO WOLVES.

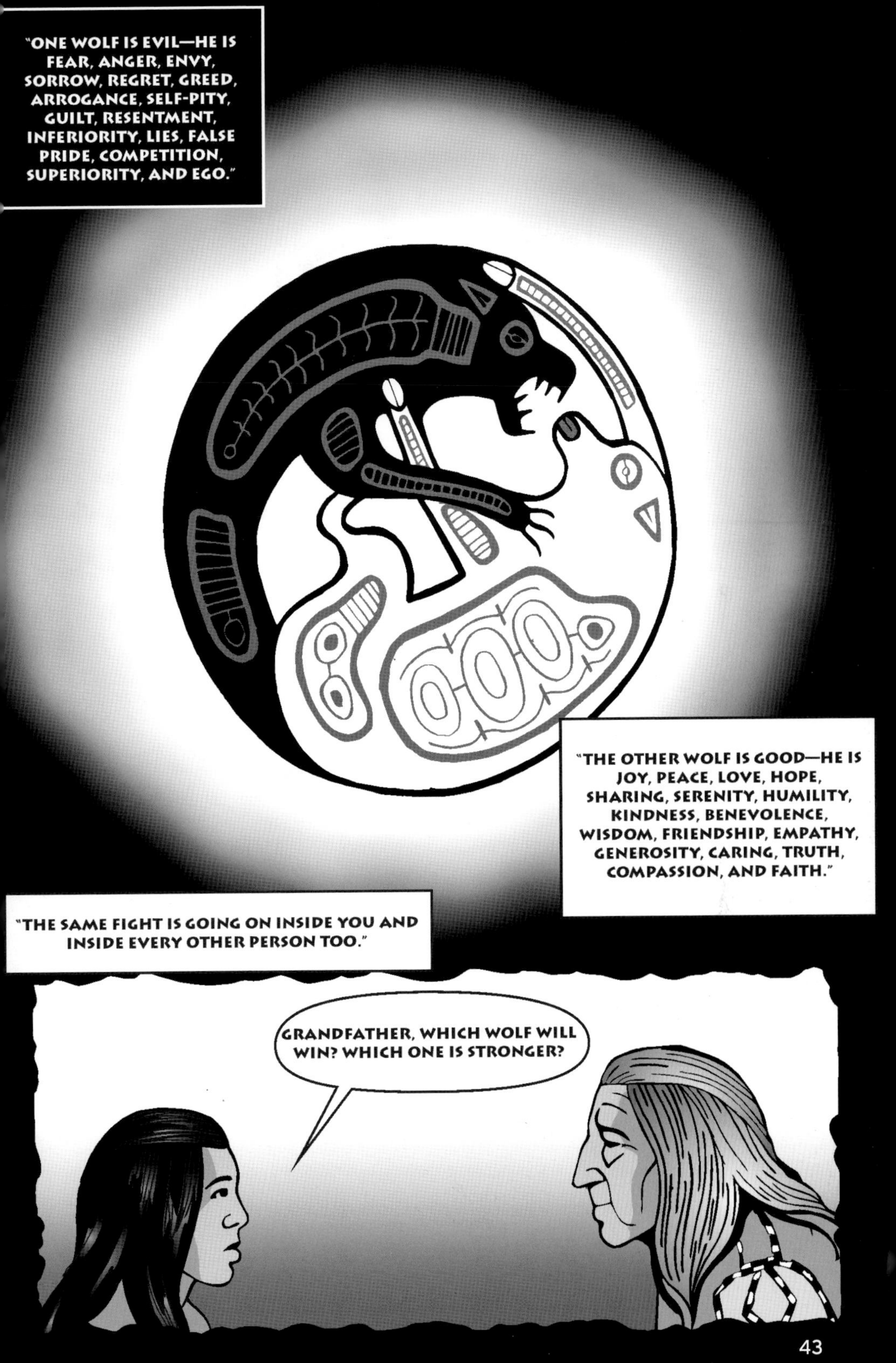
"ONE WOLF IS EVIL—HE IS FEAR, ANGER, ENVY, SORROW, REGRET, GREED, ARROGANCE, SELF-PITY, GUILT, RESENTMENT, INFERIORITY, LIES, FALSE PRIDE, COMPETITION, SUPERIORITY, AND EGO."
"THE OTHER WOLF IS GOOD—HE IS JOY, PEACE, LOVE, HOPE, SHARING, SERENITY, HUMILITY, KINDNESS, BENEVOLENCE, WISDOM, FRIENDSHIP, EMPATHY, GENEROSITY, CARING, TRUTH, COMPASSION, AND FAITH."
"THE SAME FIGHT IS GOING ON INSIDE YOU AND INSIDE EVERY OTHER PERSON TOO."
GRANDFATHER, WHICH WOLF WILL WIN? WHICH ONE IS STRONGER?

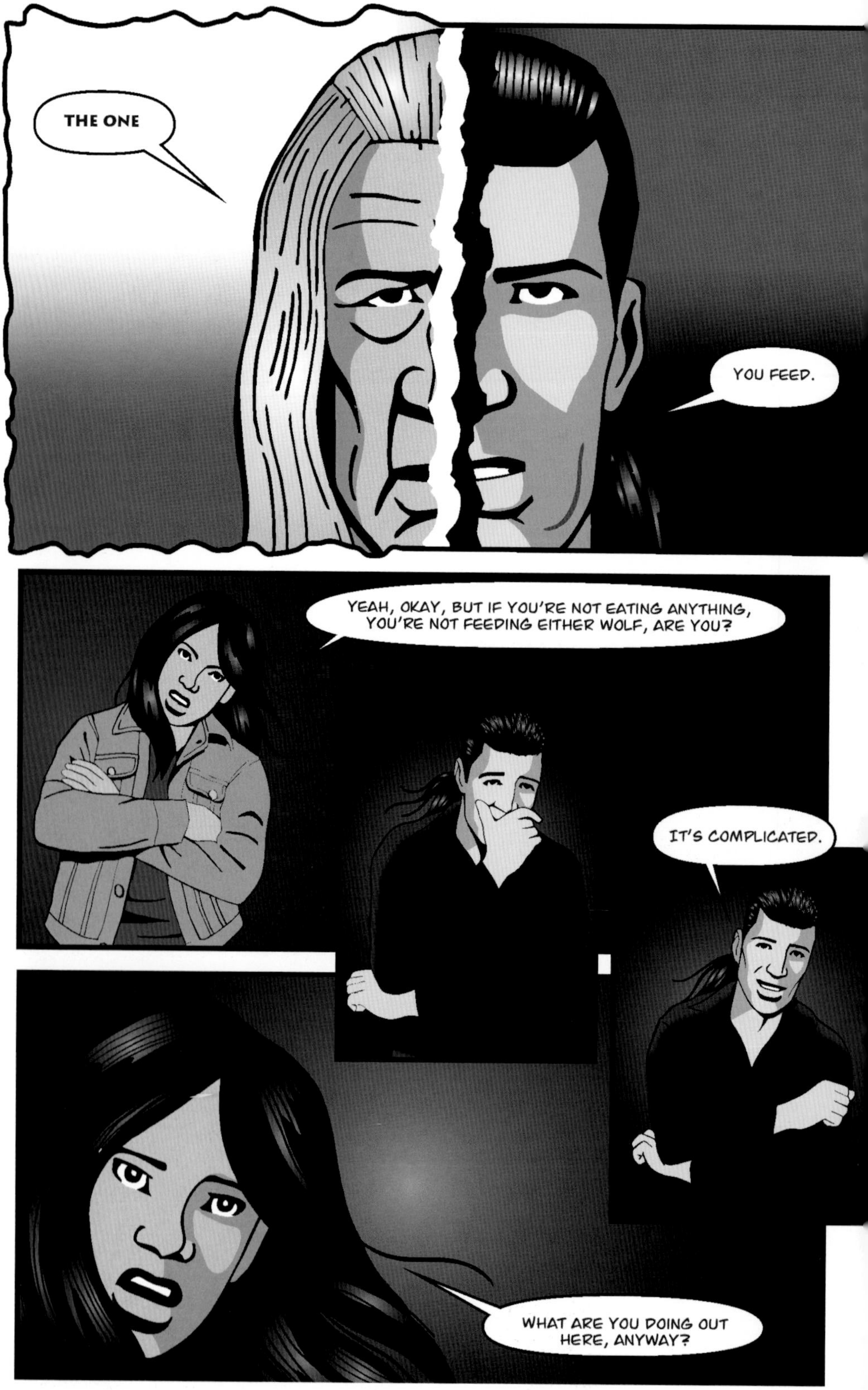
THE ONE
YOU FEED.
YEAH, OKAY, BUT IF YOU'RE NOT EATING ANYTHING, YOU'RE NOT FEEDING EITHER WOLF, ARE YOU?
IT'S COMPLICATED.
WHAT ARE YOU DOING OUT HERE, ANYWAY?

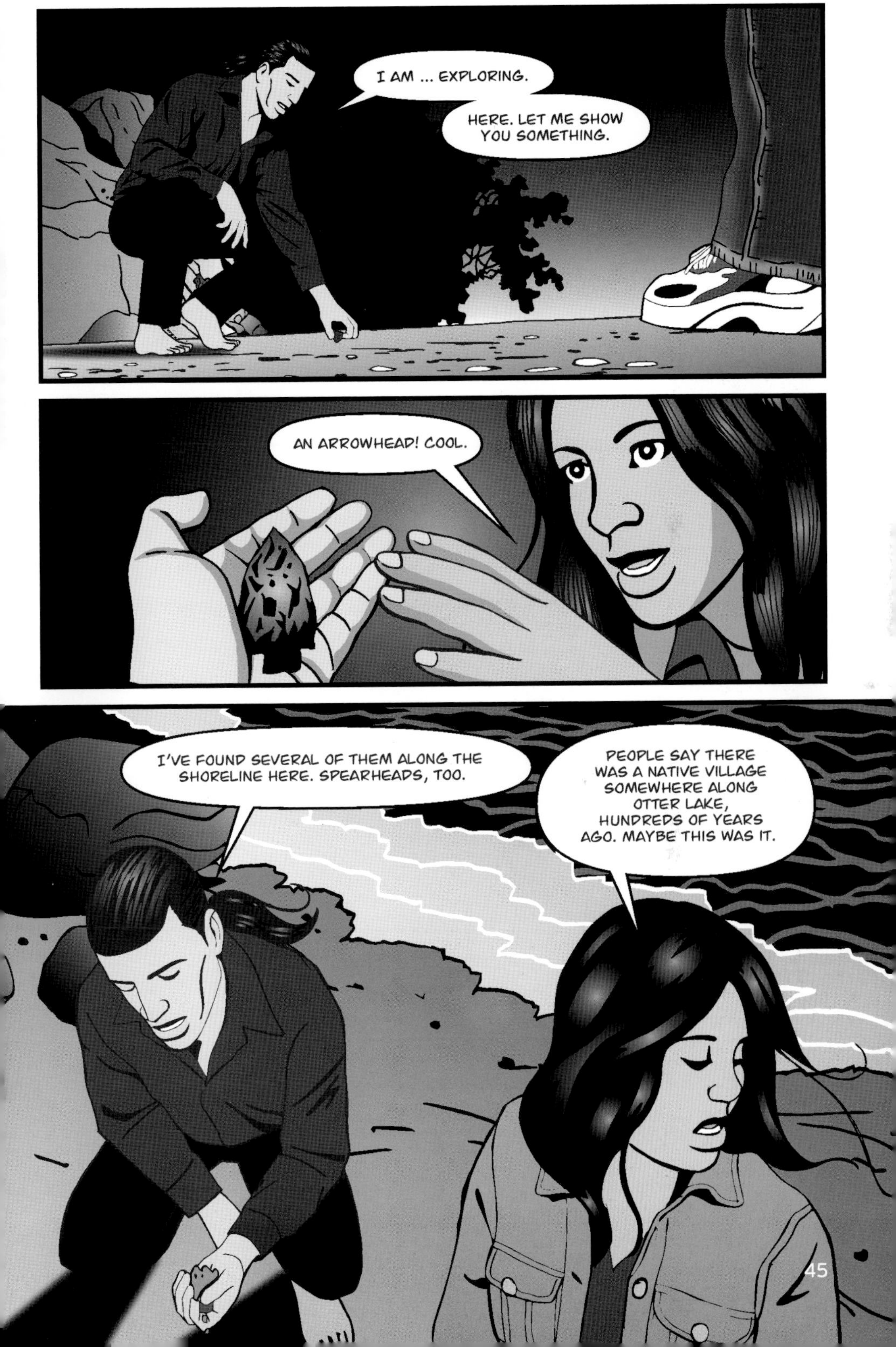
I AM ... EXPLORING.
HERE. LET ME SHOW YOU SOMETHING.
AN ARROWHEAD! COOL.
I'VE FOUND SEVERAL OF THEM ALONG THE SHORELINE HERE. SPEARHEADS, TOO.
PEOPLE SAY THERE WAS A NATIVE VILLAGE SOMEWHERE ALONG OTTER LAKE, HUNDREDS OF YEARS AGO. MAYBE THIS WAS IT.

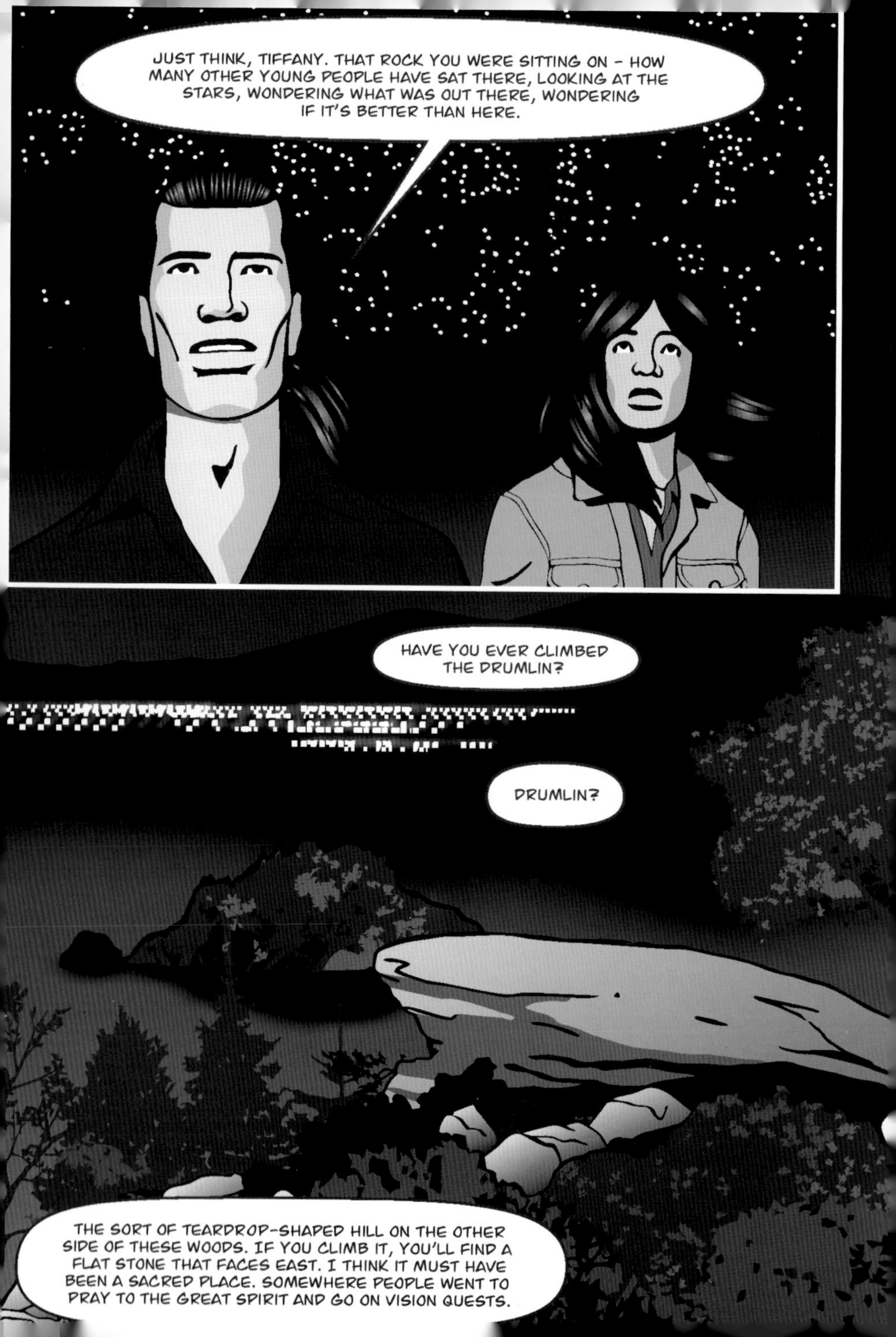
JUST THINK, TIFFANY. THAT ROCK YOU WERE SITTING ON – HOW MANY OTHER YOUNG PEOPLE HAVE SAT THERE, LOOKING AT THE STARS, WONDERING WHAT WAS OUT THERE, WONDERING IF IT'S BETTER THAN HERE.
HAVE YOU EVER CLIMBED THE DRUMLIN?
DRUMLIN?
THE SORT OF TEARDROP-SHAPED HILL ON THE OTHER SIDE OF THESE WOODS. IF YOU CLIMB IT, YOU'LL FIND A FLAT STONE THAT FACES EAST. I THINK IT MUST HAVE BEEN A SACRED PLACE. SOMEWHERE PEOPLE WENT TO PRAY TO THE GREAT SPIRIT AND GO ON VISION QUESTS.

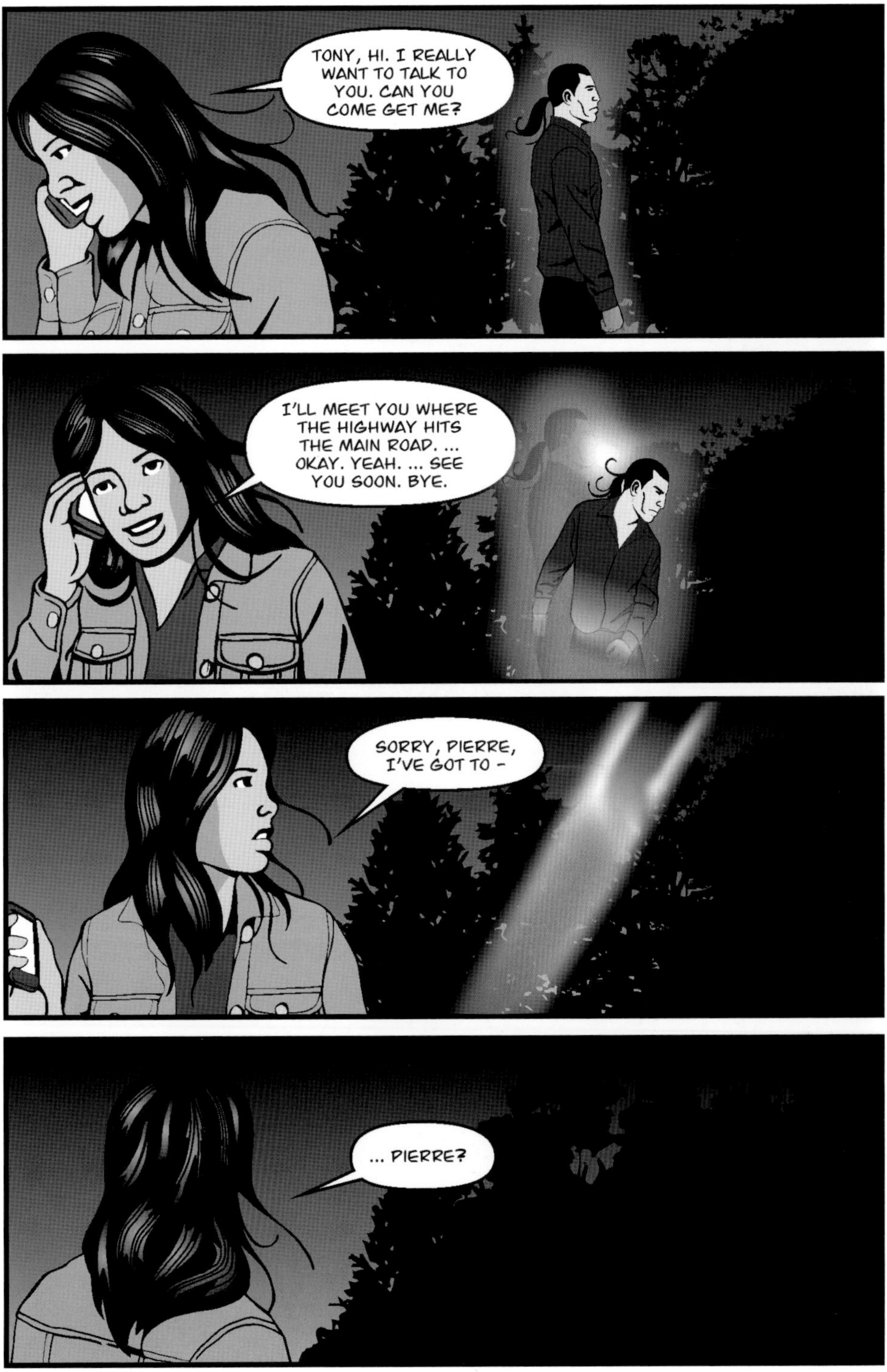
TONY, HI. I REALLY WANT TO TALK TO YOU. CAN YOU COME GET ME?
I'LL MEET YOU WHERE THE HIGHWAY HITS THE MAIN ROAD. ... OKAY. YEAH. ... SEE YOU SOON. BYE.
SORRY, PIERRE, I'VE GOT TO –
... PIERRE?

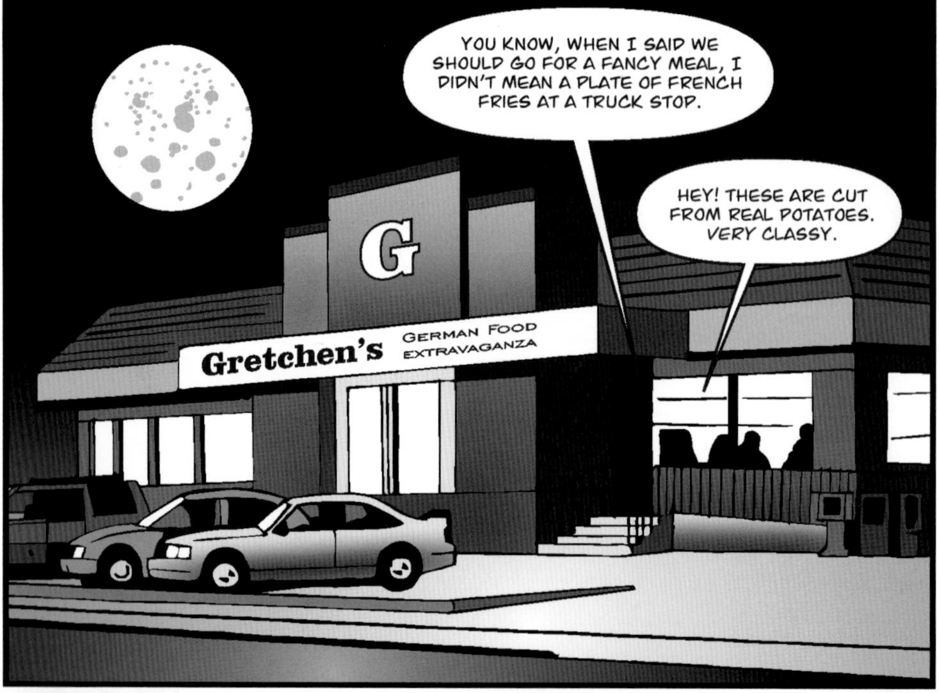
YOU KNOW, WHEN I SAID WE SHOULD GO FOR A FANCY MEAL, I DIDN'T MEAN A PLATE OF FRENCH FRIES AT A TRUCK STOP.
HEY! THESE ARE CUT FROM REAL POTATOES. VERY CLASSY.
G
Gretchen's
GERMAN FOOD
EXTRAVAGANZA

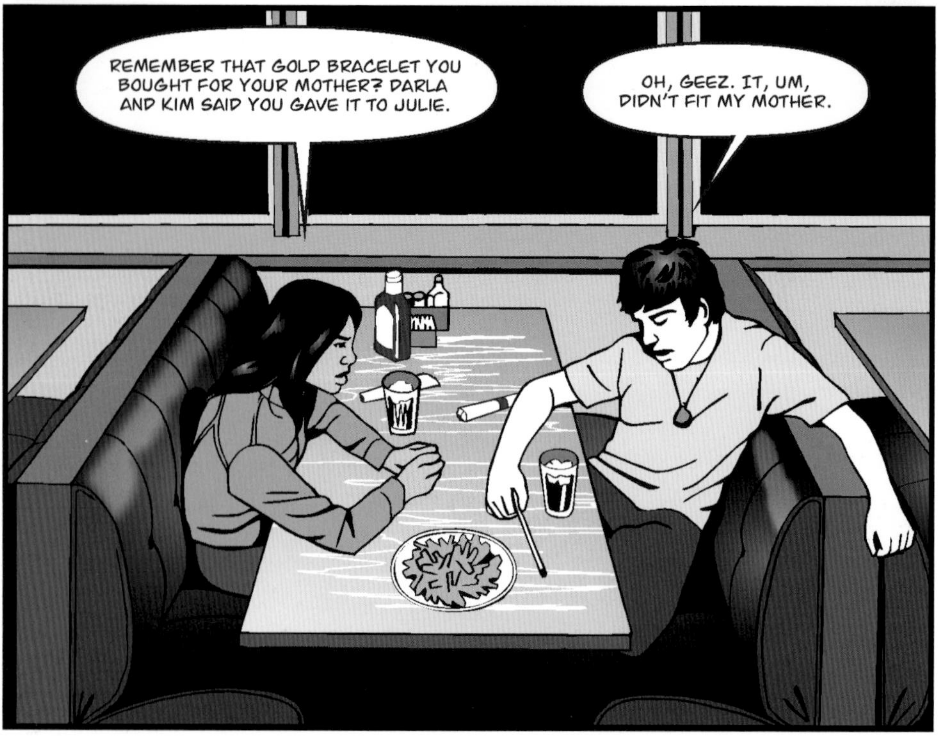
REMEMBER THAT GOLD BRACELET YOU BOUGHT FOR YOUR MOTHER? DARLA AND KIM SAID YOU GAVE IT TO JULIE.
OH, GEEZ. IT, UM, DIDN'T FIT MY MOTHER.

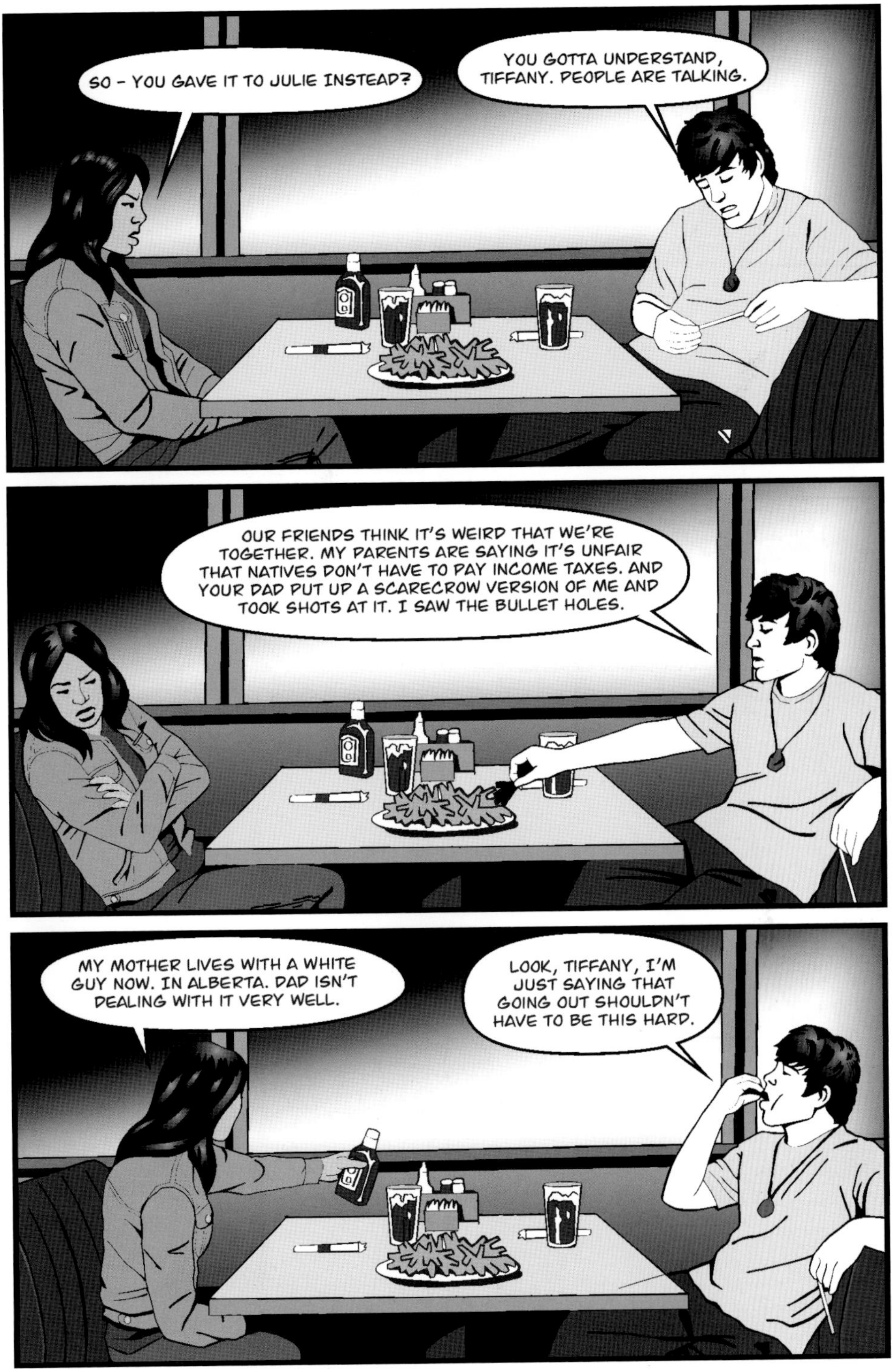
SO – YOU GAVE IT TO JULIE INSTEAD?
YOU GOTTA UNDERSTAND, TIFFANY. PEOPLE ARE TALKING.
OUR FRIENDS THINK IT'S WEIRD THAT WE'RE TOGETHER. MY PARENTS ARE SAYING IT'S UNFAIR THAT NATIVES DON'T HAVE TO PAY INCOME TAXES. AND YOUR DAD PUT UP A SCARECROW VERSION OF ME AND TOOK SHOTS AT IT. I SAW THE BULLET HOLES.
MY MOTHER LIVES WITH A WHITE GUY NOW. IN ALBERTA. DAD ISN'T DEALING WITH IT VERY WELL.
LOOK, TIFFANY, I'M JUST SAYING THAT GOING OUT SHOULDN'T HAVE TO BE THIS HARD.

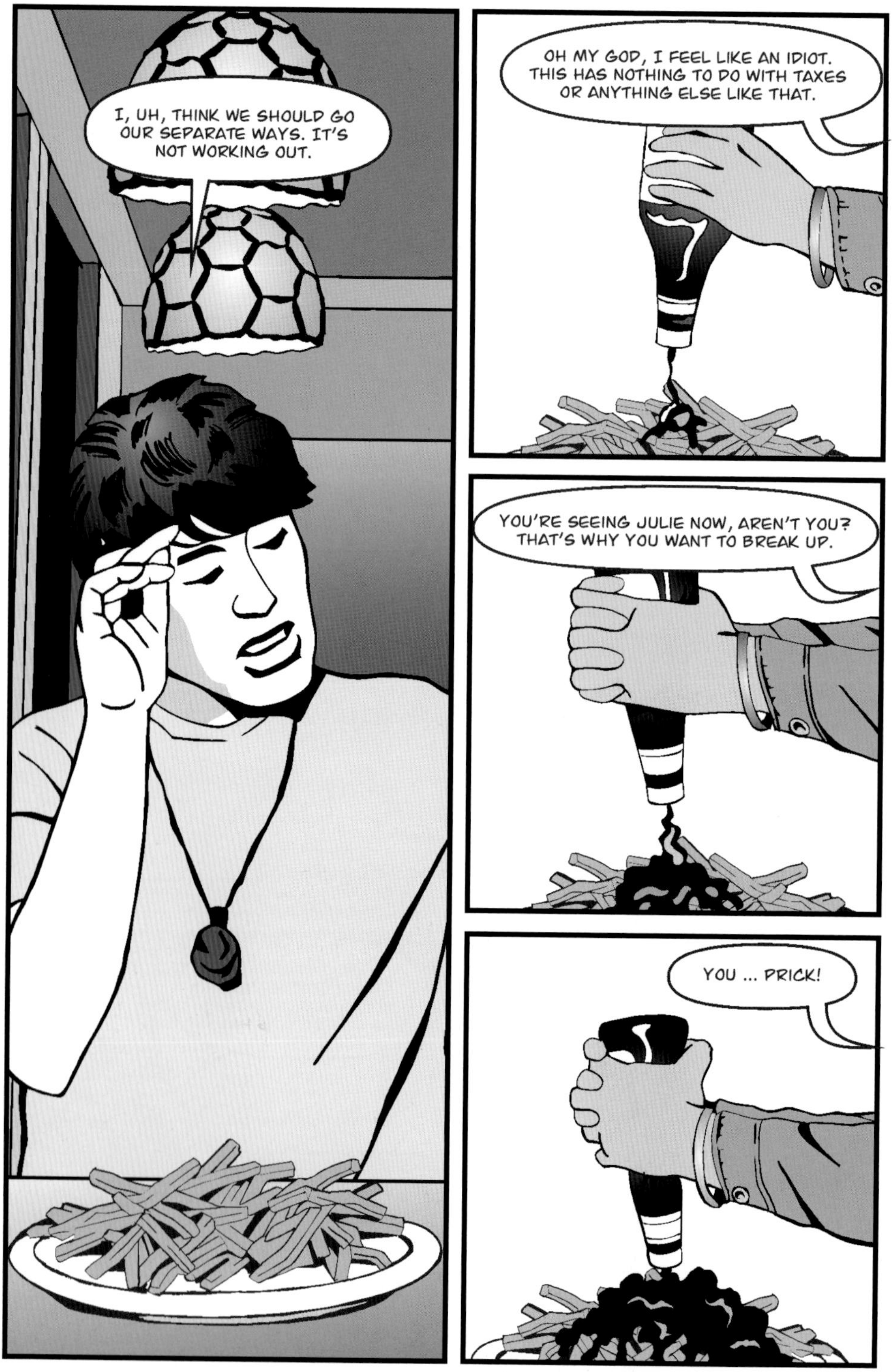
I, UH, THINK WE SHOULD GO OUR SEPARATE WAYS. IT'S NOT WORKING OUT.
OH MY GOD, I FEEL LIKE AN IDIOT. THIS HAS NOTHING TO DO WITH TAXES OR ANYTHING ELSE LIKE THAT.
YOU'RE SEEING JULIE NOW, AREN'T YOU? THAT'S WHY YOU WANT TO BREAK UP.
YOU ... PRICK!

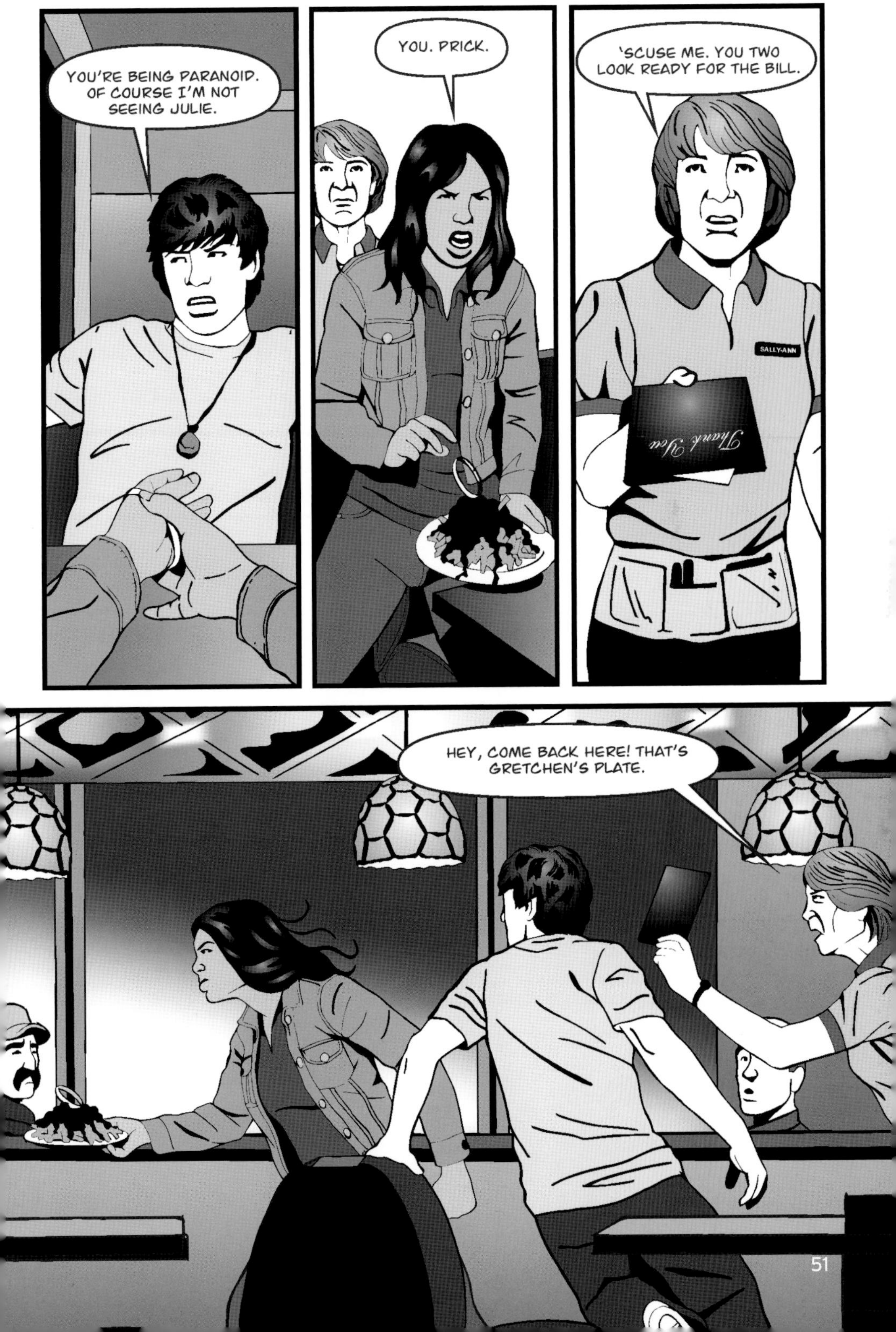
YOU'RE BEING PARANOID. OF COURSE I'M NOT SEEING JULIE.
YOU. PRICK.
'SCUSE ME. YOU TWO LOOK READY FOR THE BILL.
SALLY-ANN
HEY, COME BACK HERE! THAT'S GRETCHEN'S PLATE.

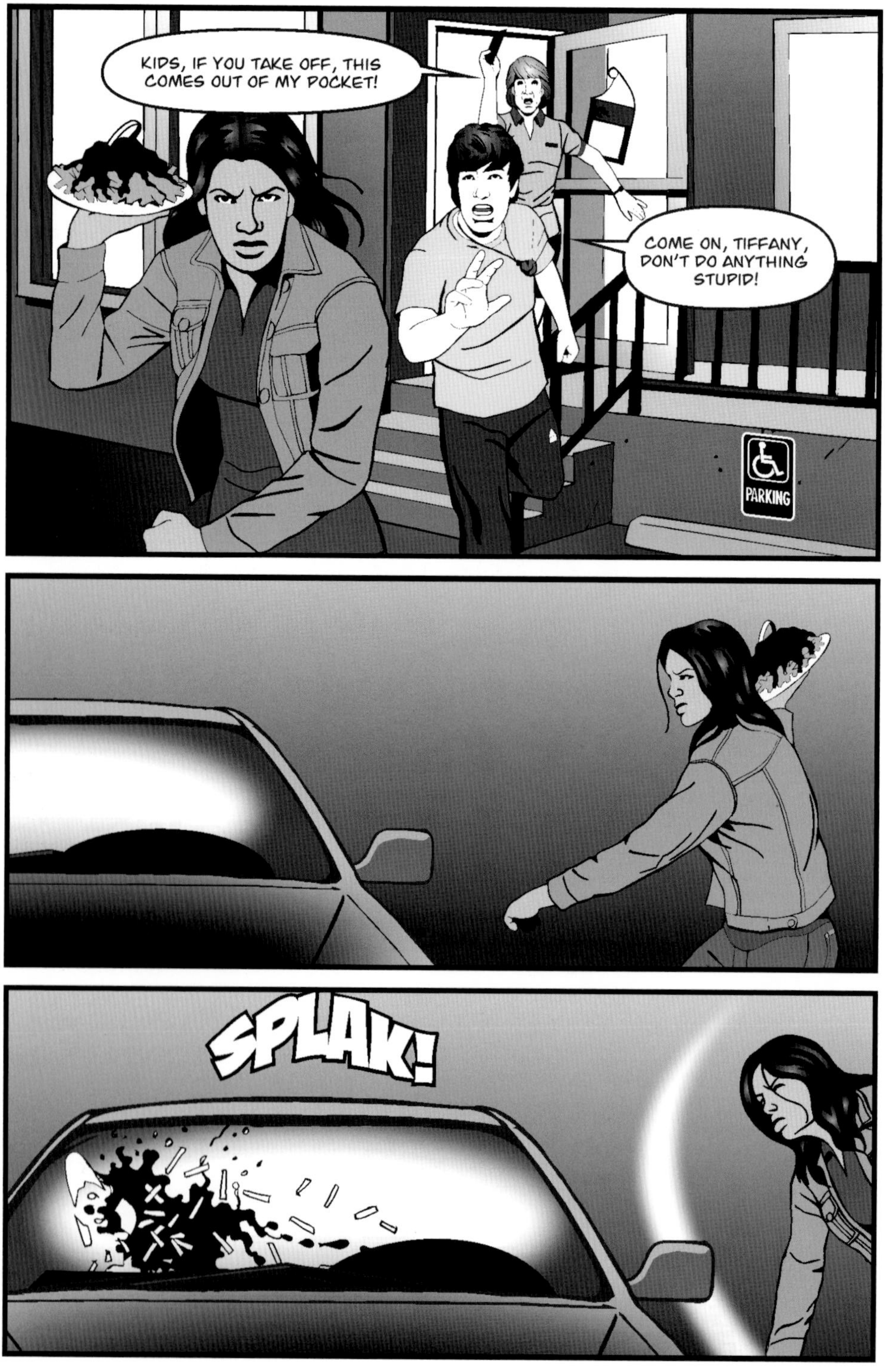
KIDS, IF YOU TAKE OFF, THIS COMES OUT OF MY POCKET!
COME ON, TIFFANY, DON'T DO ANYTHING STUPID!
PARKING
SPLAK!

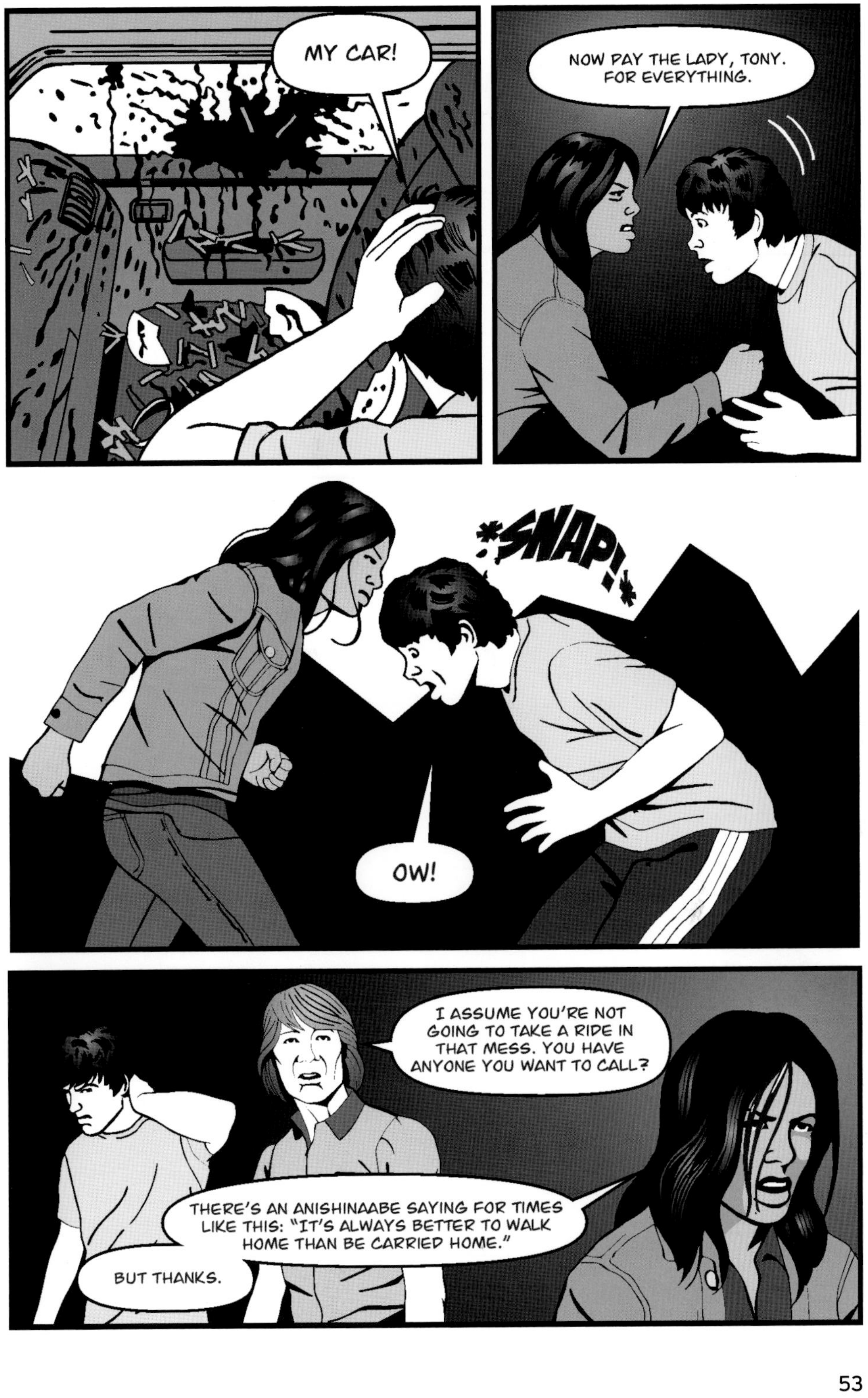
MY CAR!
NOW PAY THE LADY, TONY. FOR EVERYTHING.
SNAP!
OW!
I ASSUME YOU'RE NOT GOING TO TAKE A RIDE IN THAT MESS. YOU HAVE ANYONE YOU WANT TO CALL?
THERE'S AN ANISHINAABE SAYING FOR TIMES LIKE THIS: "IT'S ALWAYS BETTER TO WALK HOME THAN BE CARRIED HOME."
BUT THANKS.

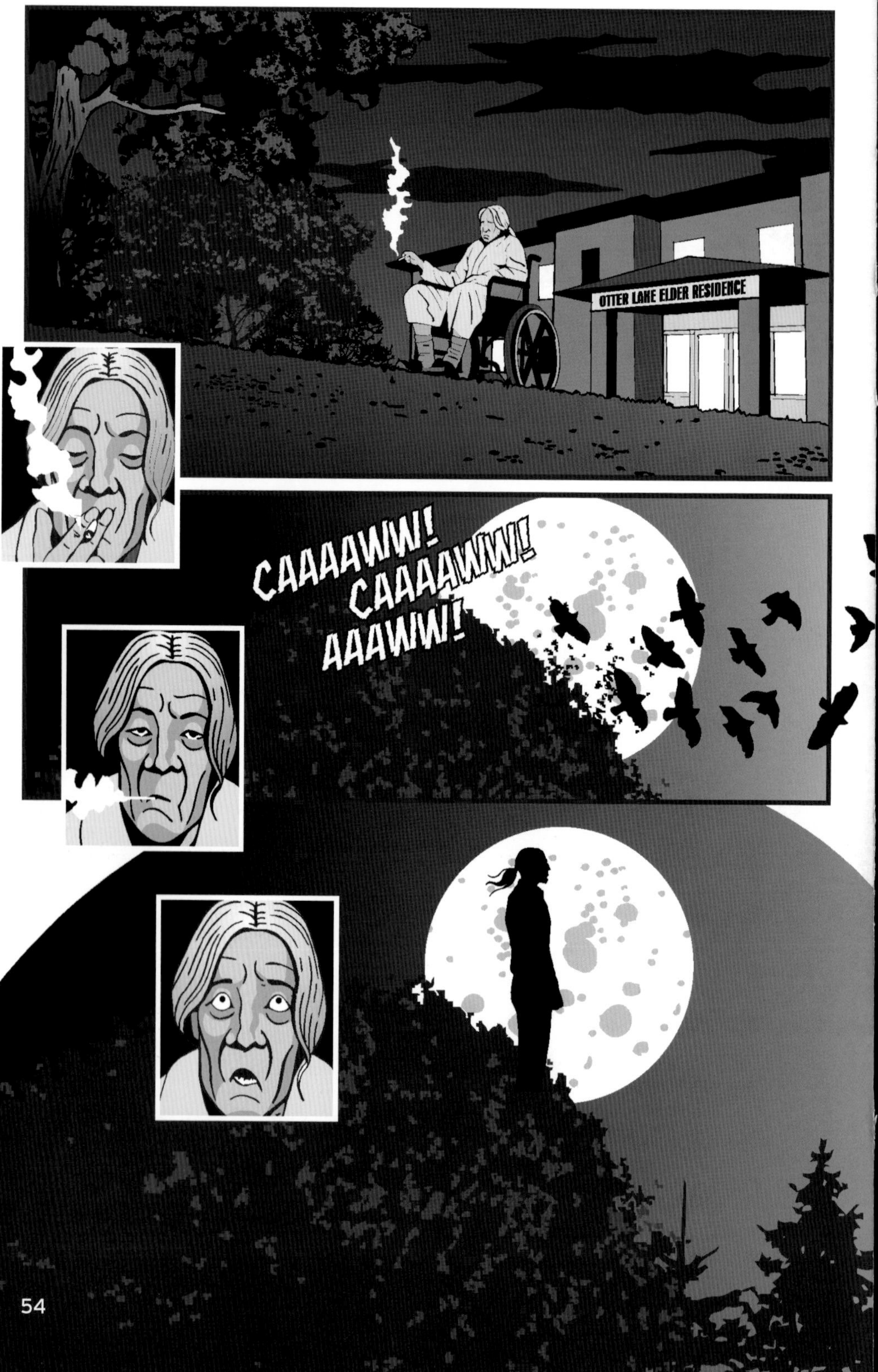
OTTER LAKE ELDER RESIDENCE
CAAAAWW!
CAAAAWW!
AAAWW!

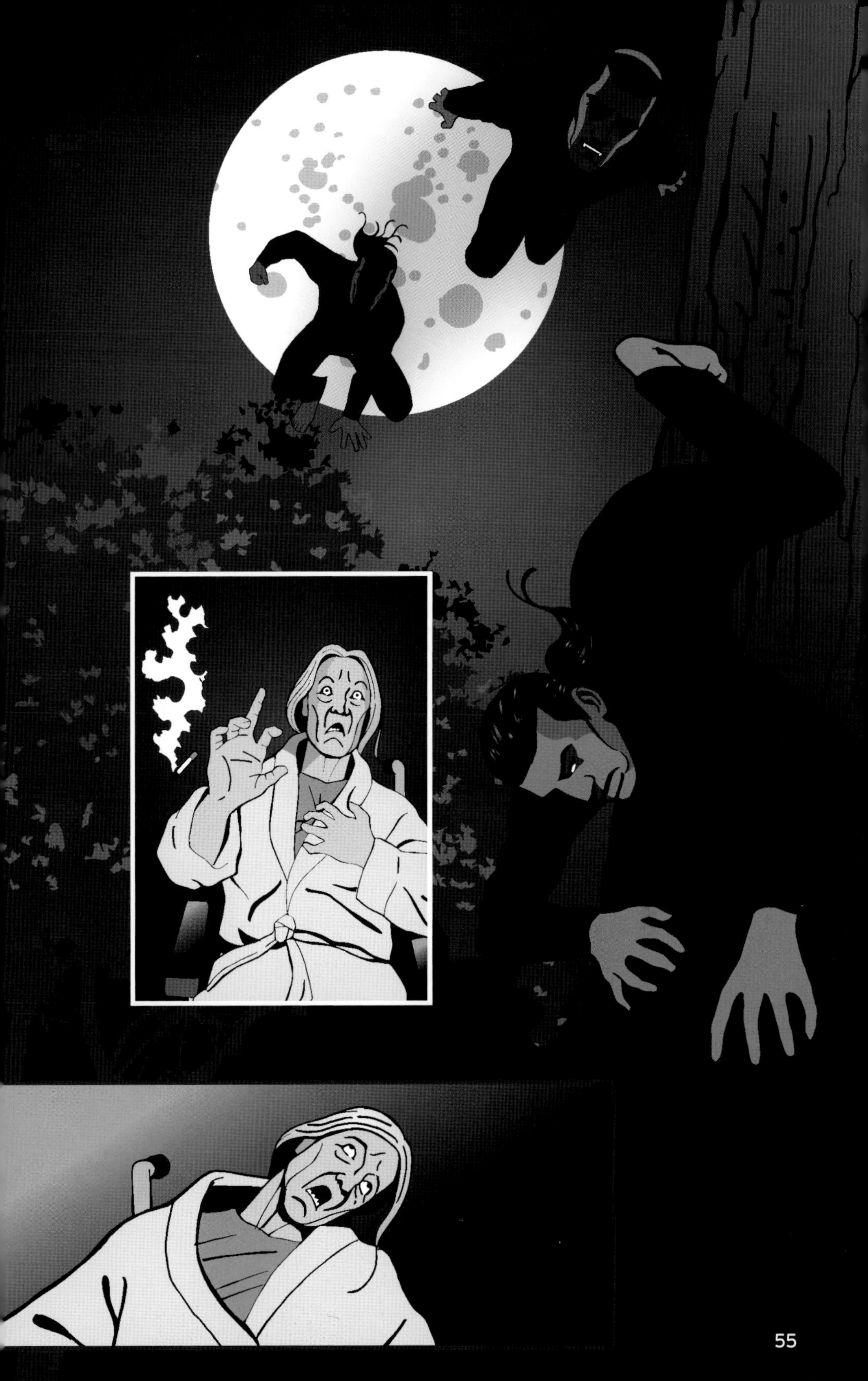

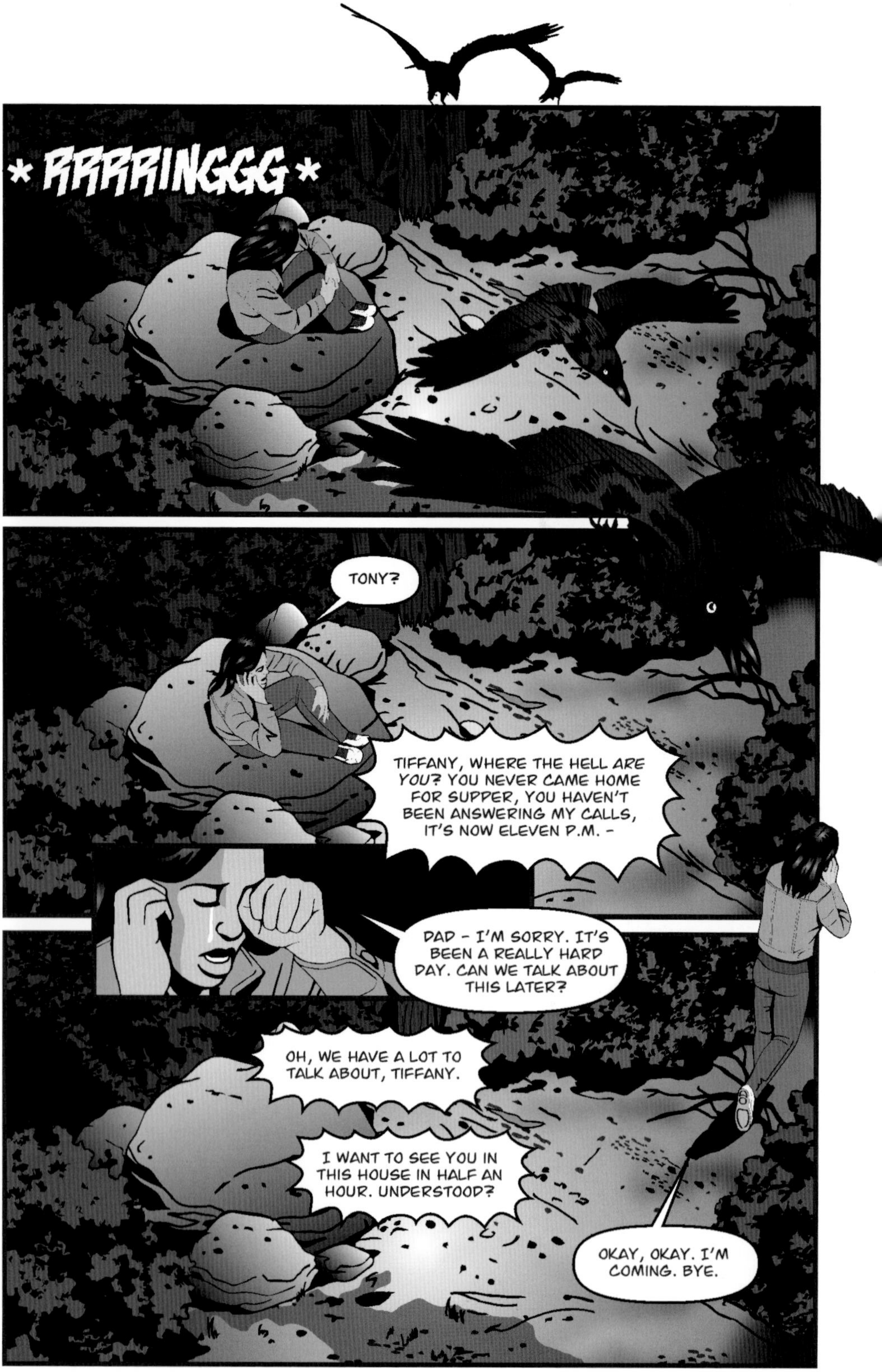
* RRRRINGGG *
TONY?
TIFFANY, WHERE THE HELL ARE YOU? YOU NEVER CAME HOME FOR SUPPER, YOU HAVEN'T BEEN ANSWERING MY CALLS, IT'S NOW ELEVEN P.M. –
DAD – I'M SORRY. IT'S BEEN A REALLY HARD DAY. CAN WE TALK ABOUT THIS LATER?
OH, WE HAVE A LOT TO TALK ABOUT, TIFFANY.
I WANT TO SEE YOU IN THIS HOUSE IN HALF AN HOUR. UNDERSTOOD?
OKAY, OKAY. I'M COMING. BYE.

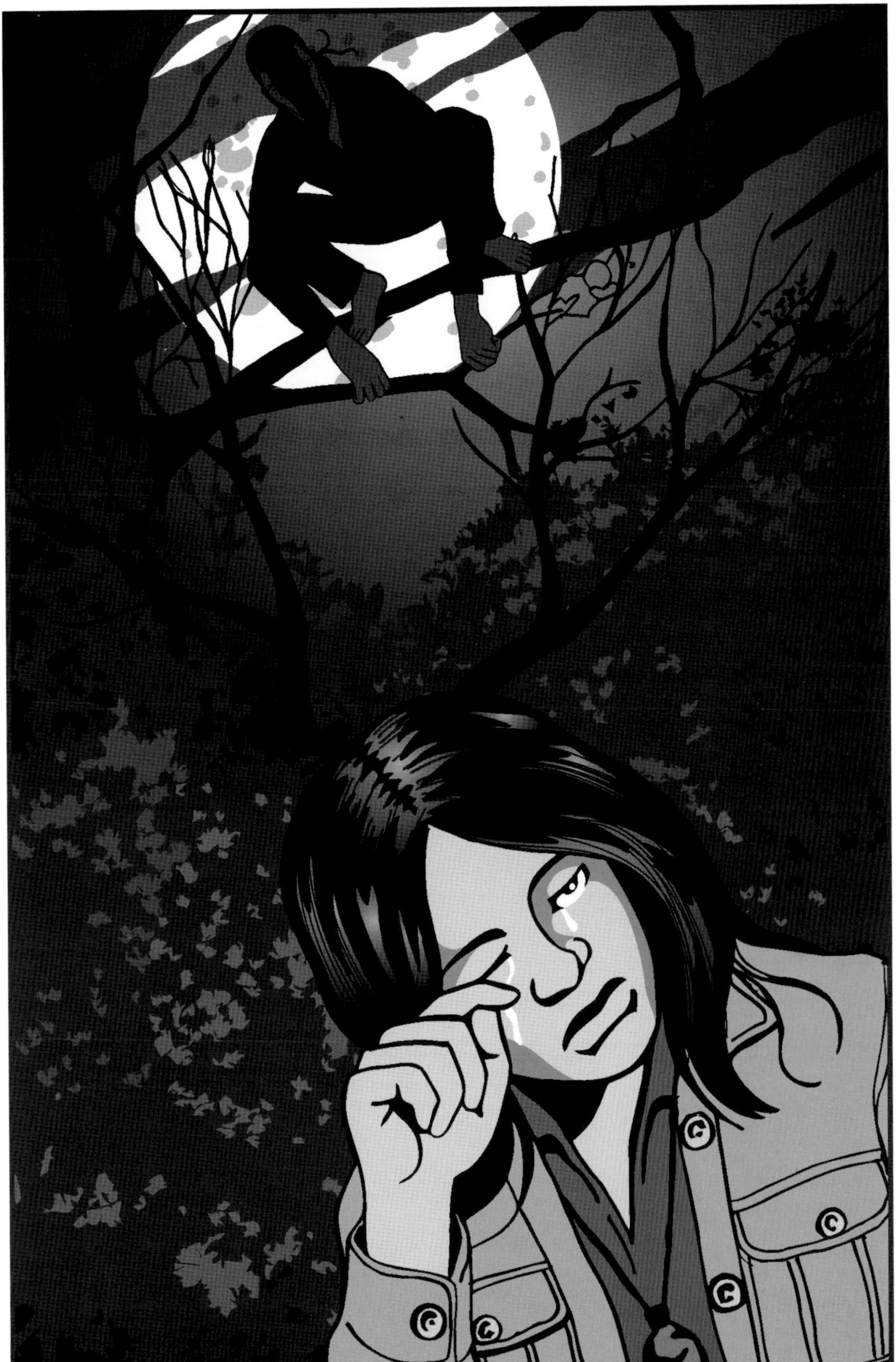

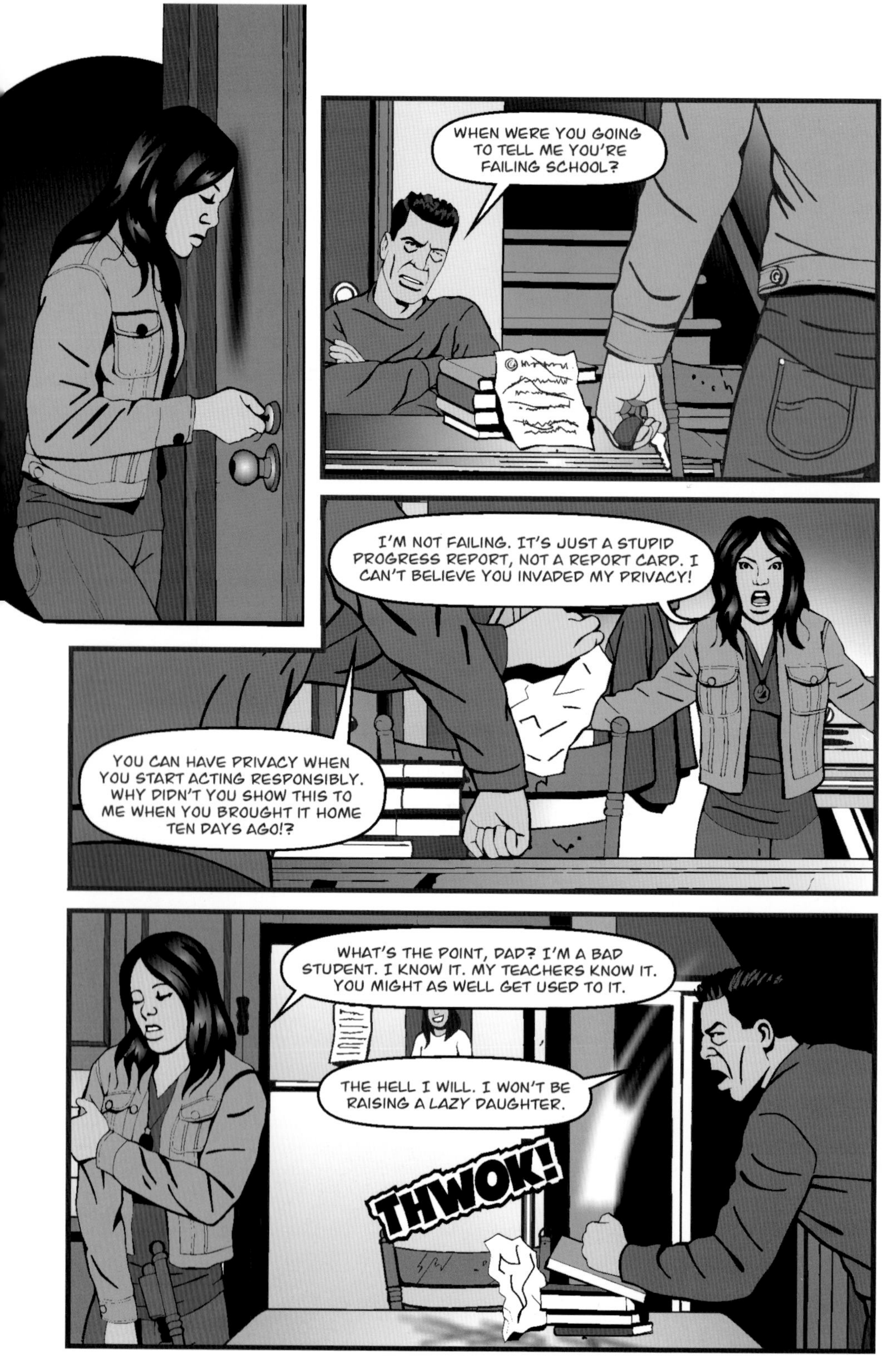

WHEN WERE YOU GOING TO TELL ME YOU'RE FAILING SCHOOL?
I'M NOT FAILING. IT'S JUST A STUPID PROGRESS REPORT, NOT A REPORT CARD. I CAN'T BELIEVE YOU INVADED MY PRIVACY!
YOU CAN HAVE PRIVACY WHEN YOU START ACTING RESPONSIBLY. WHY DIDN'T YOU SHOW THIS TO ME WHEN YOU BROUGHT IT HOME TEN DAYS AGO!?
WHAT'S THE POINT, DAD? I'M A BAD STUDENT. I KNOW IT. MY TEACHERS KNOW IT. YOU MIGHT AS WELL GET USED TO IT.
THE HELL I WILL. I WON'T BE RAISING A LAZY DAUGHTER.
THWOK!

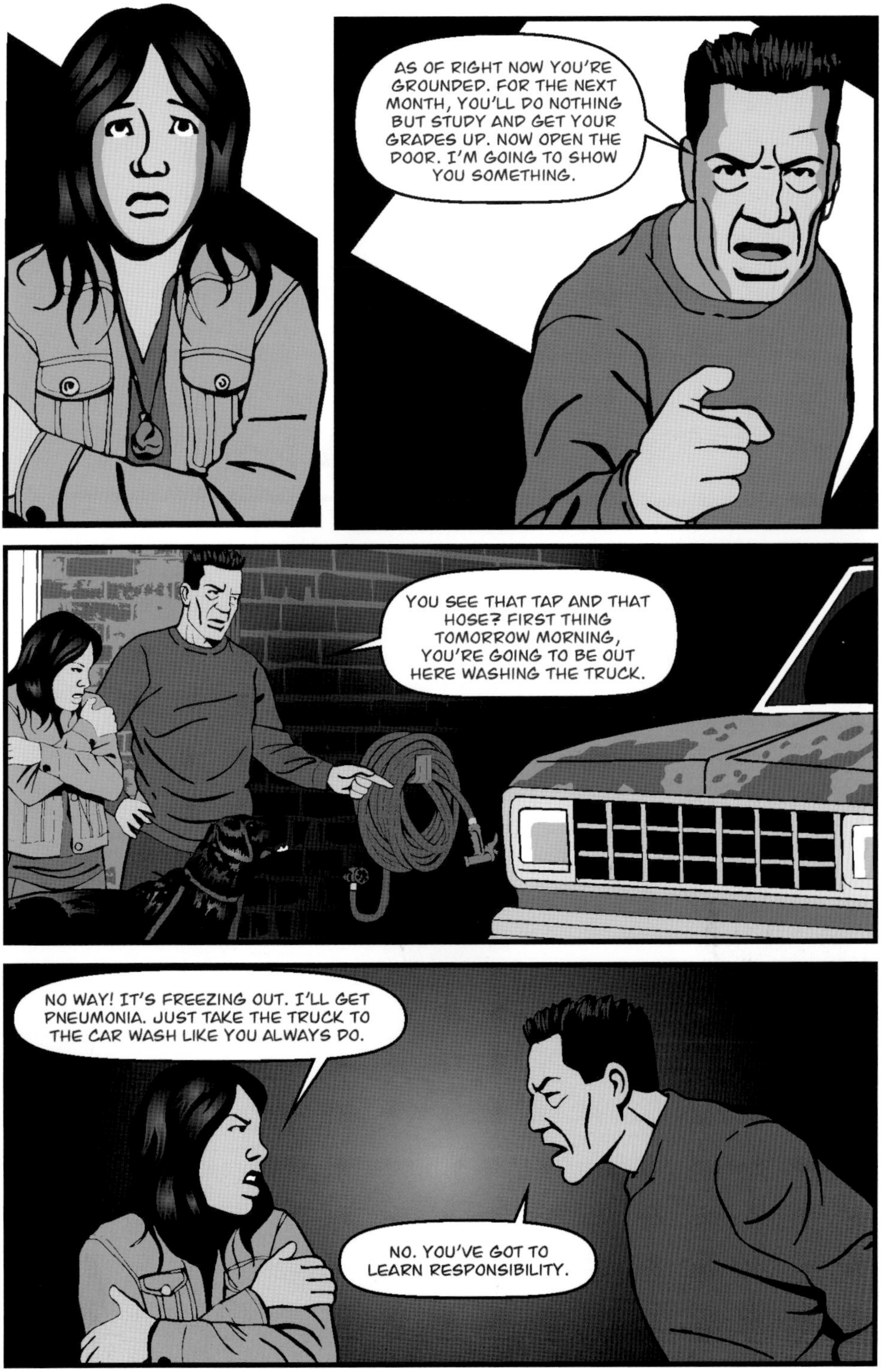
AS OF RIGHT NOW YOU'RE GROUNDED. FOR THE NEXT MONTH, YOU'LL DO NOTHING BUT STUDY AND GET YOUR GRADES UP. NOW OPEN THE DOOR. I'M GOING TO SHOW YOU SOMETHING.
YOU SEE THAT TAP AND THAT HOSE? FIRST THING TOMORROW MORNING, YOU'RE GOING TO BE OUT HERE WASHING THE TRUCK.
NO WAY! IT'S FREEZING OUT. I'LL GET PNEUMONIA. JUST TAKE THE TRUCK TO THE CAR WASH LIKE YOU ALWAYS DO.
NO. YOU'VE GOT TO LEARN RESPONSIBILITY.

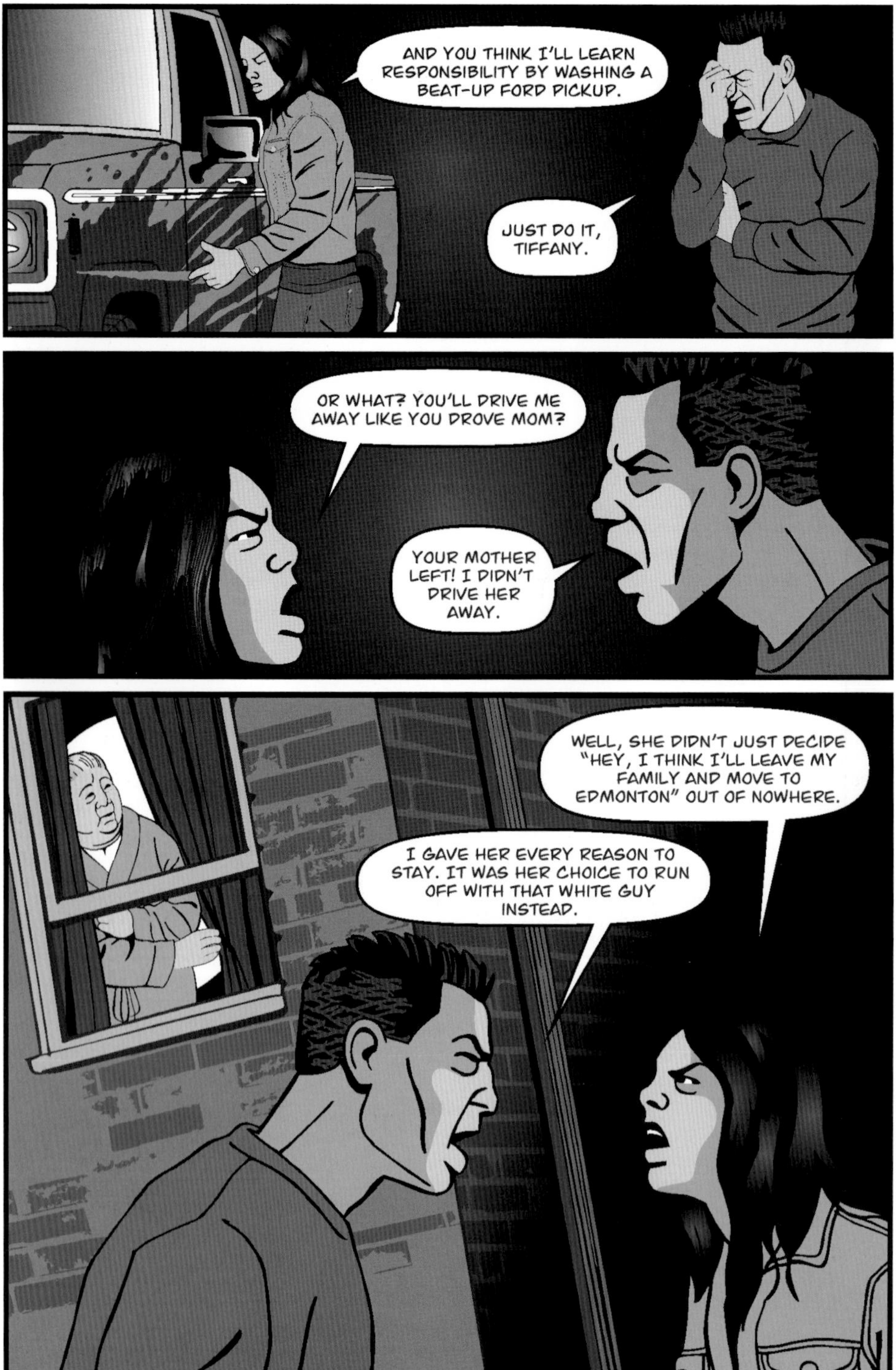
AND YOU THINK I'LL LEARN RESPONSIBILITY BY WASHING A BEAT-UP FORD PICKUP.
JUST DO IT, TIFFANY.
OR WHAT? YOU'LL DRIVE ME AWAY LIKE YOU DROVE MOM?
YOUR MOTHER LEFT! I DIDN'T DRIVE HER AWAY.
WELL, SHE DIDN'T JUST DECIDE "HEY, I THINK I'LL LEAVE MY FAMILY AND MOVE TO EDMONTON" OUT OF NOWHERE.
I GAVE HER EVERY REASON TO STAY. IT WAS HER CHOICE TO RUN OFF WITH THAT WHITE GUY INSTEAD.

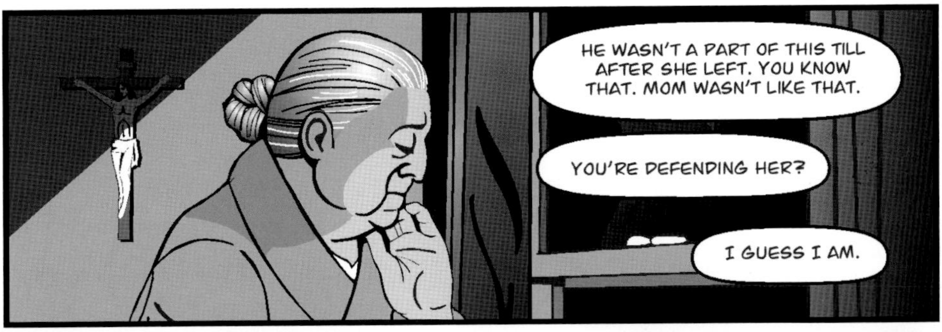
HE WASN'T A PART OF THIS TILL AFTER SHE LEFT. YOU KNOW THAT. MOM WASN'T LIKE THAT.
YOU'RE DEFENDING HER?
I GUESS I AM.

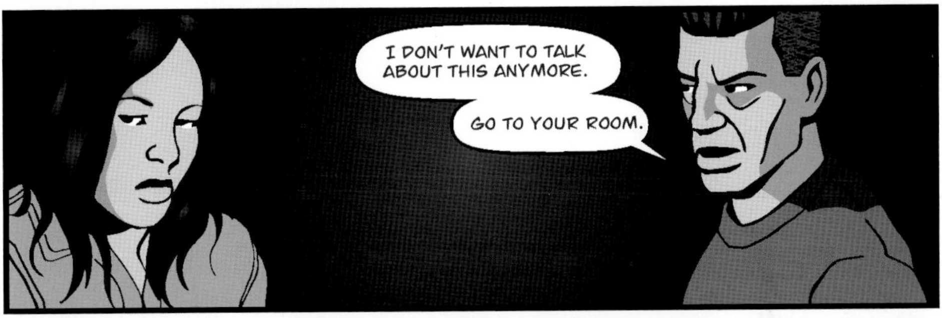
I DON'T WANT TO TALK ABOUT THIS ANYMORE.
GO TO YOUR ROOM.

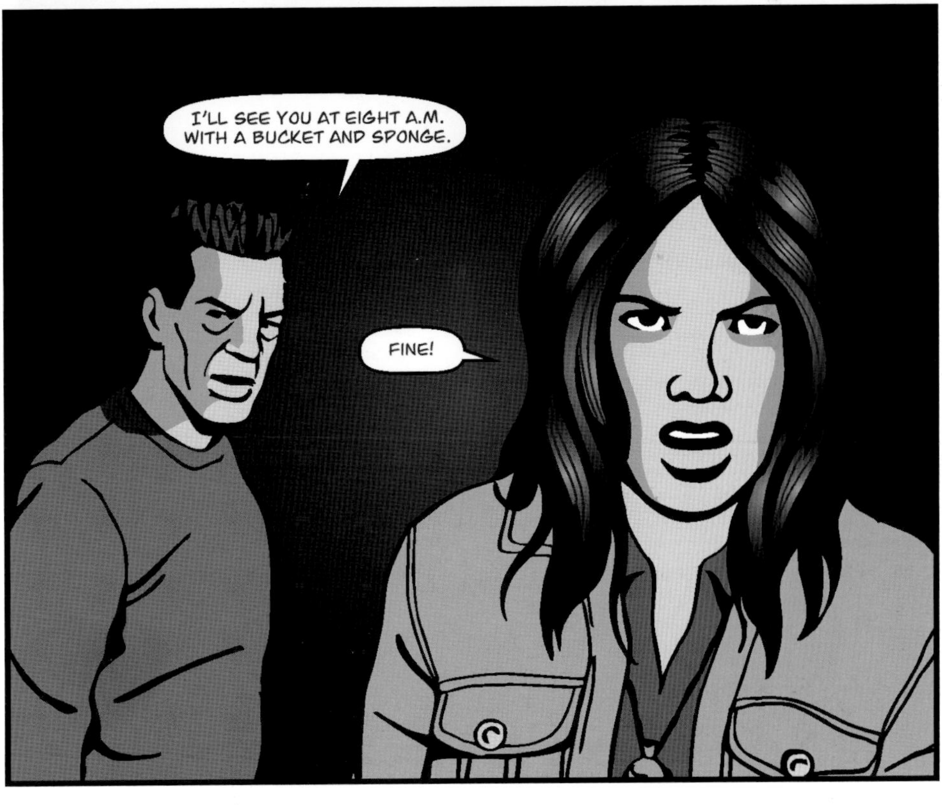
I'LL SEE YOU AT EIGHT A.M. WITH A BUCKET AND SPONGE.
FINE!

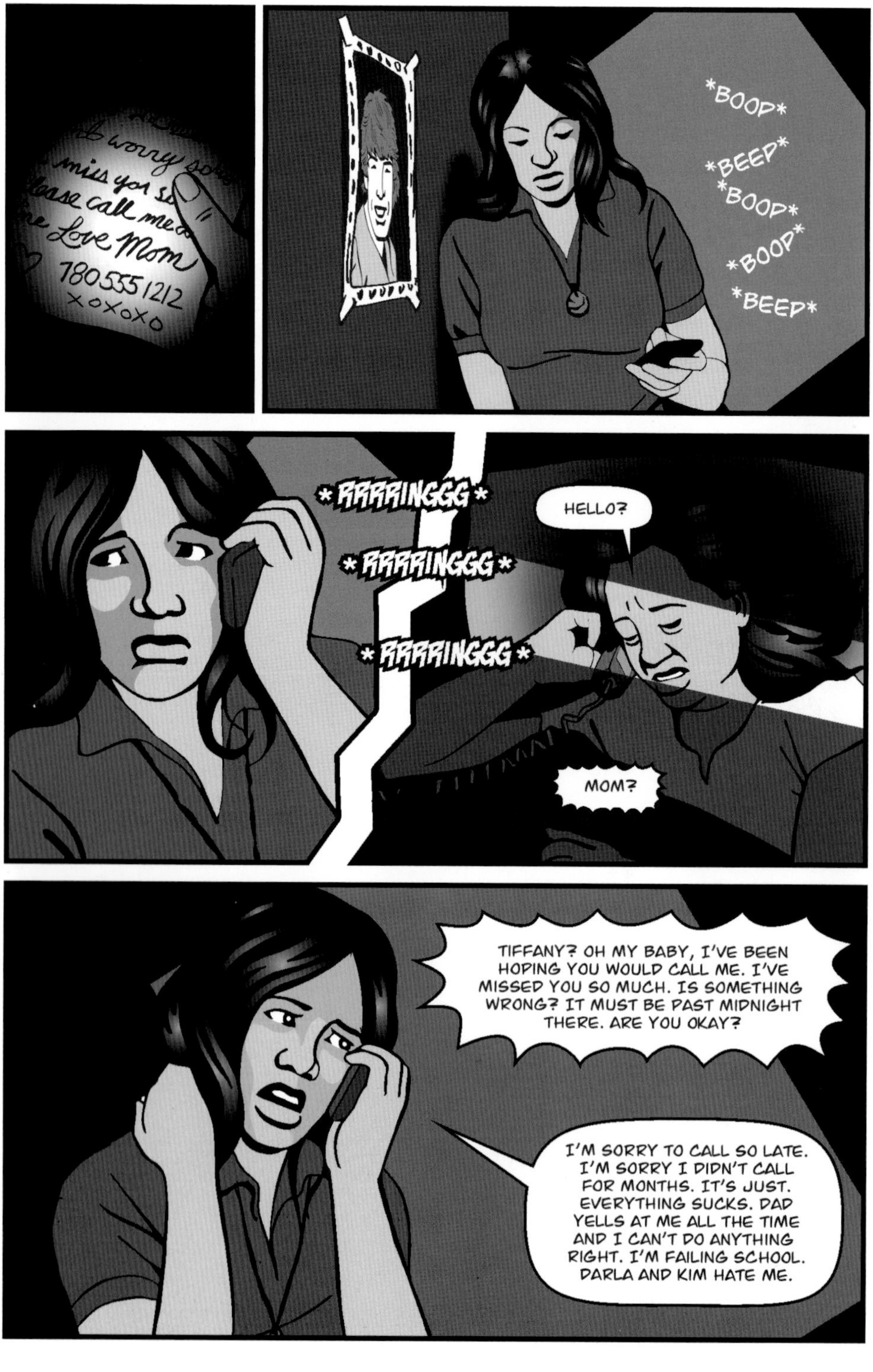
I worry so
Love Mom
7805551212
xoxoxo
BOOP
BEEP
BOOP
BOOP
BEEP
RRRRINGGG
RRRRINGGG
RRRRINGGG
HELLO?
MOM?
TIFFANY? OH MY BABY, I'VE BEEN HOPING YOU WOULD CALL ME. I'VE MISSED YOU SO MUCH. IS SOMETHING WRONG? IT MUST BE PAST MIDNIGHT THERE. ARE YOU OKAY?
I'M SORRY TO CALL SO LATE. I'M SORRY I DIDN'T CALL FOR MONTHS. IT'S JUST. EVERYTHING SUCKS. DAD YELLS AT ME ALL THE TIME AND I CAN'T DO ANYTHING RIGHT. I'M FAILING SCHOOL. DARLA AND KIM HATE ME.

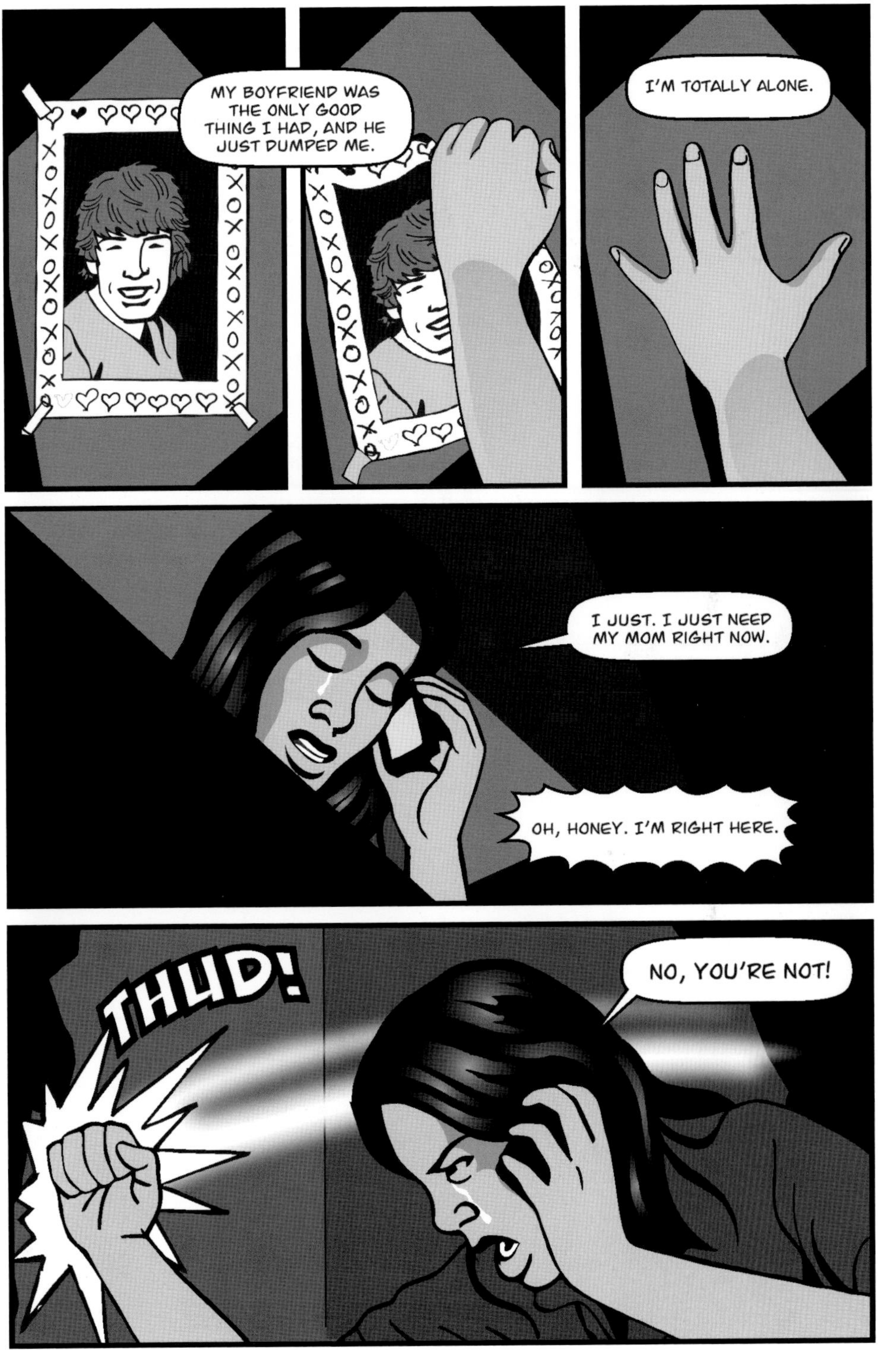
MY BOYFRIEND WAS THE ONLY GOOD THING I HAD, AND HE JUST DUMPED ME.
I'M TOTALLY ALONE.
I JUST. I JUST NEED MY MOM RIGHT NOW.
OH, HONEY. I'M RIGHT HERE.
THUD!
NO, YOU'RE NOT!

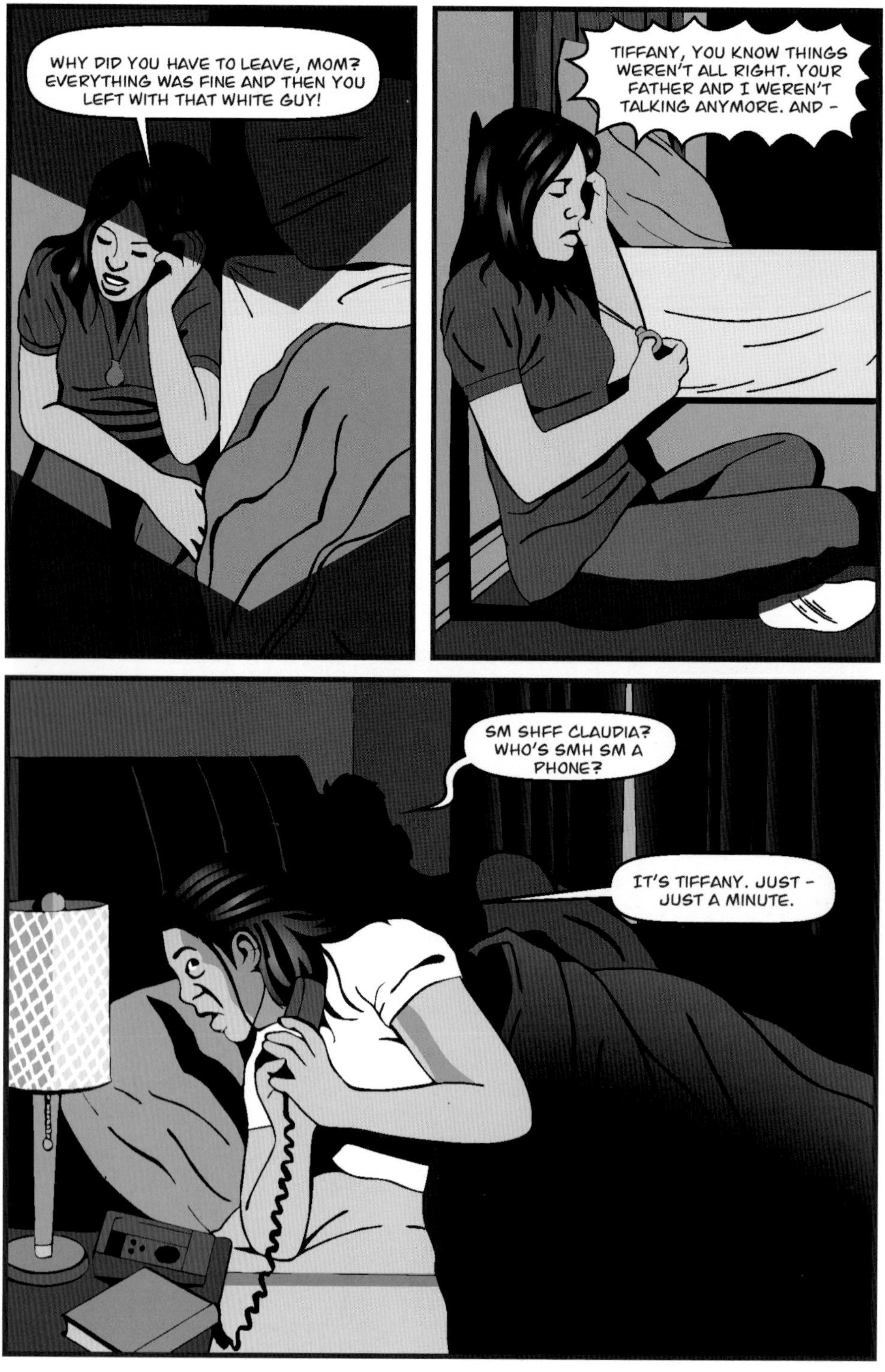
WHY DID YOU HAVE TO LEAVE, MOM? EVERYTHING WAS FINE AND THEN YOU LEFT WITH THAT WHITE GUY!
TIFFANY, YOU KNOW THINGS WEREN'T ALL RIGHT. YOUR FATHER AND I WEREN'T TALKING ANYMORE. AND -
SM SHFF CLAUDIA? WHO'S SMH SM A PHONE?
IT'S TIFFANY. JUST - JUST A MINUTE.

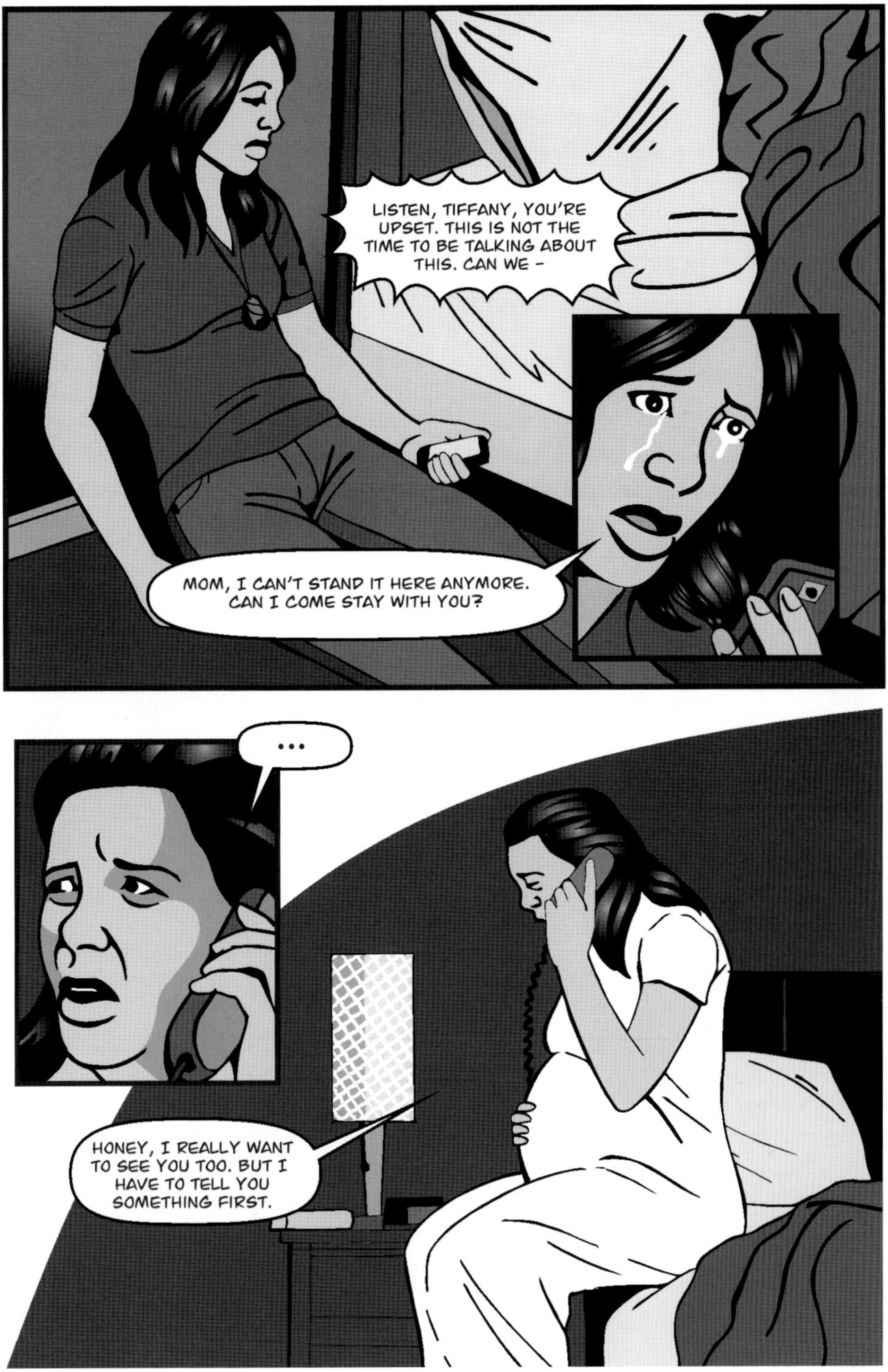
LISTEN, TIFFANY, YOU'RE UPSET. THIS IS NOT THE TIME TO BE TALKING ABOUT THIS. CAN WE –
MOM, I CAN'T STAND IT HERE ANYMORE. CAN I COME STAY WITH YOU?
...
HONEY, I REALLY WANT TO SEE YOU TOO. BUT I HAVE TO TELL YOU SOMETHING FIRST.

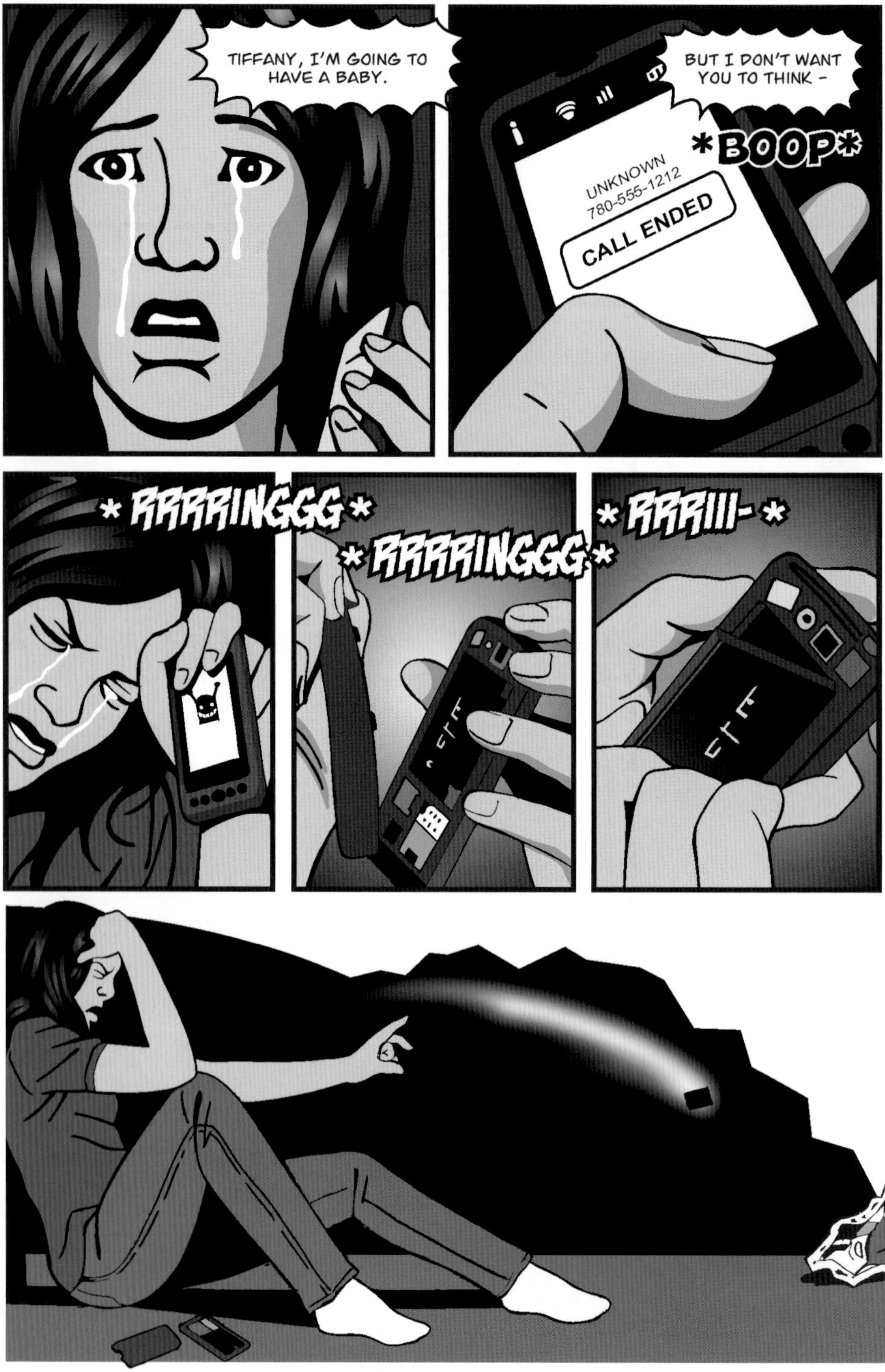
TIFFANY, I'M GOING TO HAVE A BABY.
BUT I DON'T WANT YOU TO THINK -
BOOP
UNKNOWN
780-555-1212
CALL ENDED
* RRRRINGGG *
* RRRRINGGG *
* RRRIII- *

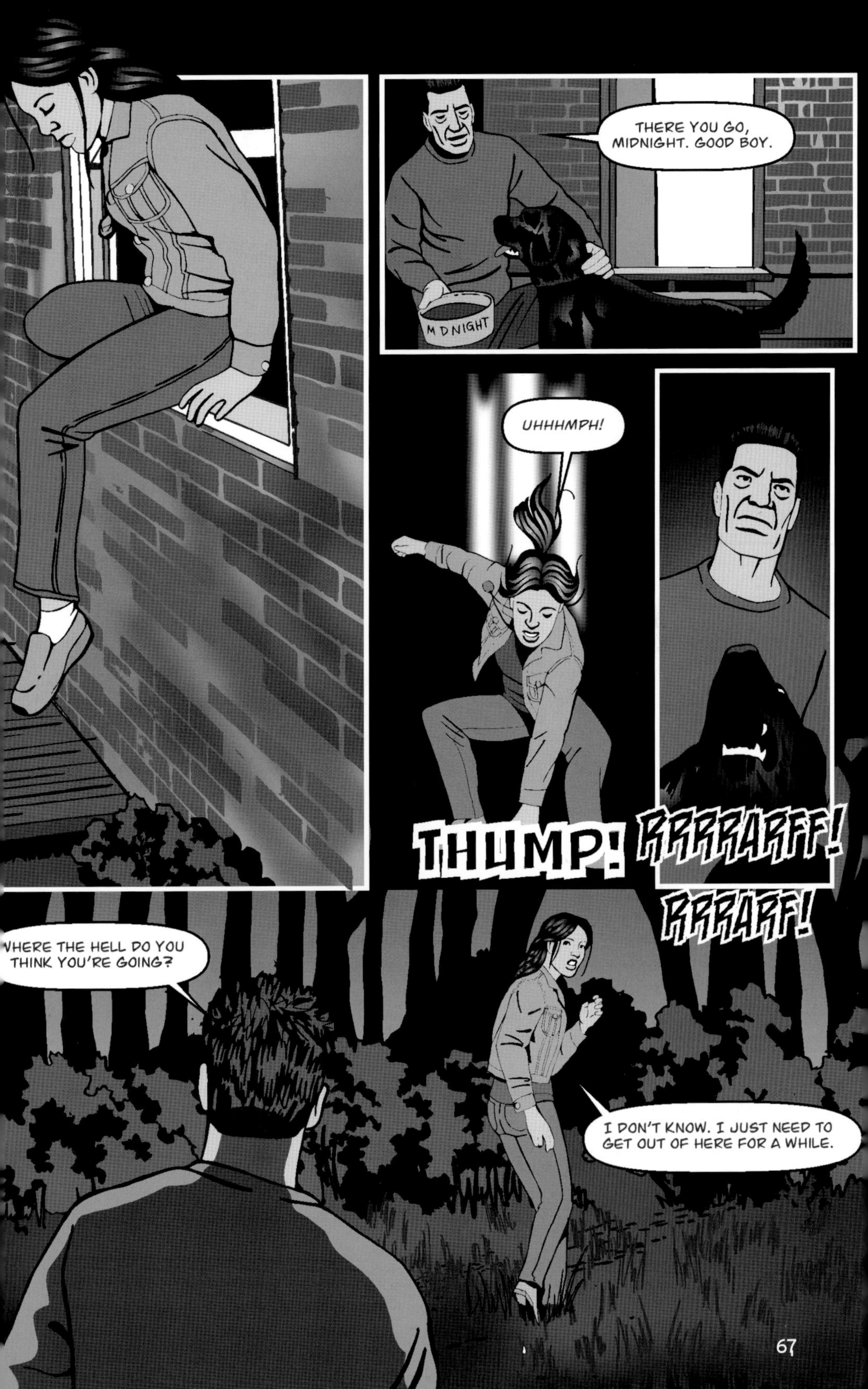

THERE YOU GO, MIDNIGHT. GOOD BOY.
M DNIGHT
UHHHMPH!
THUMP!
RRRRARFF!
RRRARF!
WHERE THE HELL DO YOU THINK YOU'RE GOING?
I DON'T KNOW. I JUST NEED TO GET OUT OF HERE FOR A WHILE.

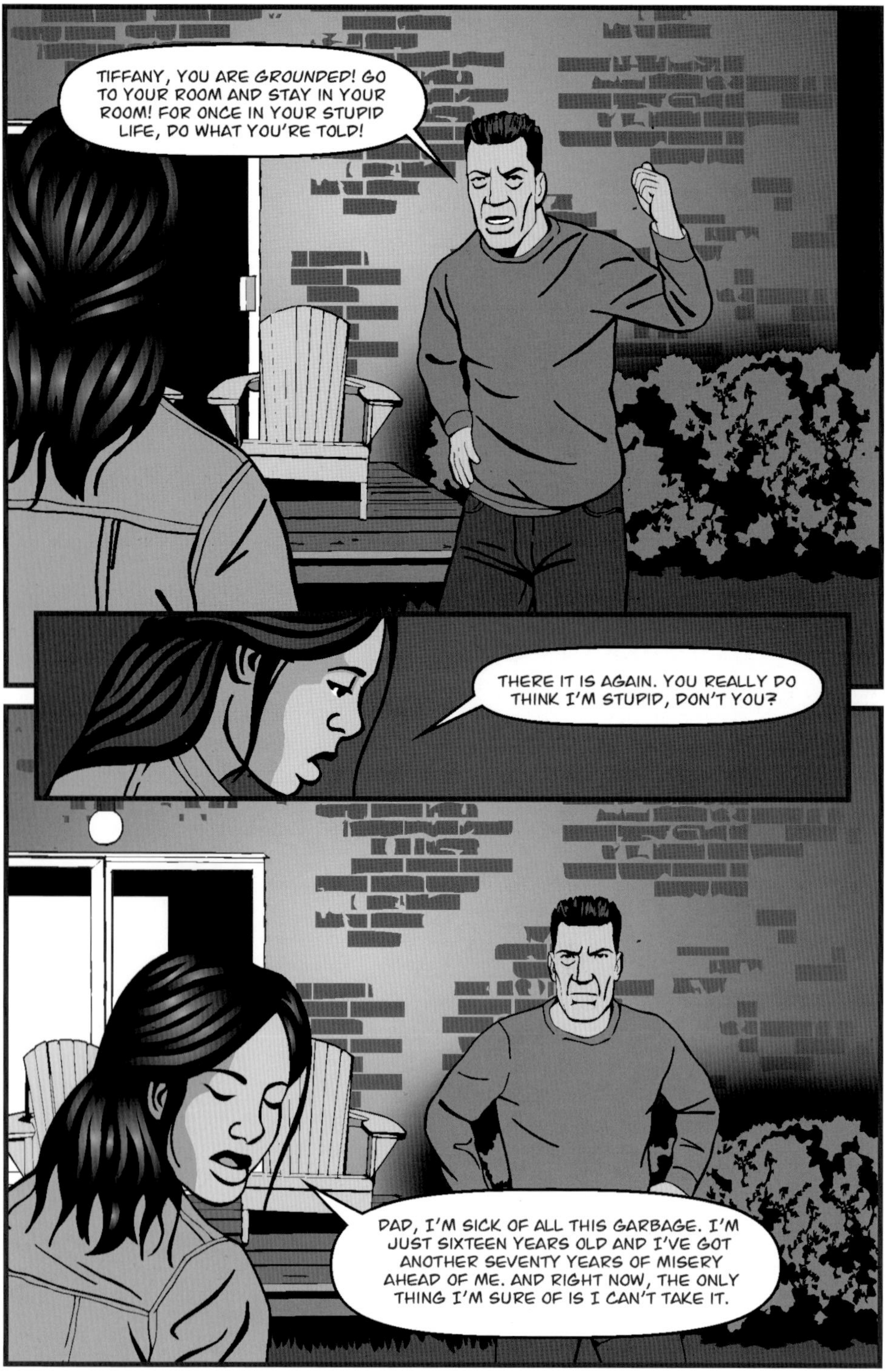
TIFFANY, YOU ARE GROUNDED! GO TO YOUR ROOM AND STAY IN YOUR ROOM! FOR ONCE IN YOUR STUPID LIFE, DO WHAT YOU'RE TOLD!
THERE IT IS AGAIN. YOU REALLY DO THINK I'M STUPID, DON'T YOU?
DAD, I'M SICK OF ALL THIS GARBAGE. I'M JUST SIXTEEN YEARS OLD AND I'VE GOT ANOTHER SEVENTY YEARS OF MISERY AHEAD OF ME. AND RIGHT NOW, THE ONLY THING I'M SURE OF IS I CAN'T TAKE IT.

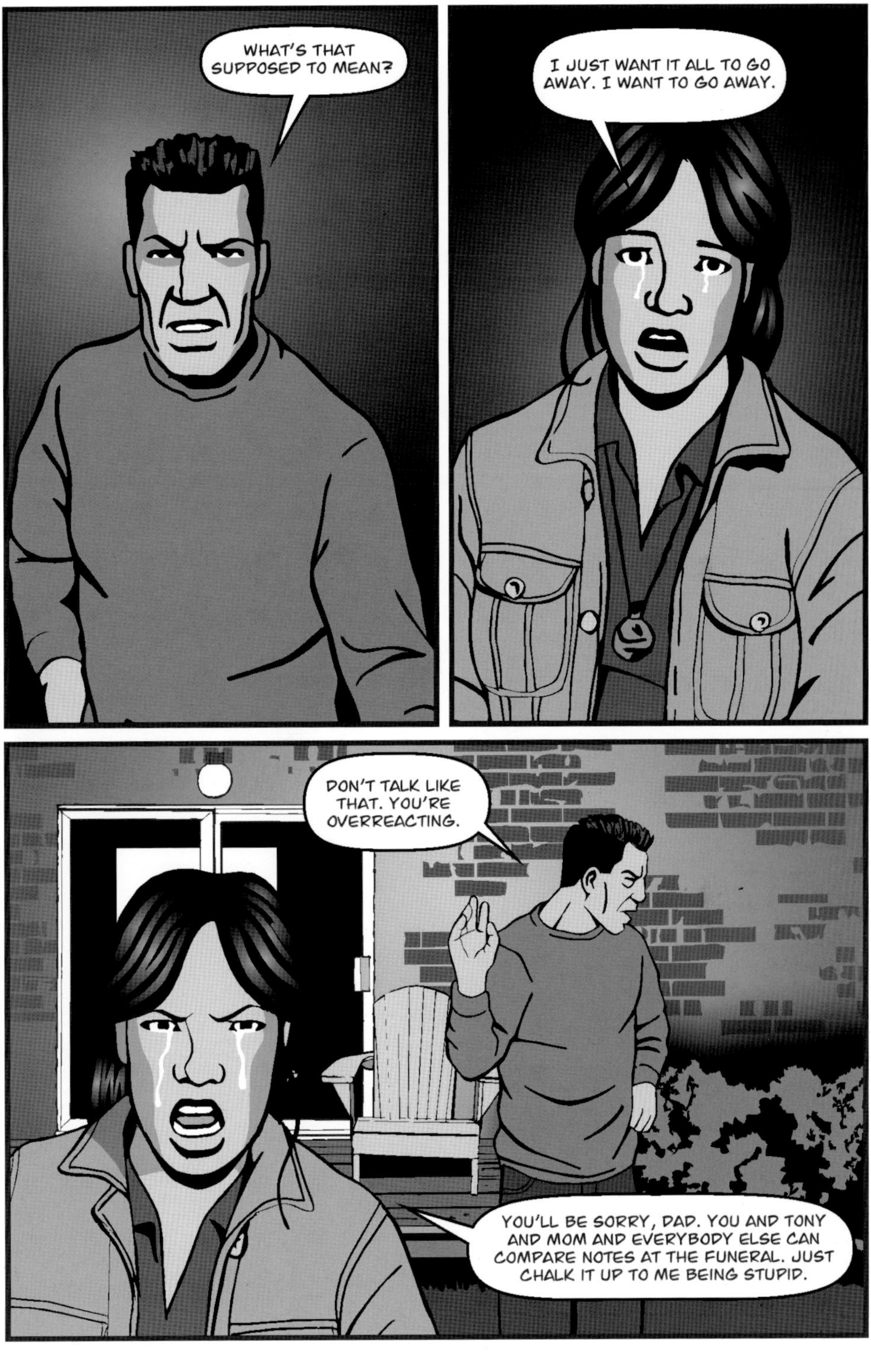
WHAT'S THAT SUPPOSED TO MEAN?
I JUST WANT IT ALL TO GO AWAY. I WANT TO GO AWAY.
DON'T TALK LIKE THAT. YOU'RE OVERREACTING.
YOU'LL BE SORRY, DAD. YOU AND TONY AND MOM AND EVERYBODY ELSE CAN COMPARE NOTES AT THE FUNERAL. JUST CHALK IT UP TO ME BEING STUPID.

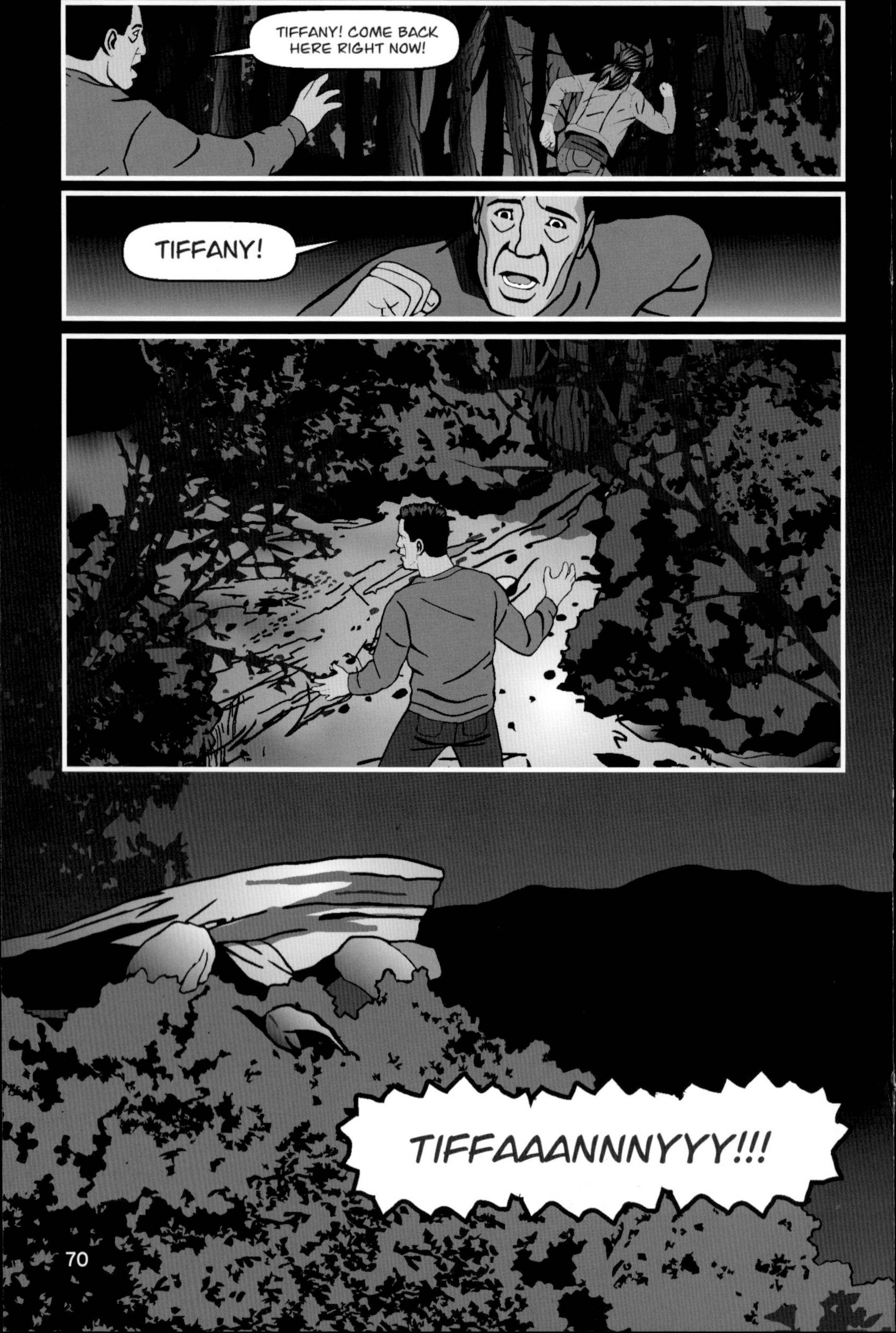
TIFFANY! COME BACK HERE RIGHT NOW!
TIFFANY!
TIFFAAANNNYYY!!!

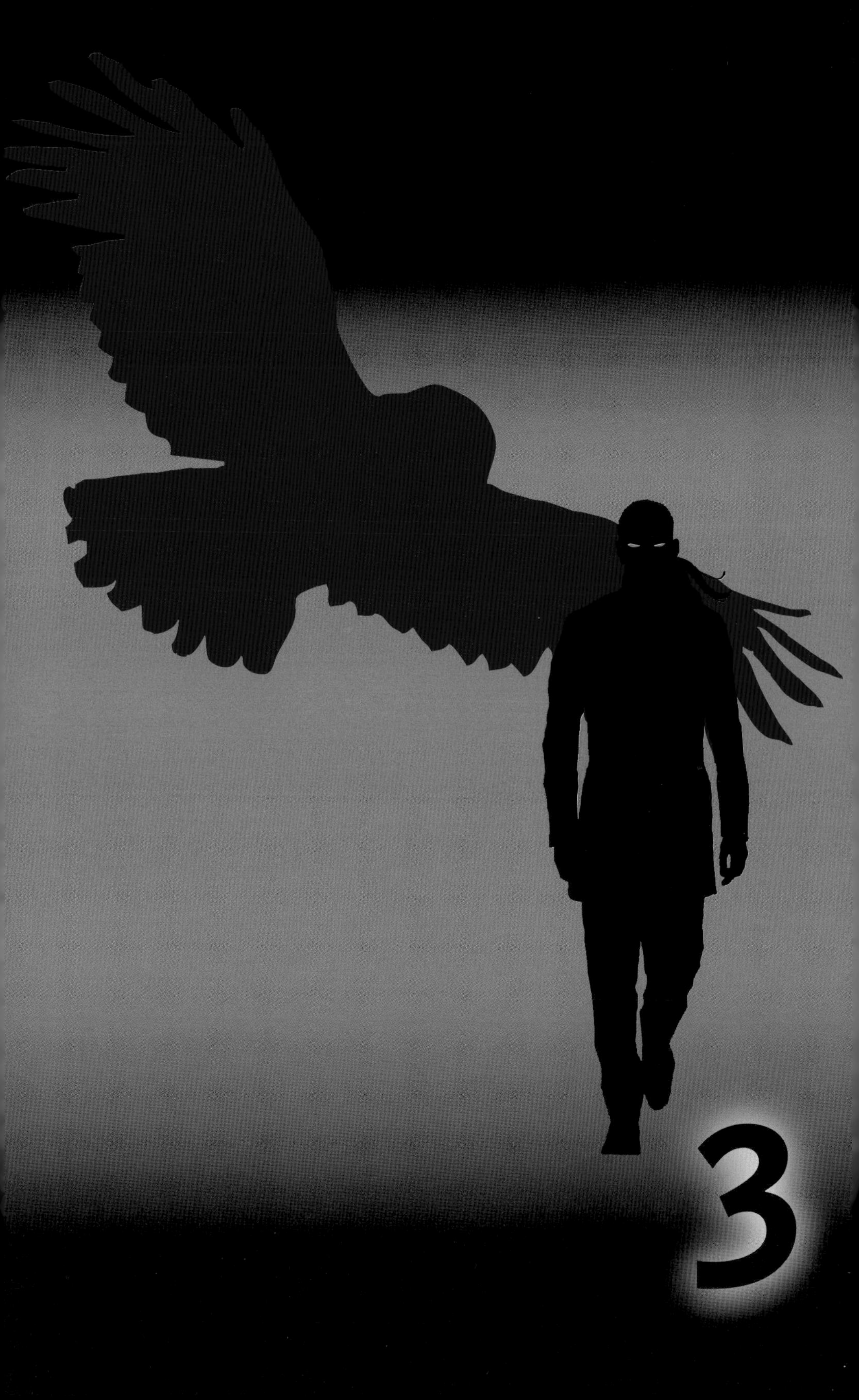
3

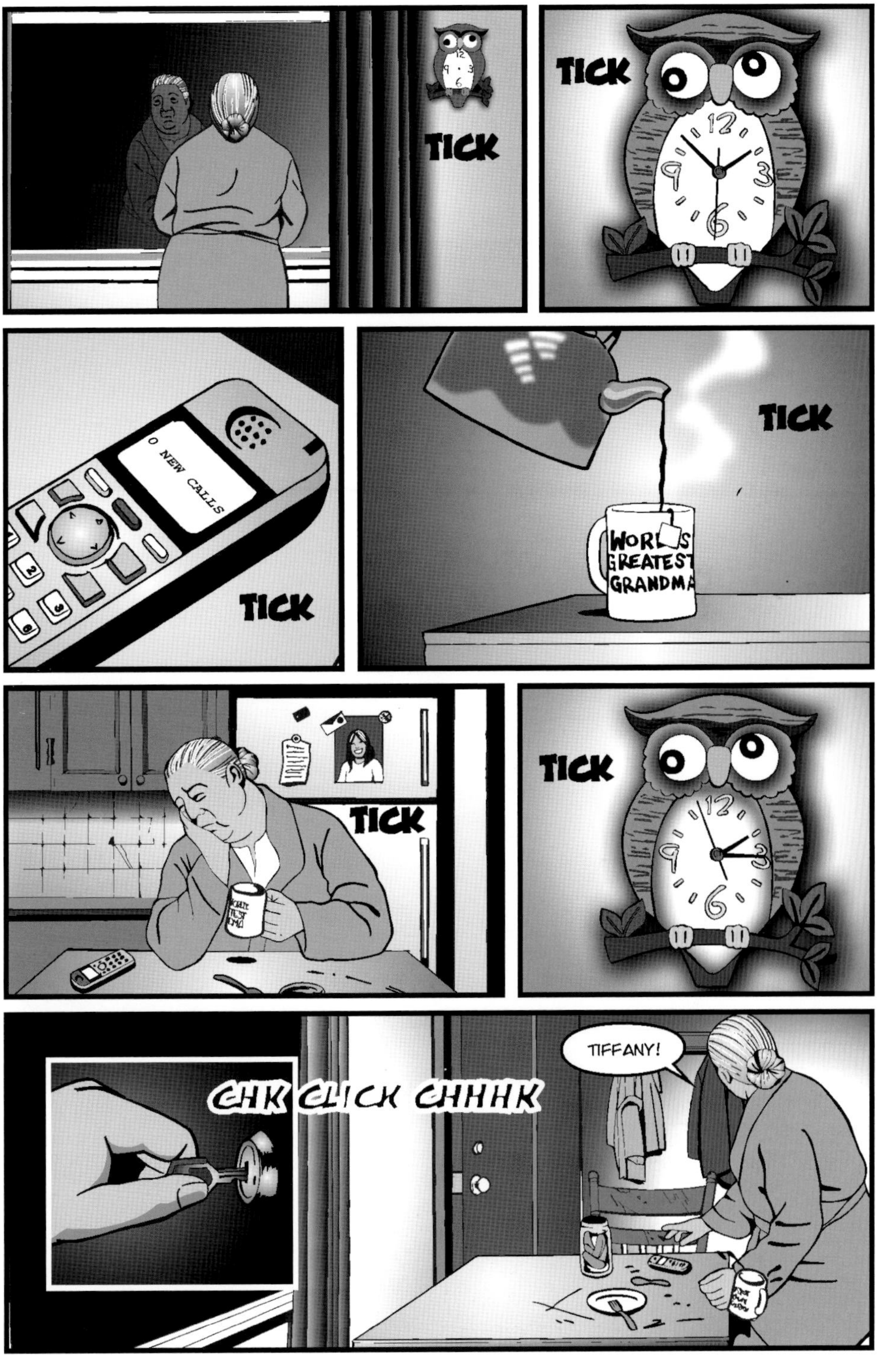
TICK
TICK
0 NEW CALLS
TICK
TICK
WORLD'S GREATEST GRANDMA
TICK
TICK
CHK CLICK CHHHK
TIFFANY!

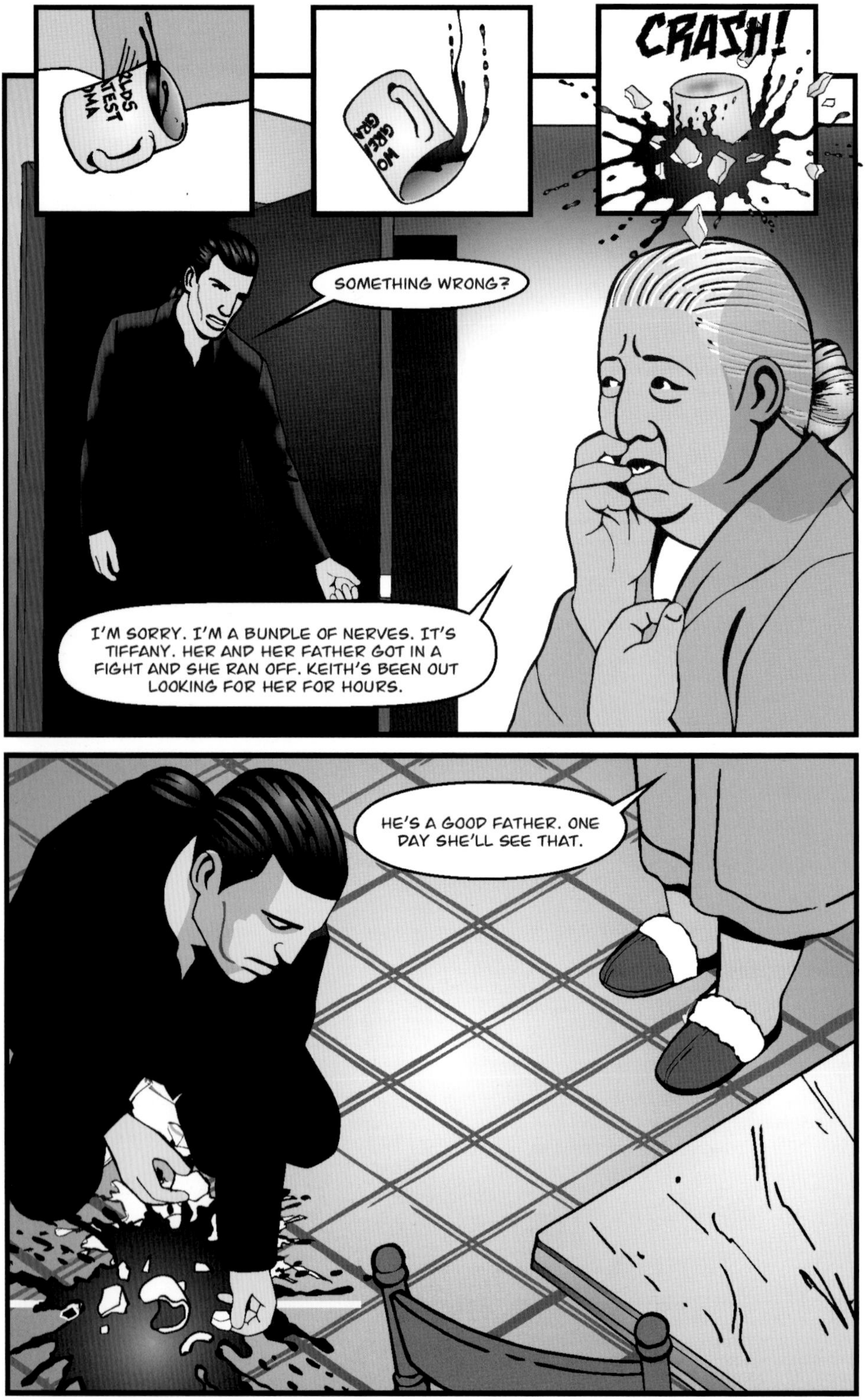
CRASH!
SOMETHING WRONG?
I'M SORRY. I'M A BUNDLE OF NERVES. IT'S TIFFANY. HER AND HER FATHER GOT IN A FIGHT AND SHE RAN OFF. KEITH'S BEEN OUT LOOKING FOR HER FOR HOURS.
HE'S A GOOD FATHER. ONE DAY SHE'LL SEE THAT.

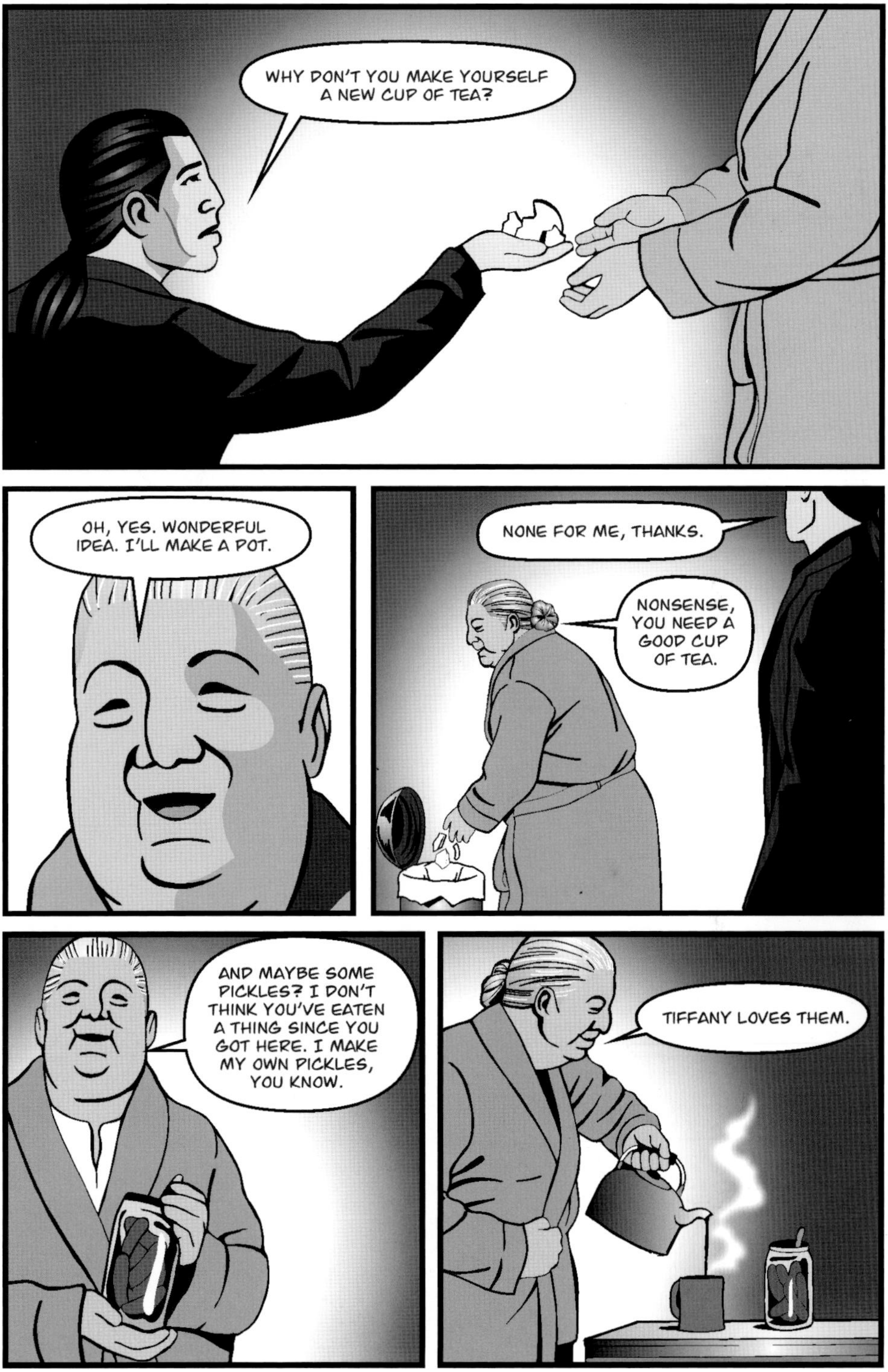
WHY DON'T YOU MAKE YOURSELF A NEW CUP OF TEA?
OH, YES. WONDERFUL IDEA. I'LL MAKE A POT.
NONE FOR ME, THANKS.
NONSENSE, YOU NEED A GOOD CUP OF TEA.
AND MAYBE SOME PICKLES? I DON'T THINK YOU'VE EATEN A THING SINCE YOU GOT HERE. I MAKE MY OWN PICKLES, YOU KNOW.
TIFFANY LOVES THEM.

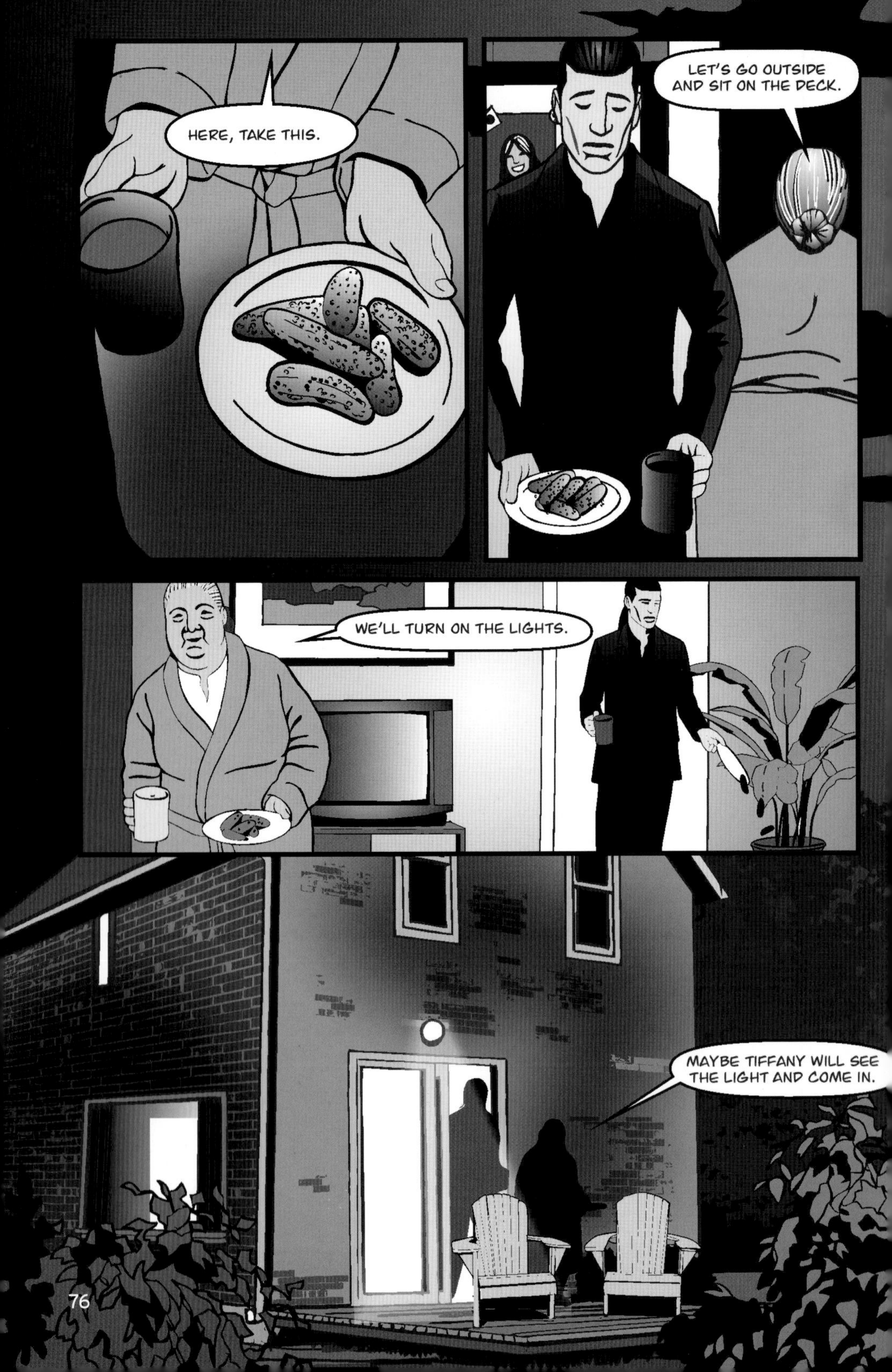
HERE, TAKE THIS.
LET'S GO OUTSIDE AND SIT ON THE DECK.
WE'LL TURN ON THE LIGHTS.
MAYBE TIFFANY WILL SEE THE LIGHT AND COME IN.

SO. PIERRE. WHY ARE YOU REALLY HERE?

AS I TOLD YOU –

I KNOW WHAT YOU TOLD ME. I DON'T BUY IT.

SOMETHING'S HAUNTING YOU, YOUNG MAN. AND I GET THE IMPRESSION YOU THINK YOU CAN GET RID OF WHATEVER IT IS BY COMING HERE.

I –

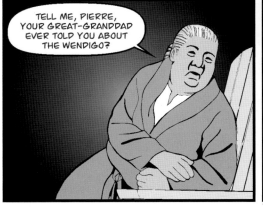

TELL ME, PIERRE, YOUR GREAT-GRANDDAD EVER TOLD YOU ABOUT THE WENDIGO?

YES.

WHAT DID HE SAY?

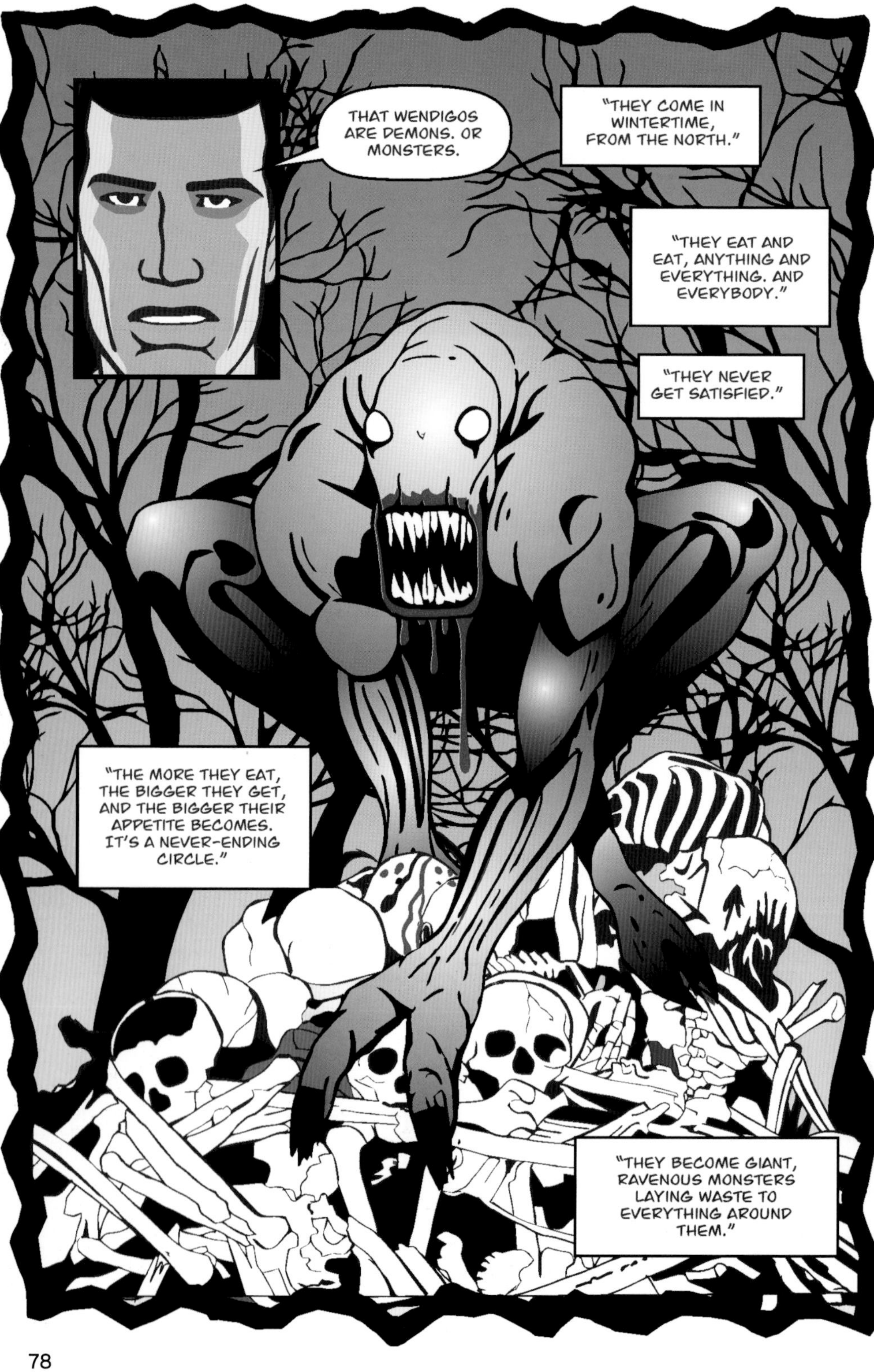
THAT WENDIGOS ARE DEMONS. OR MONSTERS.
"THEY COME IN WINTERTIME, FROM THE NORTH."
"THEY EAT AND EAT, ANYTHING AND EVERYTHING. AND EVERYBODY."
"THEY NEVER GET SATISFIED."
"THE MORE THEY EAT, THE BIGGER THEY GET, AND THE BIGGER THEIR APPETITE BECOMES. IT'S A NEVER-ENDING CIRCLE."
"THEY BECOME GIANT, RAVENOUS MONSTERS LAYING WASTE TO EVERYTHING AROUND THEM."

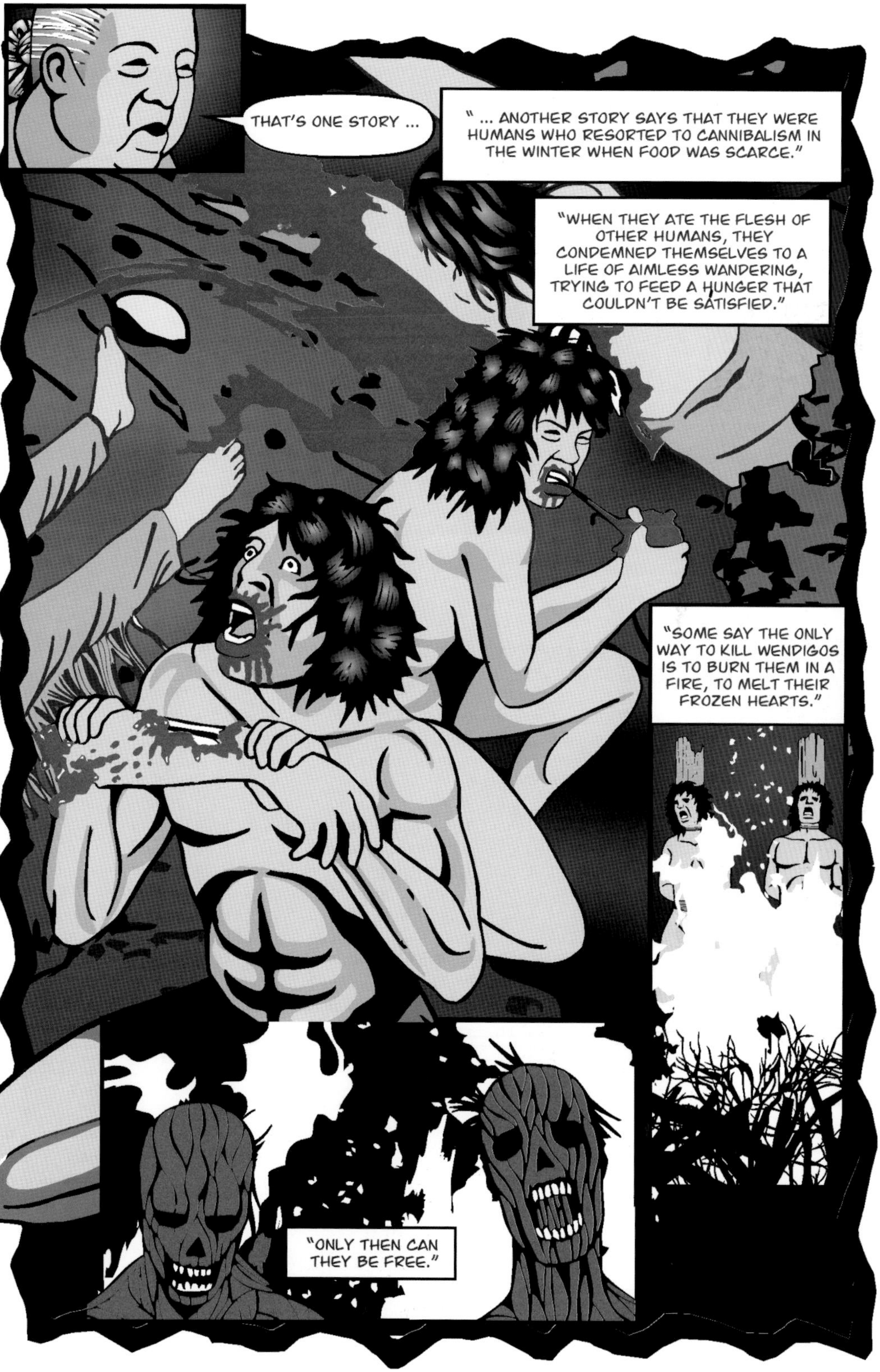
THAT'S ONE STORY ...
" ... ANOTHER STORY SAYS THAT THEY WERE HUMANS WHO RESORTED TO CANNIBALISM IN THE WINTER WHEN FOOD WAS SCARCE."
"WHEN THEY ATE THE FLESH OF OTHER HUMANS, THEY CONDEMNED THEMSELVES TO A LIFE OF AIMLESS WANDERING, TRYING TO FEED A HUNGER THAT COULDN'T BE SATISFIED."
"SOME SAY THE ONLY WAY TO KILL WENDIGOS IS TO BURN THEM IN A FIRE, TO MELT THEIR FROZEN HEARTS."
"ONLY THEN CAN THEY BE FREE."

WHY ARE YOU TELLING ME THIS NOW?

KRRACK

I DON'T KNOW. YOU'RE DOING QUITE A BIT OF WANDERING YOURSELF. AND THERE'S SOMETHING IN YOU THAT DOESN'T KNOW HOW TO GET SATISFIED.

AM I A CRAZY OLD WOMAN, OR AM I A CLEVER OLD WOMAN?

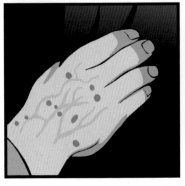

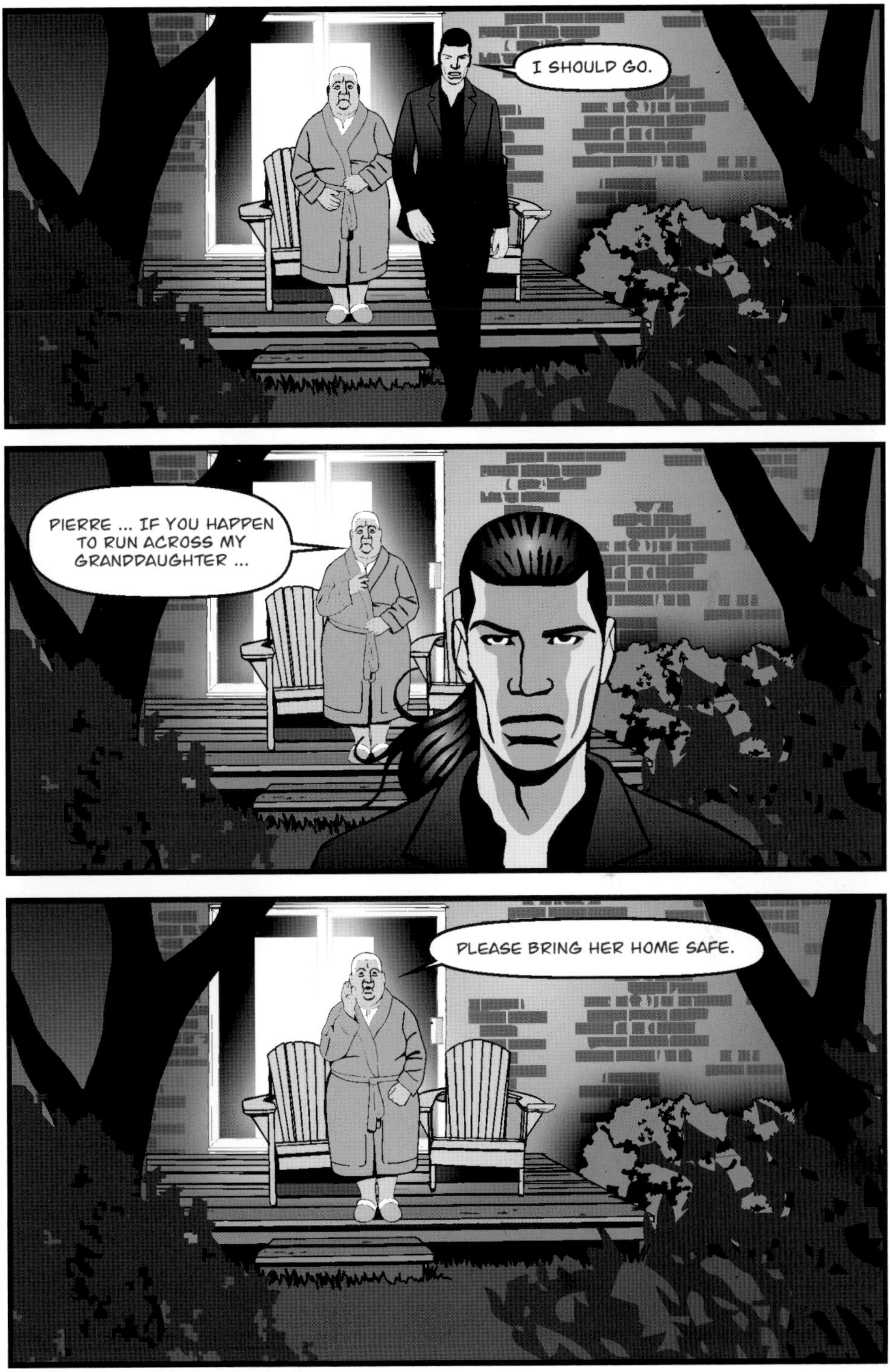
I SHOULD GO.
PIERRE ... IF YOU HAPPEN TO RUN ACROSS MY GRANDDAUGHTER ...
PLEASE BRING HER HOME SAFE.

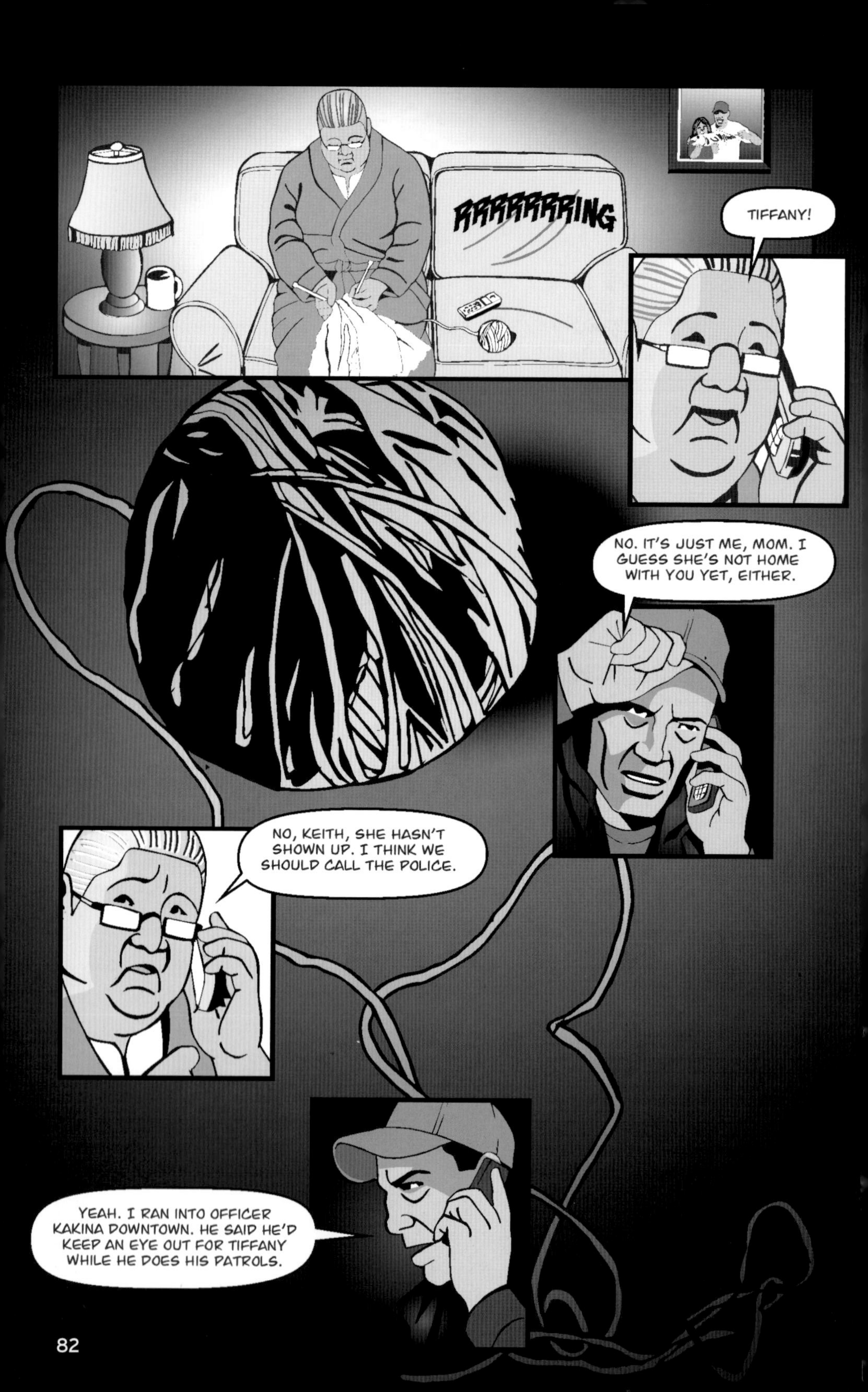
RRRRRRRING
TIFFANY!
NO. IT'S JUST ME, MOM. I GUESS SHE'S NOT HOME WITH YOU YET, EITHER.
NO, KEITH, SHE HASN'T SHOWN UP. I THINK WE SHOULD CALL THE POLICE.
YEAH. I RAN INTO OFFICER KAKINA DOWNTOWN. HE SAID HE'D KEEP AN EYE OUT FOR TIFFANY WHILE HE DOES HIS PATROLS.

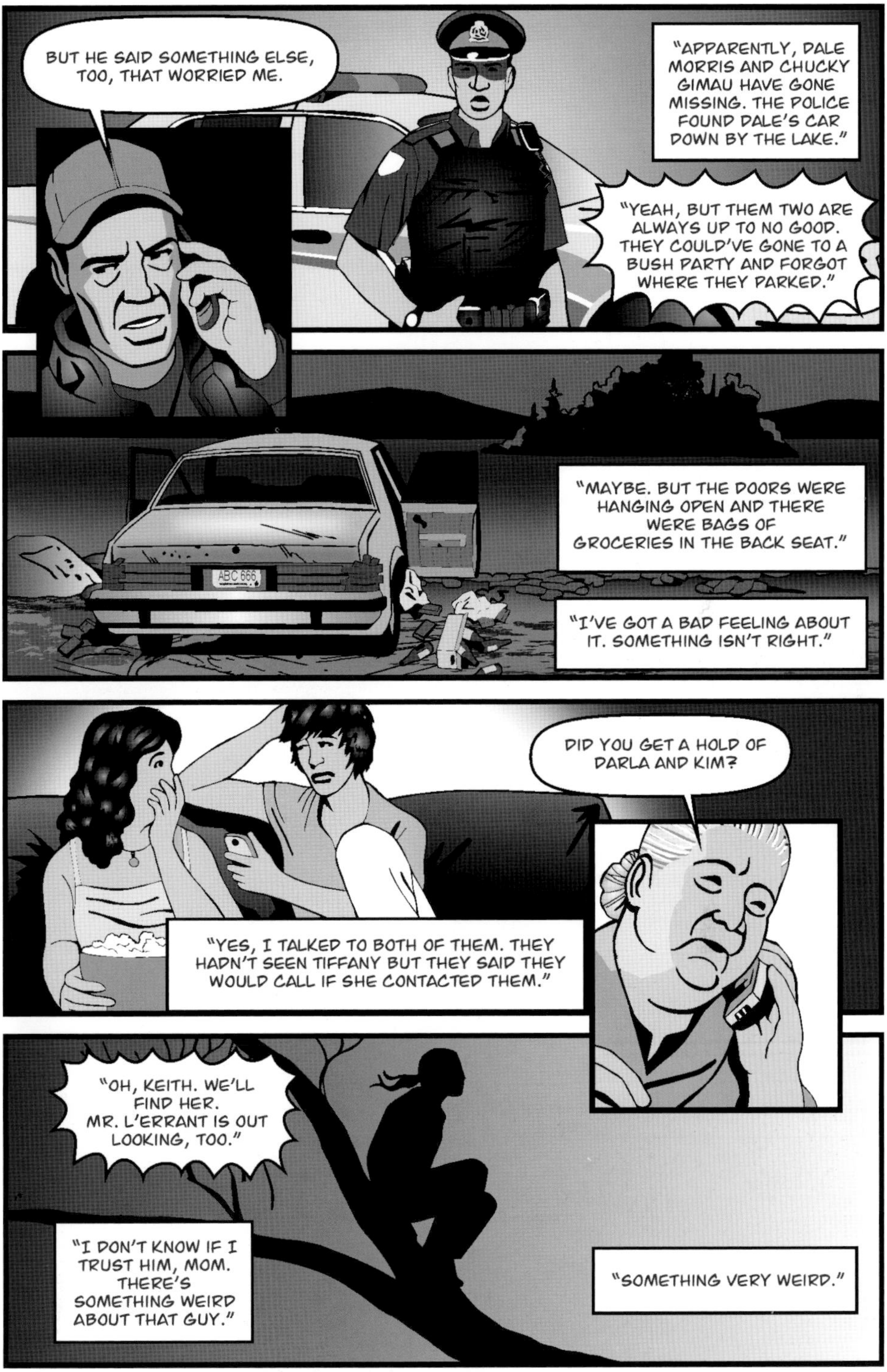
BUT HE SAID SOMETHING ELSE, TOO, THAT WORRIED ME.
"APPARENTLY, DALE MORRIS AND CHUCKY GIMAU HAVE GONE MISSING. THE POLICE FOUND DALE'S CAR DOWN BY THE LAKE."
"YEAH, BUT THEM TWO ARE ALWAYS UP TO NO GOOD. THEY COULD'VE GONE TO A BUSH PARTY AND FORGOT WHERE THEY PARKED."
ABC 666
"MAYBE. BUT THE DOORS WERE HANGING OPEN AND THERE WERE BAGS OF GROCERIES IN THE BACK SEAT."
"I'VE GOT A BAD FEELING ABOUT IT. SOMETHING ISN'T RIGHT."
DID YOU GET A HOLD OF DARLA AND KIM?
"YES, I TALKED TO BOTH OF THEM. THEY HADN'T SEEN TIFFANY BUT THEY SAID THEY WOULD CALL IF SHE CONTACTED THEM."
"OH, KEITH. WE'LL FIND HER. MR. L'ERRANT IS OUT LOOKING, TOO."
"I DON'T KNOW IF I TRUST HIM, MOM. THERE'S SOMETHING WEIRD ABOUT THAT GUY."
"SOMETHING VERY WEIRD."

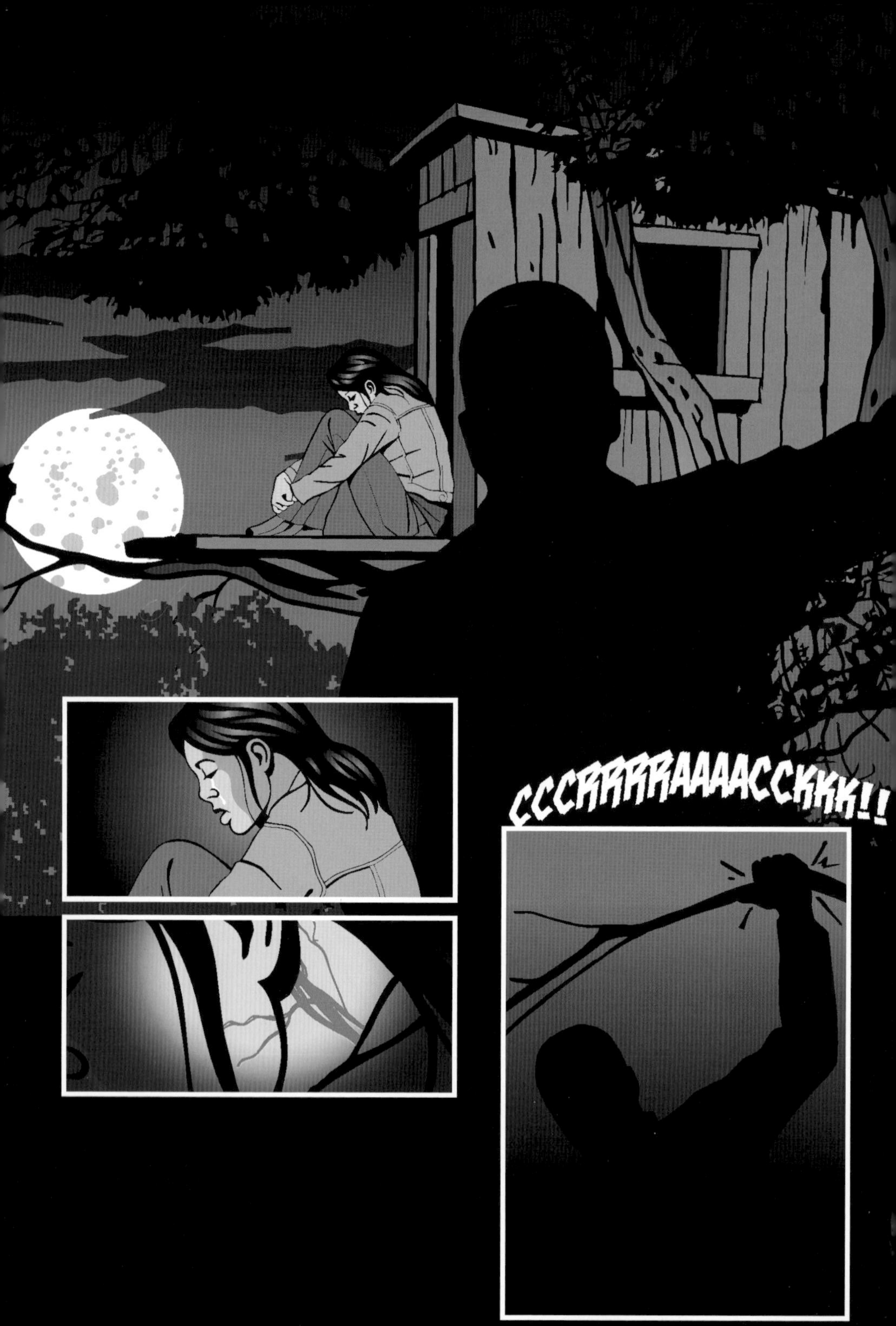
CCCRRRRAAAACCKKK!!

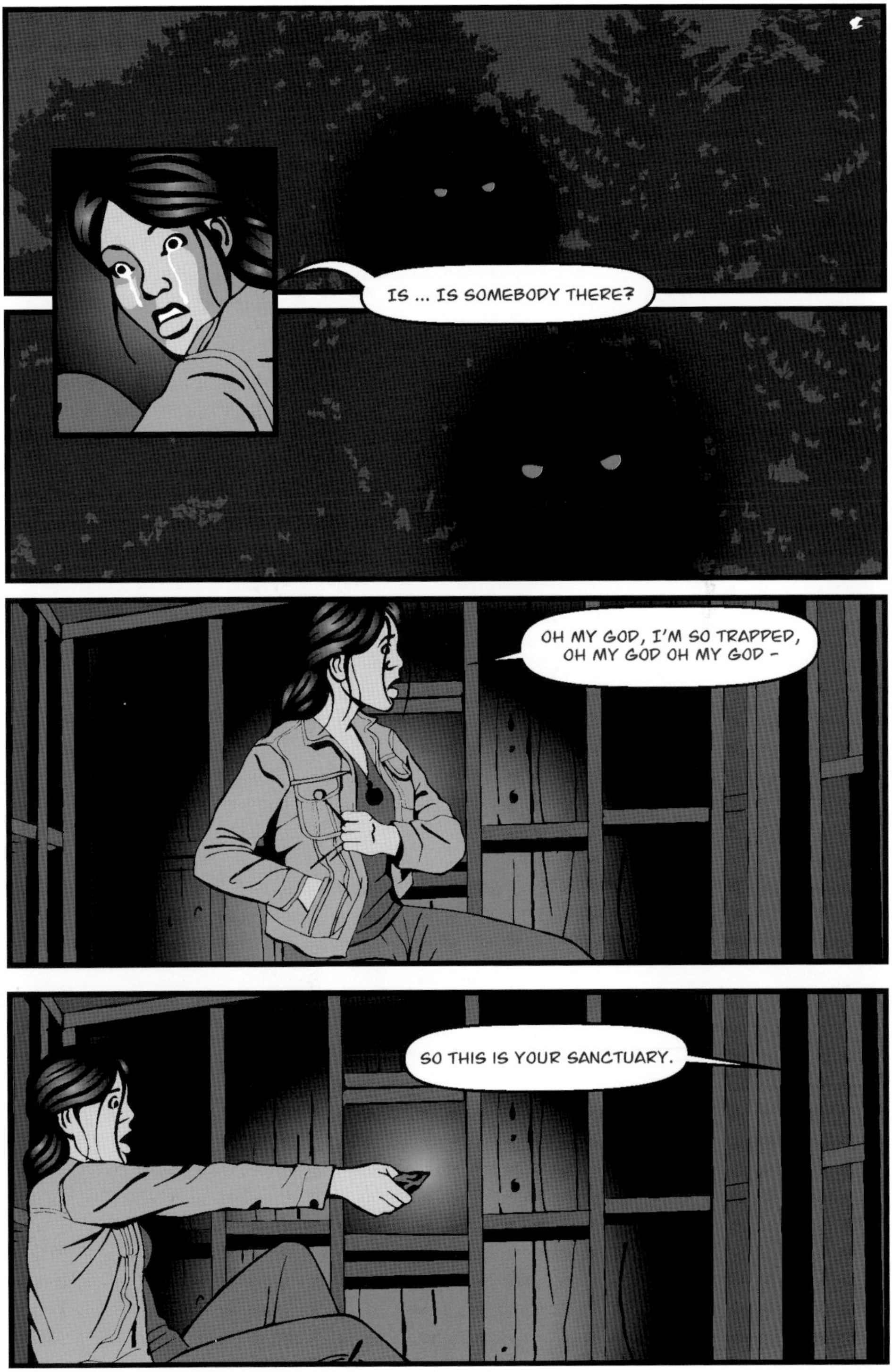
IS ... IS SOMEBODY THERE?
OH MY GOD, I'M SO TRAPPED, OH MY GOD OH MY GOD -
SO THIS IS YOUR SANCTUARY.

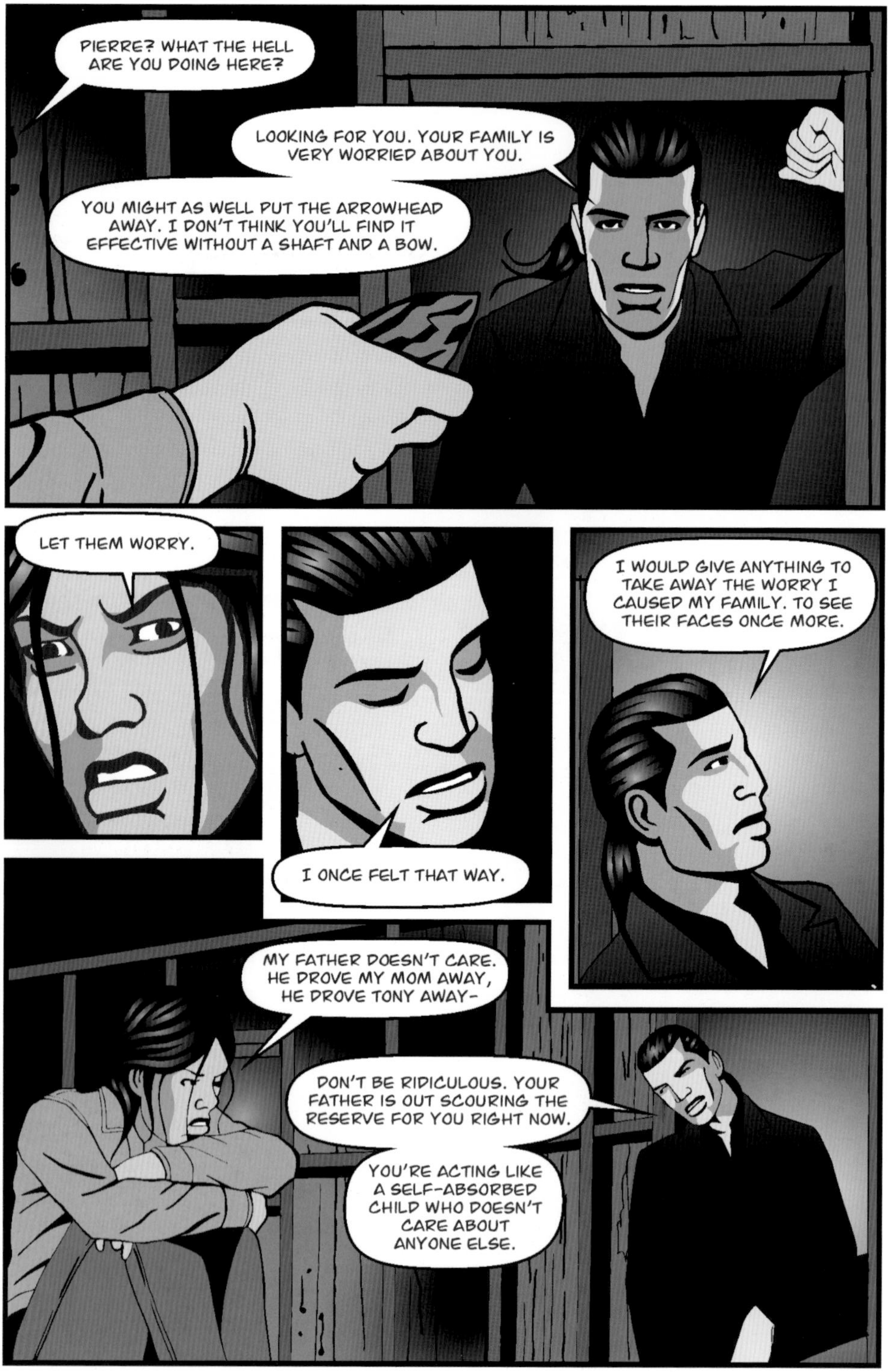
PIERRE? WHAT THE HELL ARE YOU DOING HERE?
LOOKING FOR YOU. YOUR FAMILY IS VERY WORRIED ABOUT YOU.
YOU MIGHT AS WELL PUT THE ARROWHEAD AWAY. I DON'T THINK YOU'LL FIND IT EFFECTIVE WITHOUT A SHAFT AND A BOW.
LET THEM WORRY.
I ONCE FELT THAT WAY.
I WOULD GIVE ANYTHING TO TAKE AWAY THE WORRY I CAUSED MY FAMILY. TO SEE THEIR FACES ONCE MORE.
MY FATHER DOESN'T CARE. HE DROVE MY MOM AWAY, HE DROVE TONY AWAY-
DON'T BE RIDICULOUS. YOUR FATHER IS OUT SCOURING THE RESERVE FOR YOU RIGHT NOW.
YOU'RE ACTING LIKE A SELF-ABSORBED CHILD WHO DOESN'T CARE ABOUT ANYONE ELSE.

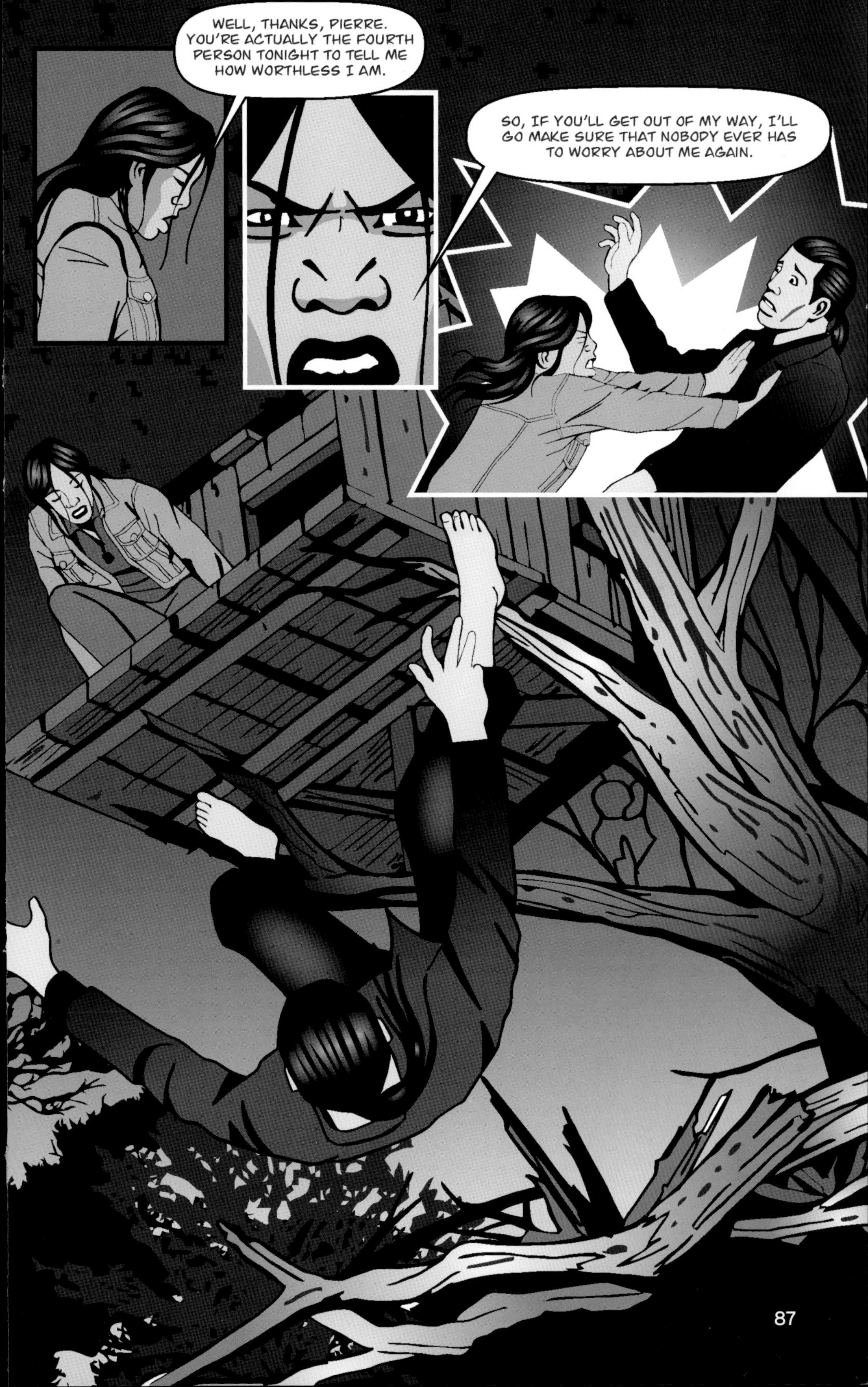
WELL, THANKS, PIERRE. YOU'RE ACTUALLY THE FOURTH PERSON TONIGHT TO TELL ME HOW WORTHLESS I AM.
SO, IF YOU'LL GET OUT OF MY WAY, I'LL GO MAKE SURE THAT NOBODY EVER HAS TO WORRY ABOUT ME AGAIN.

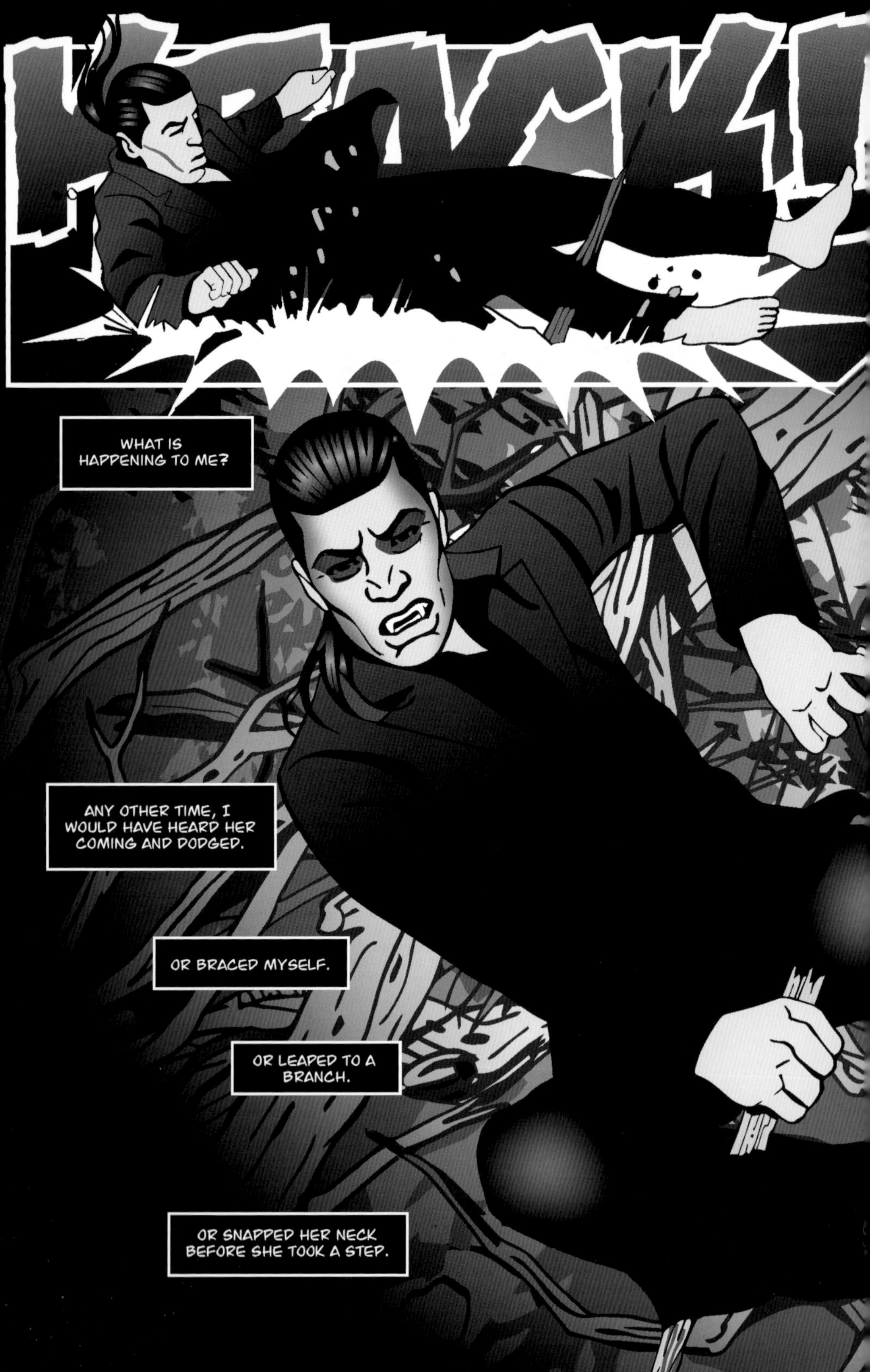
WHAT IS HAPPENING TO ME?
ANY OTHER TIME, I WOULD HAVE HEARD HER COMING AND DODGED.
OR BRACED MYSELF.
OR LEAPED TO A BRANCH.
OR SNAPPED HER NECK BEFORE SHE TOOK A STEP.

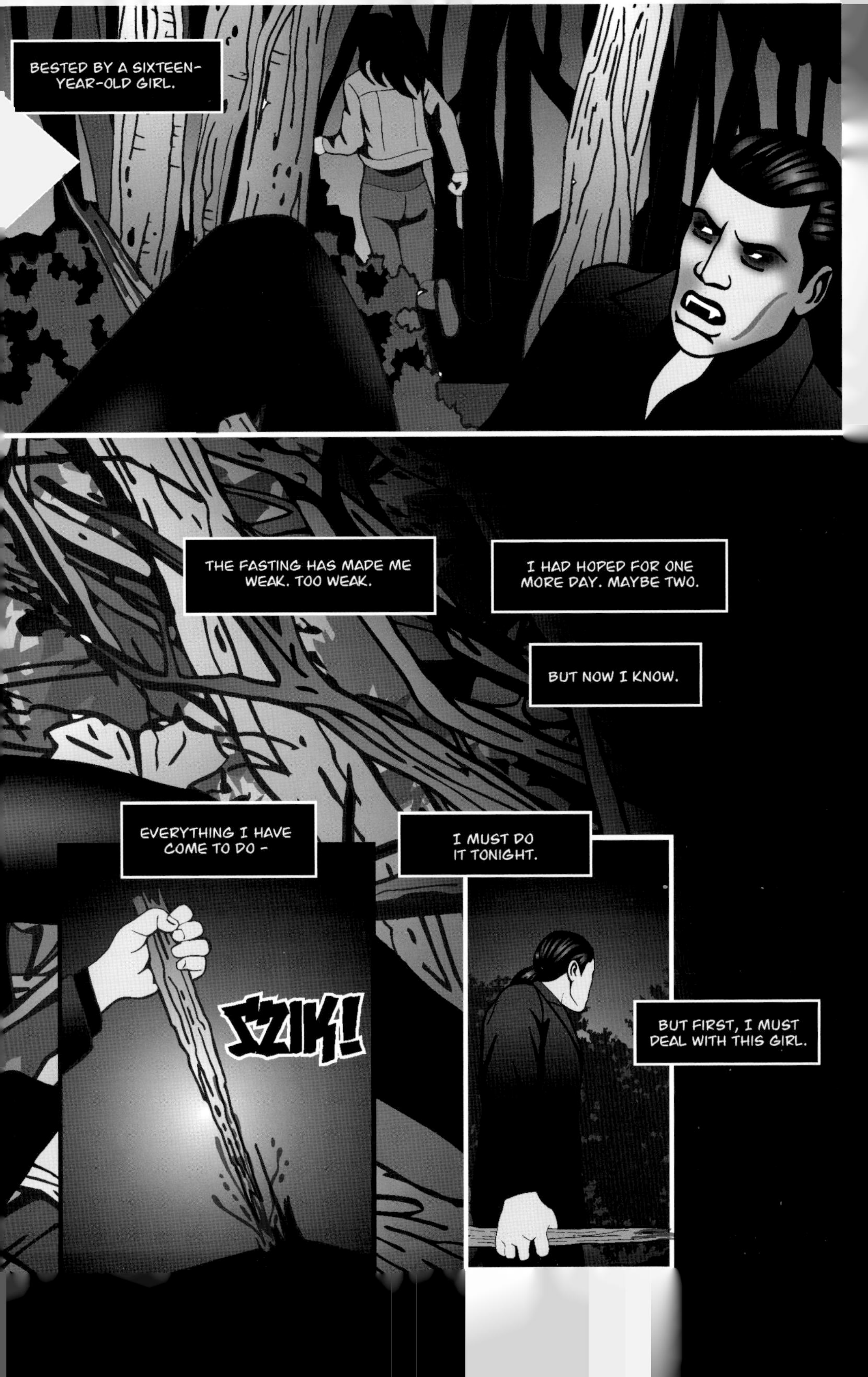
BESTED BY A SIXTEEN-YEAR-OLD GIRL.
THE FASTING HAS MADE ME WEAK. TOO WEAK.
I HAD HOPED FOR ONE MORE DAY. MAYBE TWO.
BUT NOW I KNOW.
EVERYTHING I HAVE COME TO DO -
SZIK!
I MUST DO IT TONIGHT.
BUT FIRST, I MUST DEAL WITH THIS GIRL.

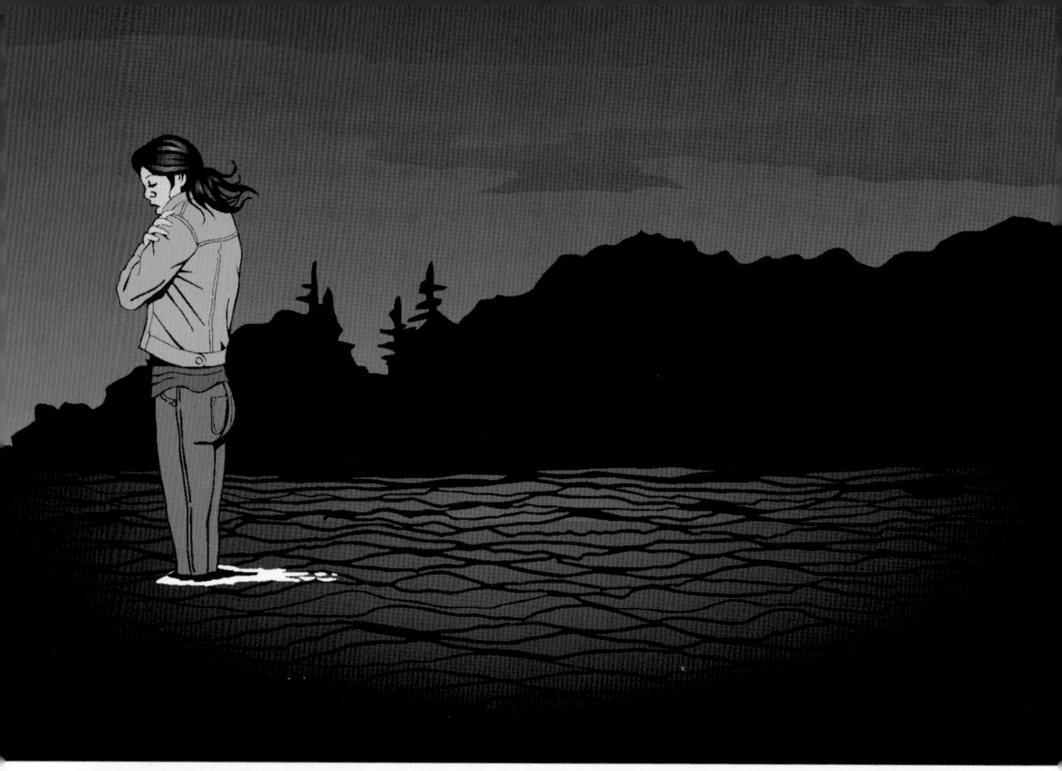

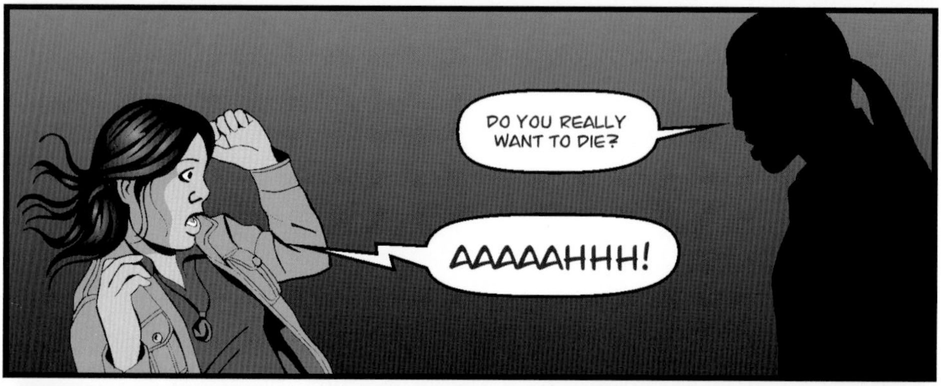
DO YOU REALLY WANT TO DIE?
AAAAAHHH!

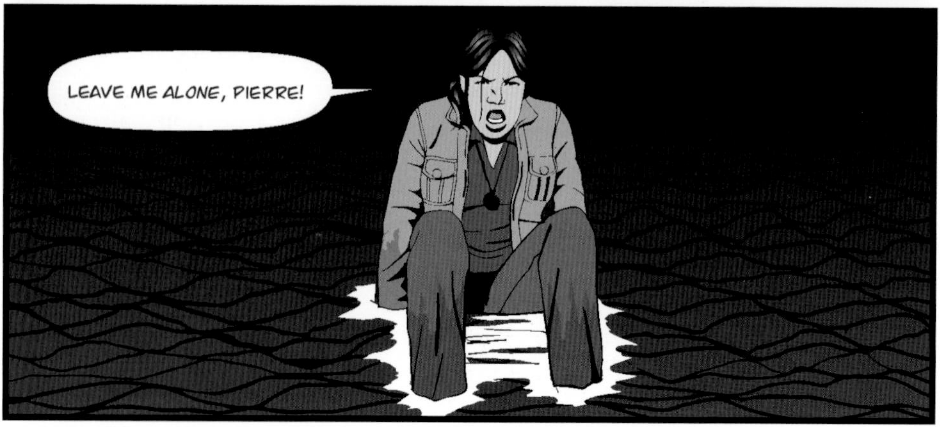
LEAVE ME ALONE, PIERRE!

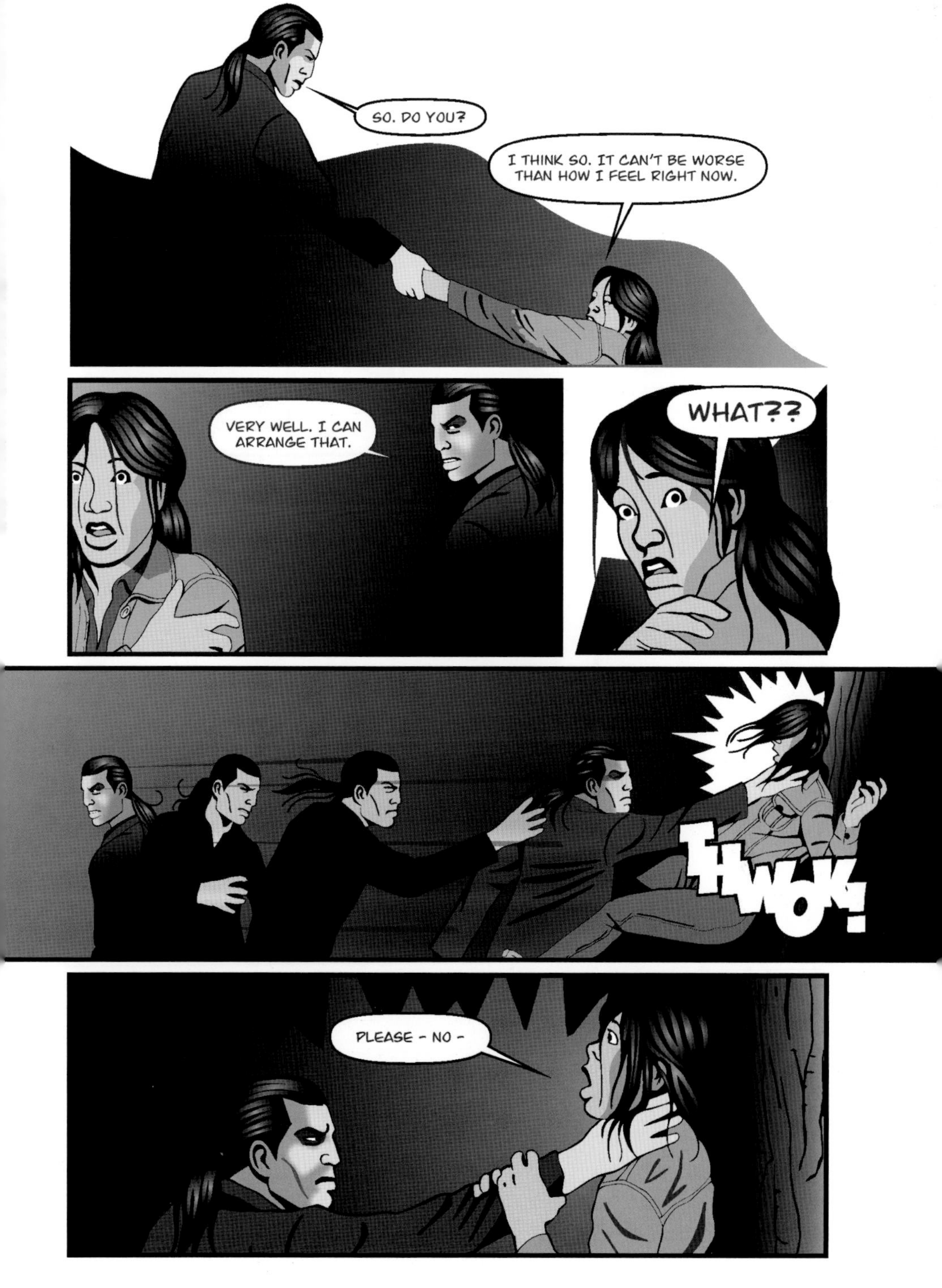
SO. DO YOU?
I THINK SO. IT CAN'T BE WORSE THAN HOW I FEEL RIGHT NOW.
VERY WELL. I CAN ARRANGE THAT.
WHAT??
THWOK!
PLEASE - NO -

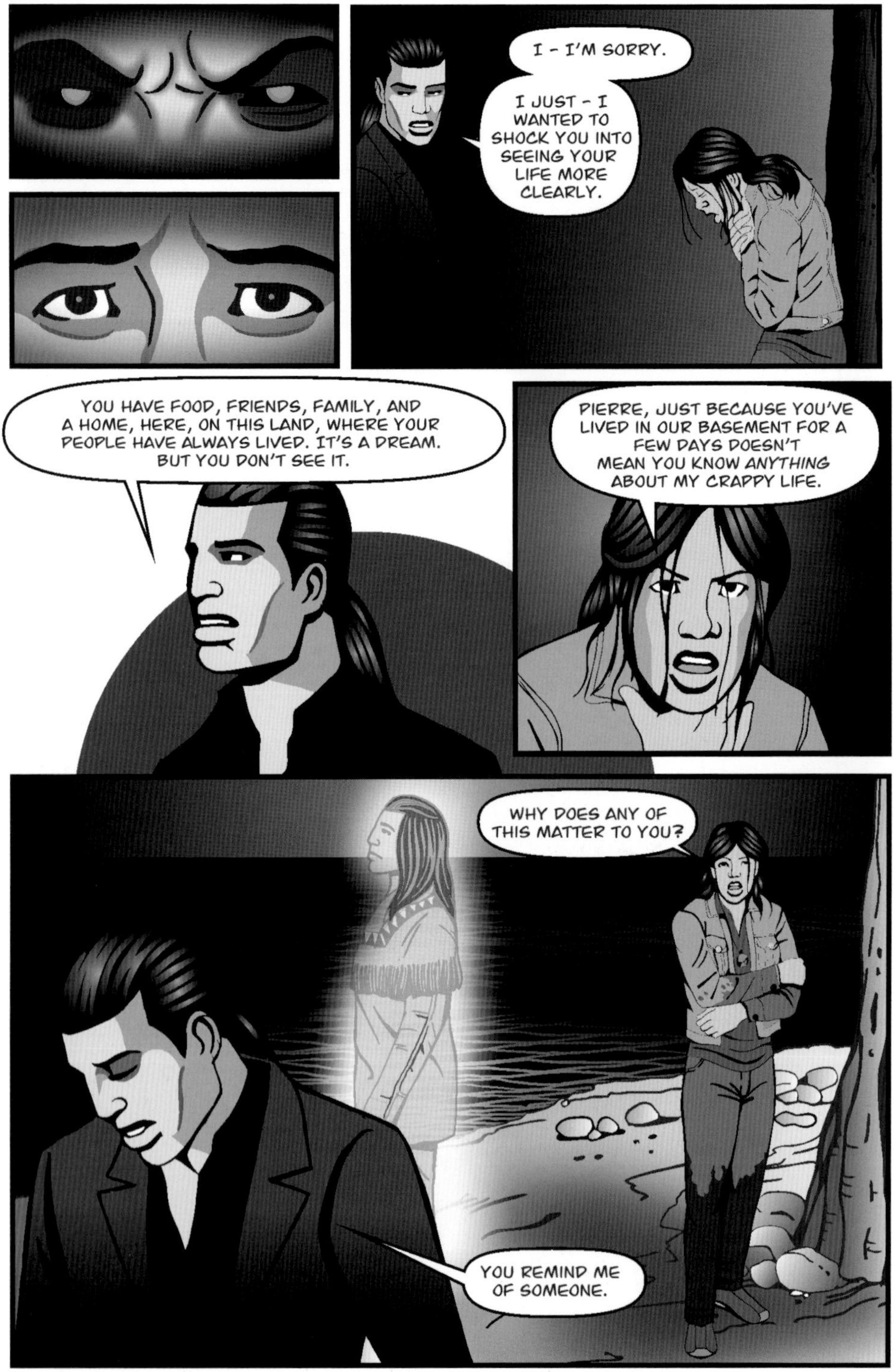
I - I'M SORRY.
I JUST - I WANTED TO SHOCK YOU INTO SEEING YOUR LIFE MORE CLEARLY.
YOU HAVE FOOD, FRIENDS, FAMILY, AND A HOME, HERE, ON THIS LAND, WHERE YOUR PEOPLE HAVE ALWAYS LIVED. IT'S A DREAM. BUT YOU DON'T SEE IT.
PIERRE, JUST BECAUSE YOU'VE LIVED IN OUR BASEMENT FOR A FEW DAYS DOESN'T MEAN YOU KNOW ANYTHING ABOUT MY CRAPPY LIFE.
WHY DOES ANY OF THIS MATTER TO YOU?
YOU REMIND ME OF SOMEONE.

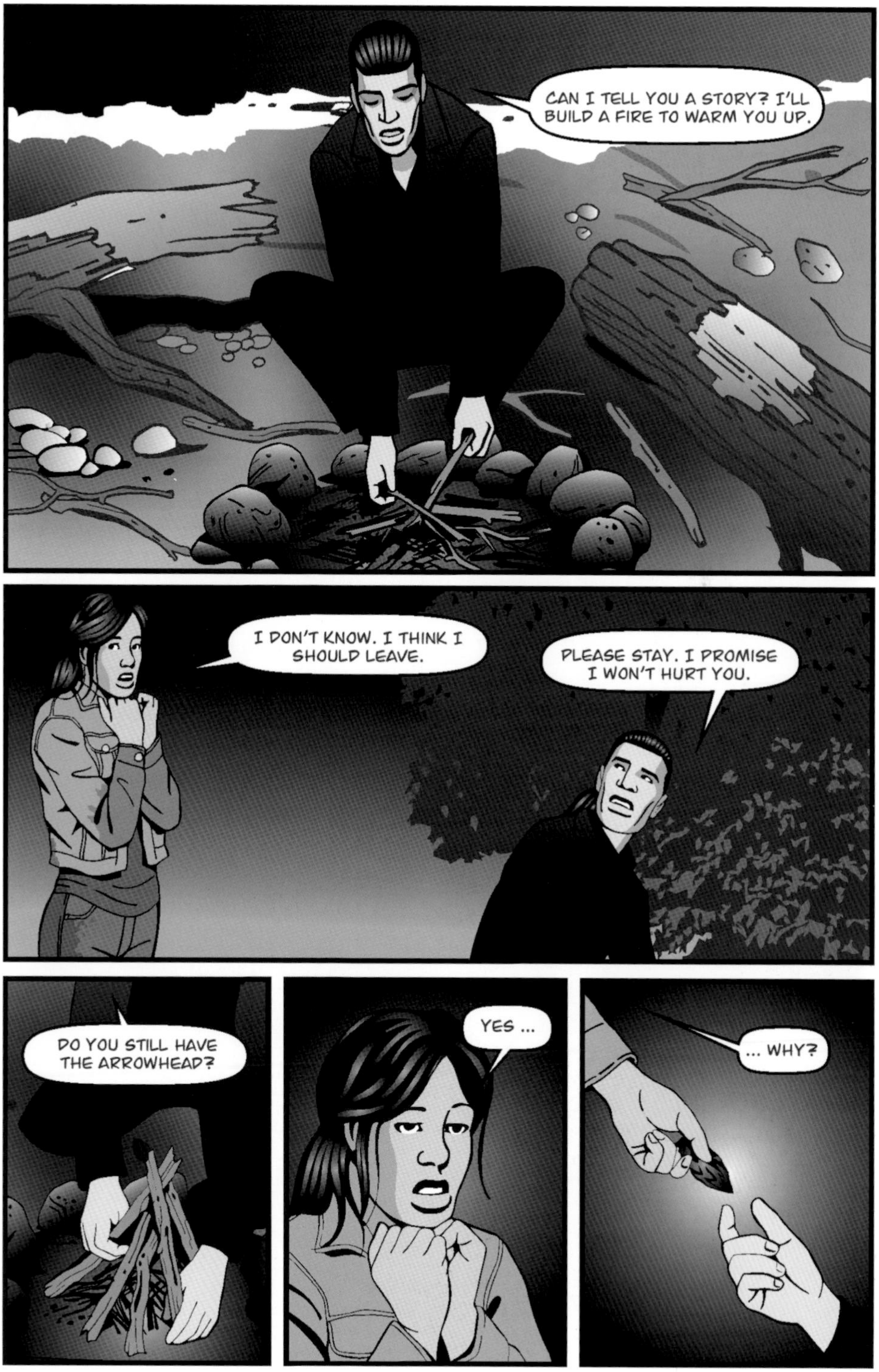
CAN I TELL YOU A STORY? I'LL BUILD A FIRE TO WARM YOU UP.
I DON'T KNOW. I THINK I SHOULD LEAVE.
PLEASE STAY. I PROMISE I WON'T HURT YOU.
DO YOU STILL HAVE THE ARROWHEAD?
YES ...
... WHY?

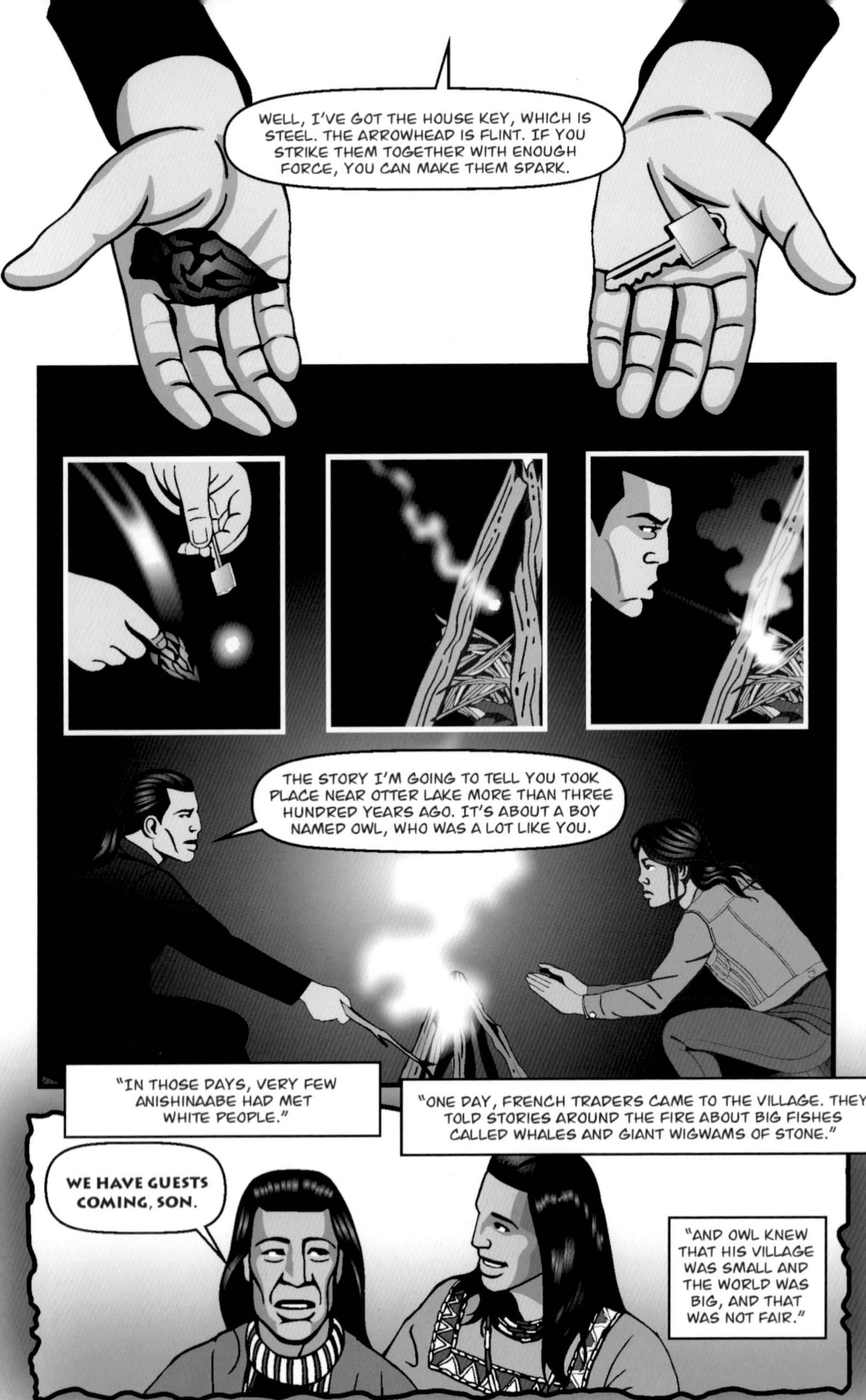
WELL, I'VE GOT THE HOUSE KEY, WHICH IS STEEL. THE ARROWHEAD IS FLINT. IF YOU STRIKE THEM TOGETHER WITH ENOUGH FORCE, YOU CAN MAKE THEM SPARK.
THE STORY I'M GOING TO TELL YOU TOOK PLACE NEAR OTTER LAKE MORE THAN THREE HUNDRED YEARS AGO. IT'S ABOUT A BOY NAMED OWL, WHO WAS A LOT LIKE YOU.
"IN THOSE DAYS, VERY FEW ANISHINAABE HAD MET WHITE PEOPLE."
"ONE DAY, FRENCH TRADERS CAME TO THE VILLAGE. THEY TOLD STORIES AROUND THE FIRE ABOUT BIG FISHES CALLED WHALES AND GIANT WIGWAMS OF STONE."
WE HAVE GUESTS COMING, SON.
"AND OWL KNEW THAT HIS VILLAGE WAS SMALL AND THE WORLD WAS BIG, AND THAT WAS NOT FAIR."

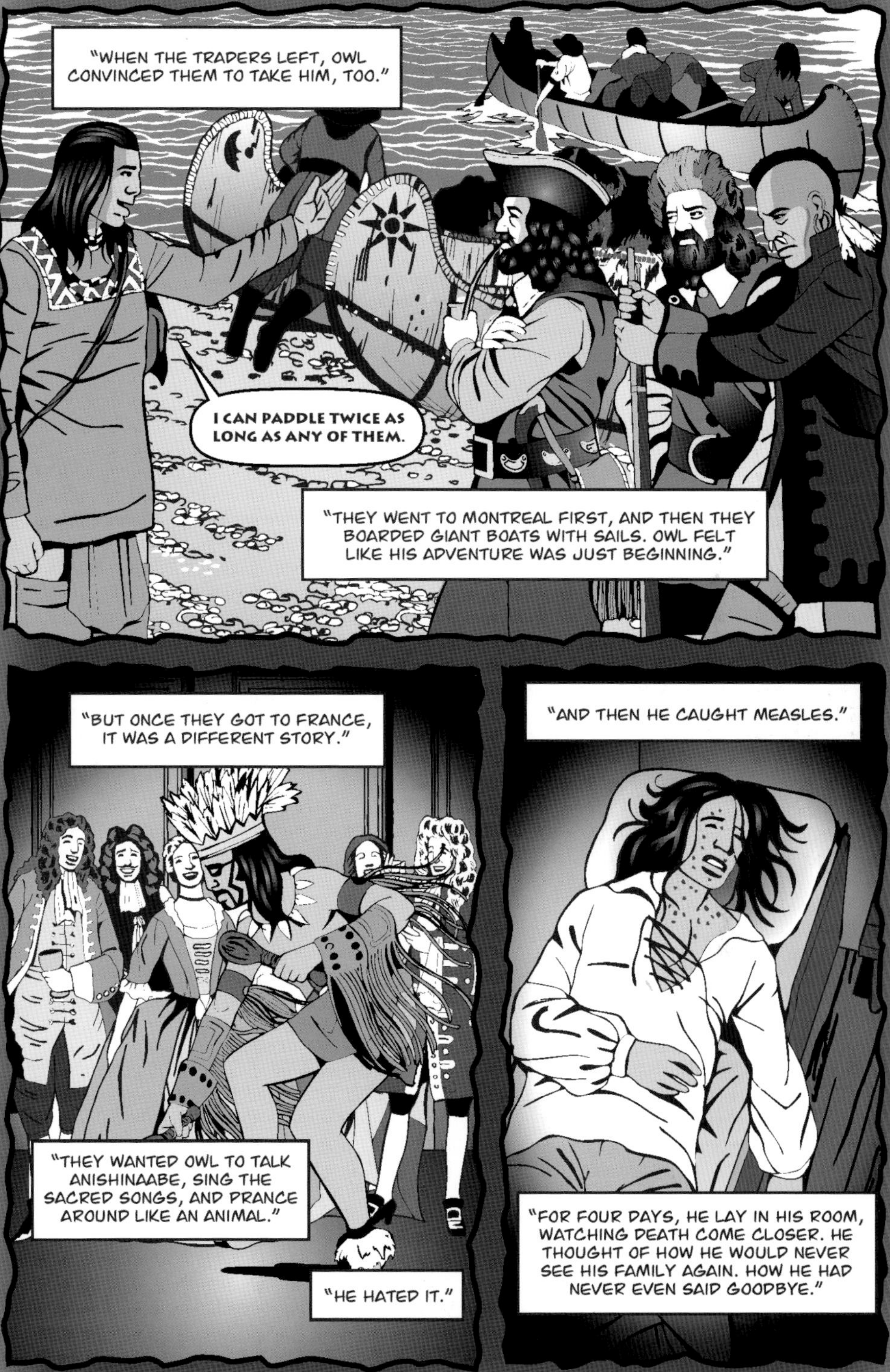
"WHEN THE TRADERS LEFT, OWL CONVINCED THEM TO TAKE HIM, TOO."
I CAN PADDLE TWICE AS LONG AS ANY OF THEM.
"THEY WENT TO MONTREAL FIRST, AND THEN THEY BOARDED GIANT BOATS WITH SAILS. OWL FELT LIKE HIS ADVENTURE WAS JUST BEGINNING."
"BUT ONCE THEY GOT TO FRANCE, IT WAS A DIFFERENT STORY."
"THEY WANTED OWL TO TALK ANISHINAABE, SING THE SACRED SONGS, AND PRANCE AROUND LIKE AN ANIMAL."
"HE HATED IT."
"AND THEN HE CAUGHT MEASLES."
"FOR FOUR DAYS, HE LAY IN HIS ROOM, WATCHING DEATH COME CLOSER. HE THOUGHT OF HOW HE WOULD NEVER SEE HIS FAMILY AGAIN. HOW HE HAD NEVER EVEN SAID GOODBYE."

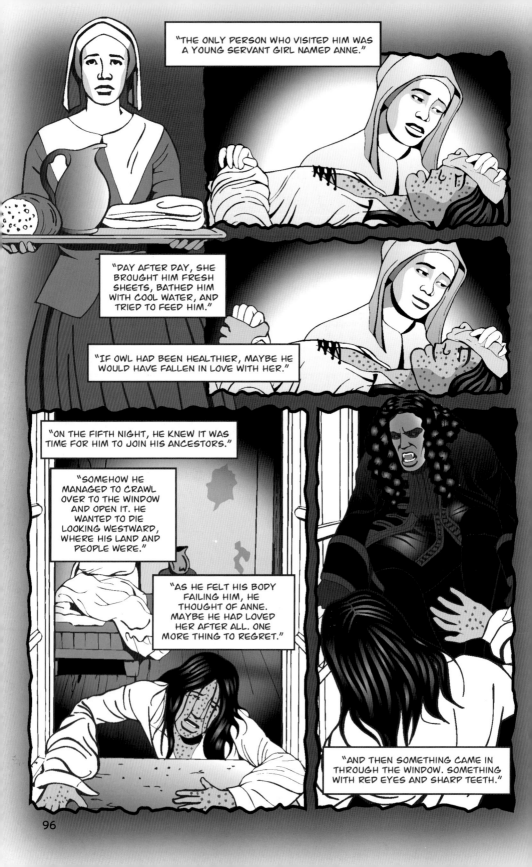

"THE ONLY PERSON WHO VISITED HIM WAS A YOUNG SERVANT GIRL NAMED ANNE."

"DAY AFTER DAY, SHE BROUGHT HIM FRESH SHEETS, BATHED HIM WITH COOL WATER, AND TRIED TO FEED HIM."

"IF OWL HAD BEEN HEALTHIER, MAYBE HE WOULD HAVE FALLEN IN LOVE WITH HER."

"ON THE FIFTH NIGHT, HE KNEW IT WAS TIME FOR HIM TO JOIN HIS ANCESTORS."

"SOMEHOW HE MANAGED TO CRAWL OVER TO THE WINDOW AND OPEN IT. HE WANTED TO DIE LOOKING WESTWARD, WHERE HIS LAND AND PEOPLE WERE."

"AS HE FELT HIS BODY FAILING HIM, HE THOUGHT OF ANNE. MAYBE HE HAD LOVED HER AFTER ALL. ONE MORE THING TO REGRET."

"AND THEN SOMETHING CAME IN THROUGH THE WINDOW. SOMETHING WITH RED EYES AND SHARP TEETH."

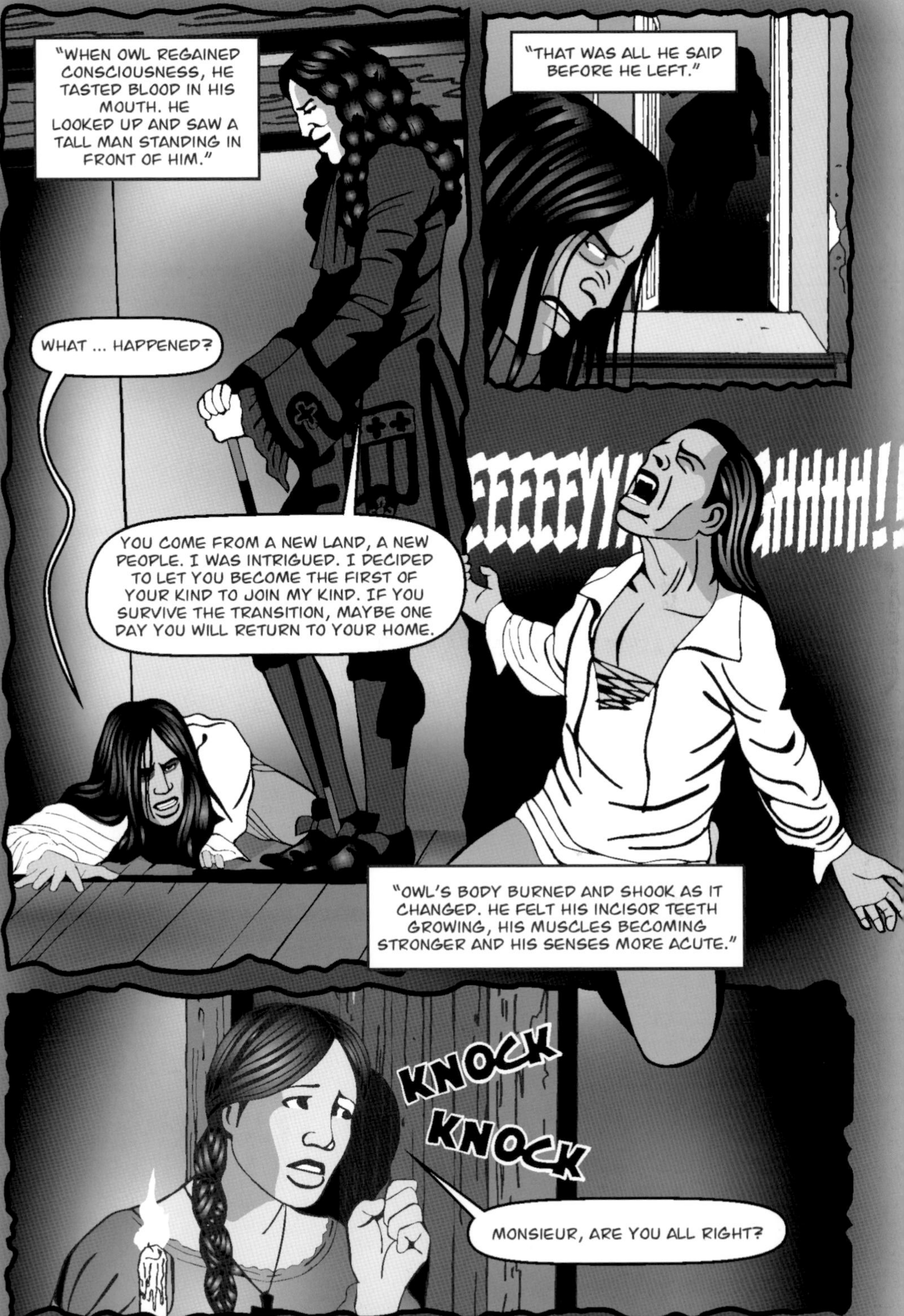
"WHEN OWL REGAINED CONSCIOUSNESS, HE TASTED BLOOD IN HIS MOUTH. HE LOOKED UP AND SAW A TALL MAN STANDING IN FRONT OF HIM."
WHAT ... HAPPENED?
YOU COME FROM A NEW LAND, A NEW PEOPLE. I WAS INTRIGUED. I DECIDED TO LET YOU BECOME THE FIRST OF YOUR KIND TO JOIN MY KIND. IF YOU SURVIVE THE TRANSITION, MAYBE ONE DAY YOU WILL RETURN TO YOUR HOME.
"THAT WAS ALL HE SAID BEFORE HE LEFT."
"OWL'S BODY BURNED AND SHOOK AS IT CHANGED. HE FELT HIS INCISOR TEETH GROWING, HIS MUSCLES BECOMING STRONGER AND HIS SENSES MORE ACUTE."
KNOCK
KNOCK
MONSIEUR, ARE YOU ALL RIGHT?

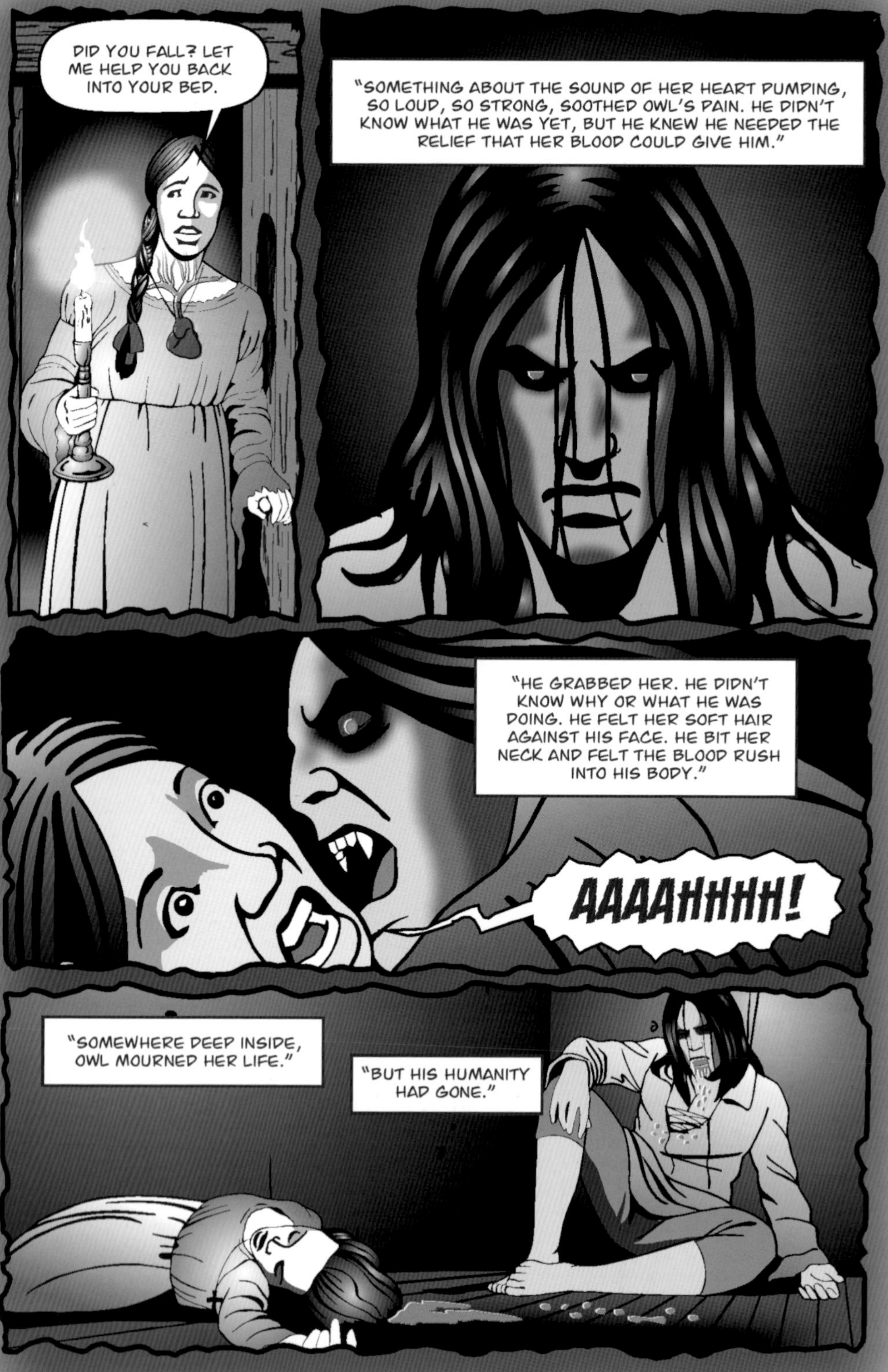
DID YOU FALL? LET ME HELP YOU BACK INTO YOUR BED.
"SOMETHING ABOUT THE SOUND OF HER HEART PUMPING, SO LOUD, SO STRONG, SOOTHED OWL'S PAIN. HE DIDN'T KNOW WHAT HE WAS YET, BUT HE KNEW HE NEEDED THE RELIEF THAT HER BLOOD COULD GIVE HIM."
"HE GRABBED HER. HE DIDN'T KNOW WHY OR WHAT HE WAS DOING. HE FELT HER SOFT HAIR AGAINST HIS FACE. HE BIT HER NECK AND FELT THE BLOOD RUSH INTO HIS BODY."
AAAAHHHH!
"SOMEWHERE DEEP INSIDE, OWL MOURNED HER LIFE."
"BUT HIS HUMANITY HAD GONE."

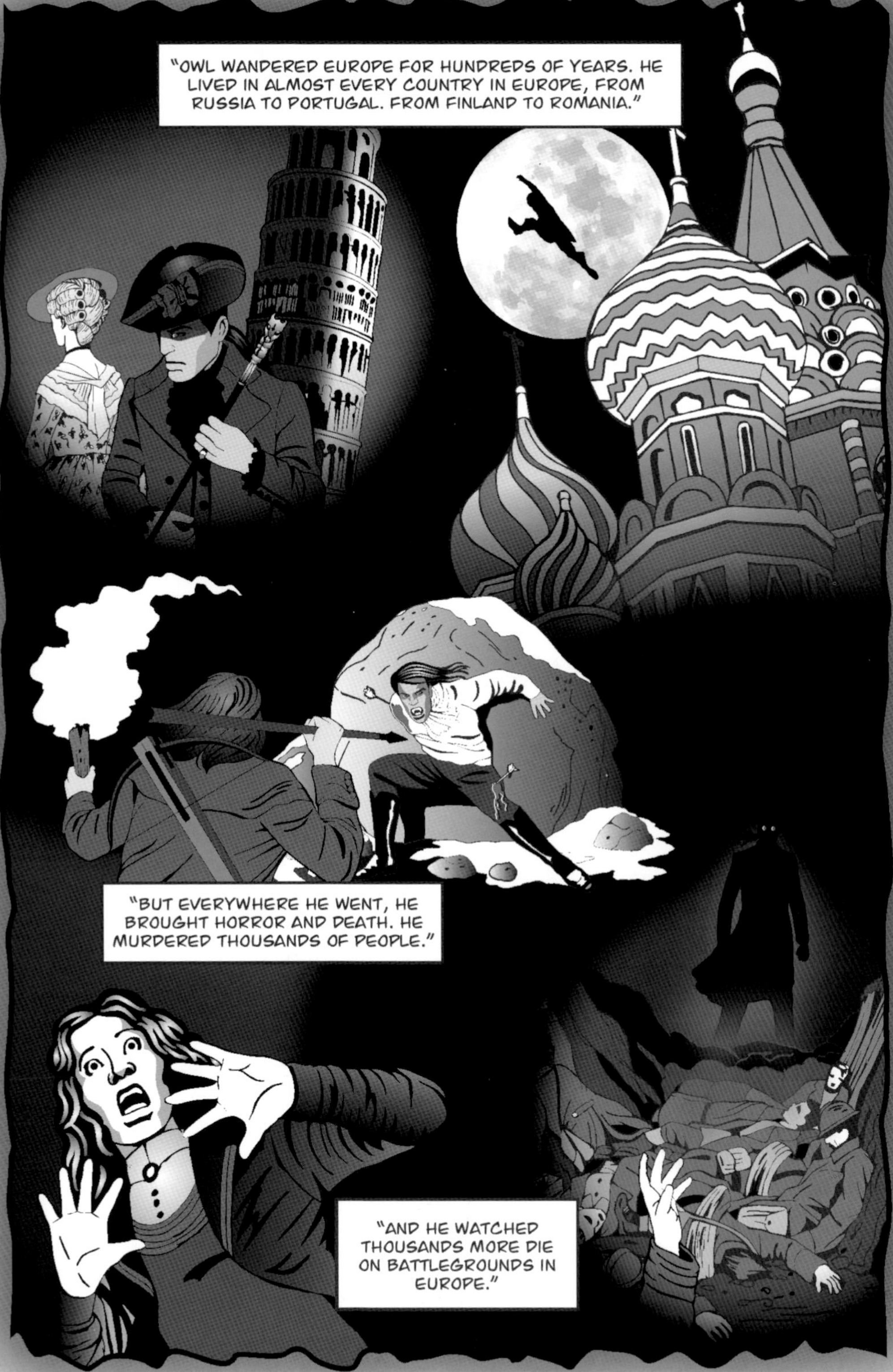
"OWL WANDERED EUROPE FOR HUNDREDS OF YEARS. HE LIVED IN ALMOST EVERY COUNTRY IN EUROPE, FROM RUSSIA TO PORTUGAL. FROM FINLAND TO ROMANIA."
"BUT EVERYWHERE HE WENT, HE BROUGHT HORROR AND DEATH. HE MURDERED THOUSANDS OF PEOPLE."
"AND HE WATCHED THOUSANDS MORE DIE ON BATTLEGROUNDS IN EUROPE."

BUT AS BROKEN AS OWL BECAME, HE NEVER FORGOT WHAT IT HAD BEEN LIKE TO FEEL WHOLE. HE NEVER FORGOT THE SNAP OF PINE IN A CAMPFIRE, THE LAUGHTER OF HIS PEOPLE, THE VILLAGE HE HAD ONCE THOUGHT OF AS BORING.

DID HE EVER GO HOME?

YES. BUT HE KNEW THAT RETURNING TO CANADA MEANT HIS DEATH. HE COULDN'T GO HOME AS THE MONSTER HE HAD BECOME.

"SO OWL BEGAN TO FAST, TO PURIFY HIMSELF, AS WAS THE CUSTOM OF HIS PEOPLE. HE CAME BACK TO HIS VILLAGE AND FOUND A SPOT THAT WAS SPECIAL TO HIM, ON TOP OF A HILL."

"HE CARRIED UP CERTAIN SACRED OBJECTS IN ADVANCE. A COPPER BOWL WITH SAGE. A POUCH OF LOOSE TOBACCO."

"WHEN THE TIME CAME, HE WENT TO HIS SPOT TO WATCH THE SUN RISE AND END HIS EXISTENCE WHERE IT HAD BEGUN."

SO, WHAT ARE YOU TRYING TO TELL ME? SUICIDE IS OKAY FOR A VAMPIRE BUT NOT FOR ME?

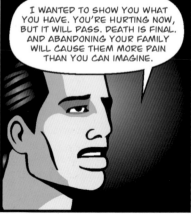

I WANTED TO SHOW YOU WHAT YOU HAVE. YOU'RE HURTING NOW, BUT IT WILL PASS. DEATH IS FINAL. AND ABANDONING YOUR FAMILY WILL CAUSE THEM MORE PAIN THAN YOU CAN IMAGINE.

THE REST OF THE STORY I TOLD FOR MY OWN SAKE.

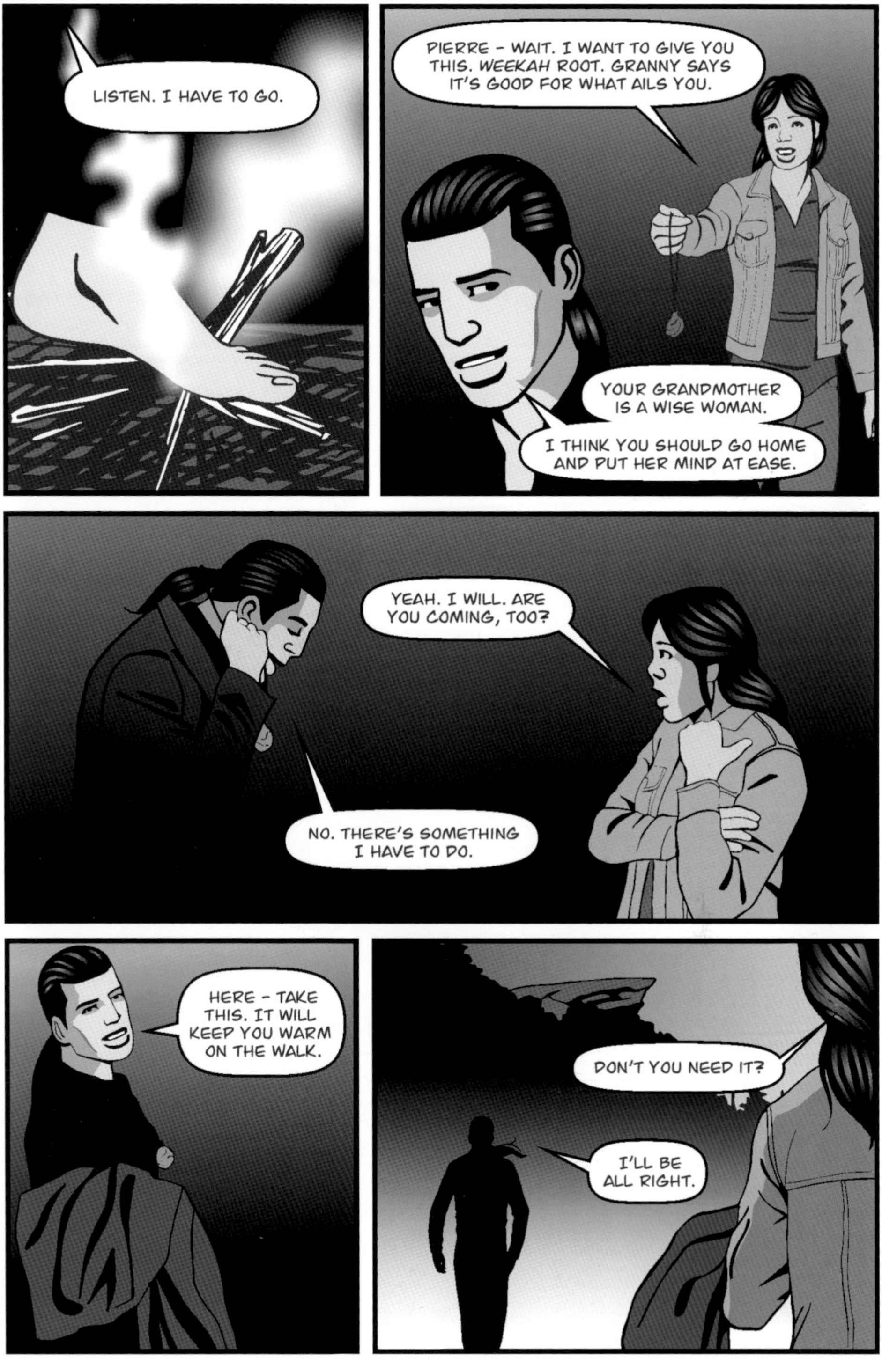
LISTEN. I HAVE TO GO.
PIERRE – WAIT. I WANT TO GIVE YOU THIS. *WEEKAH* ROOT. GRANNY SAYS IT'S GOOD FOR WHAT AILS YOU.
YOUR GRANDMOTHER IS A WISE WOMAN.
I THINK YOU SHOULD GO HOME AND PUT HER MIND AT EASE.
YEAH. I WILL. ARE YOU COMING, TOO?
NO. THERE'S SOMETHING I HAVE TO DO.
HERE – TAKE THIS. IT WILL KEEP YOU WARM ON THE WALK.
DON'T YOU NEED IT?
I'LL BE ALL RIGHT.

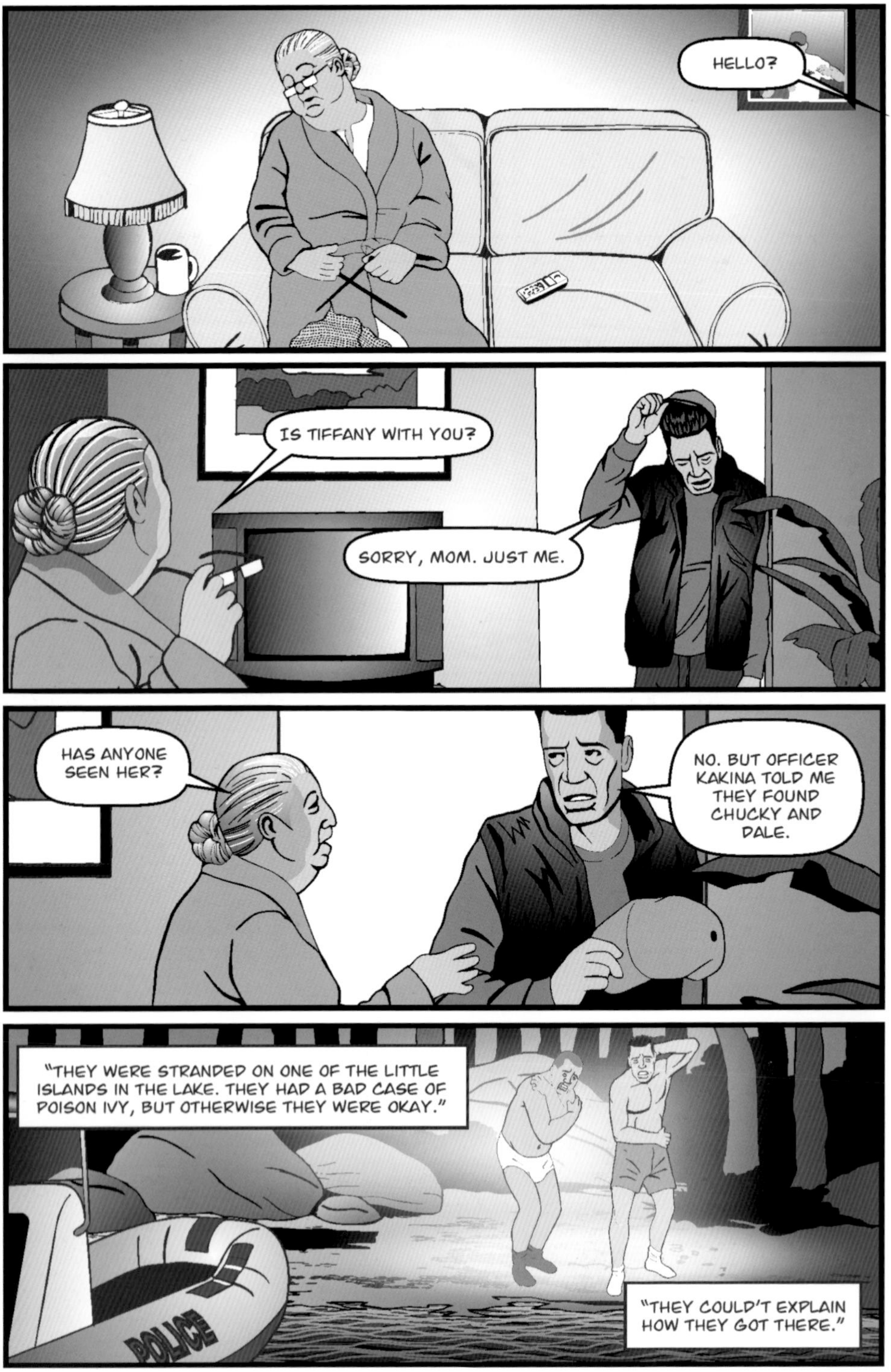
HELLO?
IS TIFFANY WITH YOU?
SORRY, MOM. JUST ME.
HAS ANYONE SEEN HER?
NO. BUT OFFICER KAKINA TOLD ME THEY FOUND CHUCKY AND DALE.
"THEY WERE STRANDED ON ONE OF THE LITTLE ISLANDS IN THE LAKE. THEY HAD A BAD CASE OF POISON IVY, BUT OTHERWISE THEY WERE OKAY."
POLICE
"THEY COULD'T EXPLAIN HOW THEY GOT THERE."

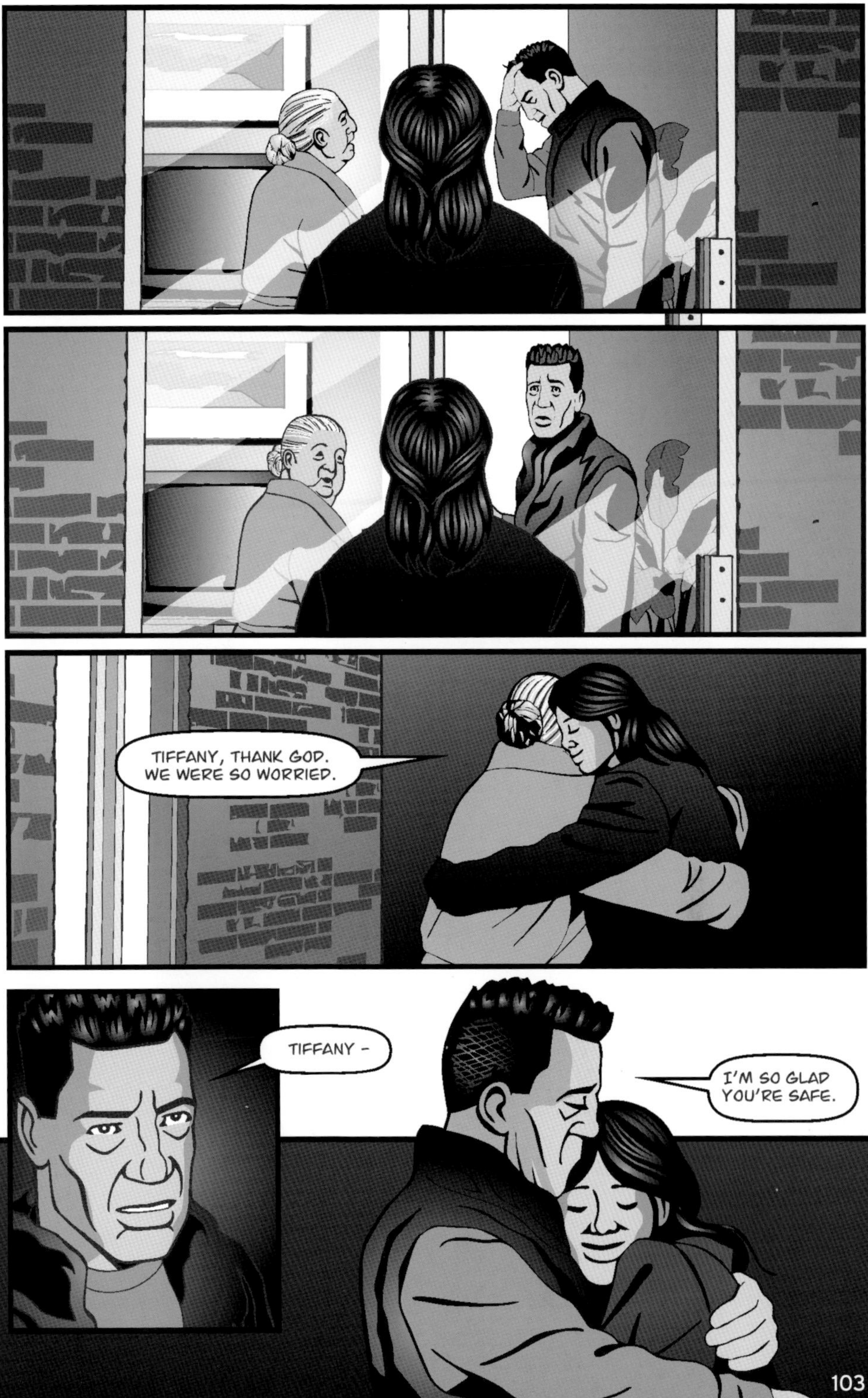
TIFFANY, THANK GOD. WE WERE SO WORRIED.
TIFFANY -
I'M SO GLAD YOU'RE SAFE.

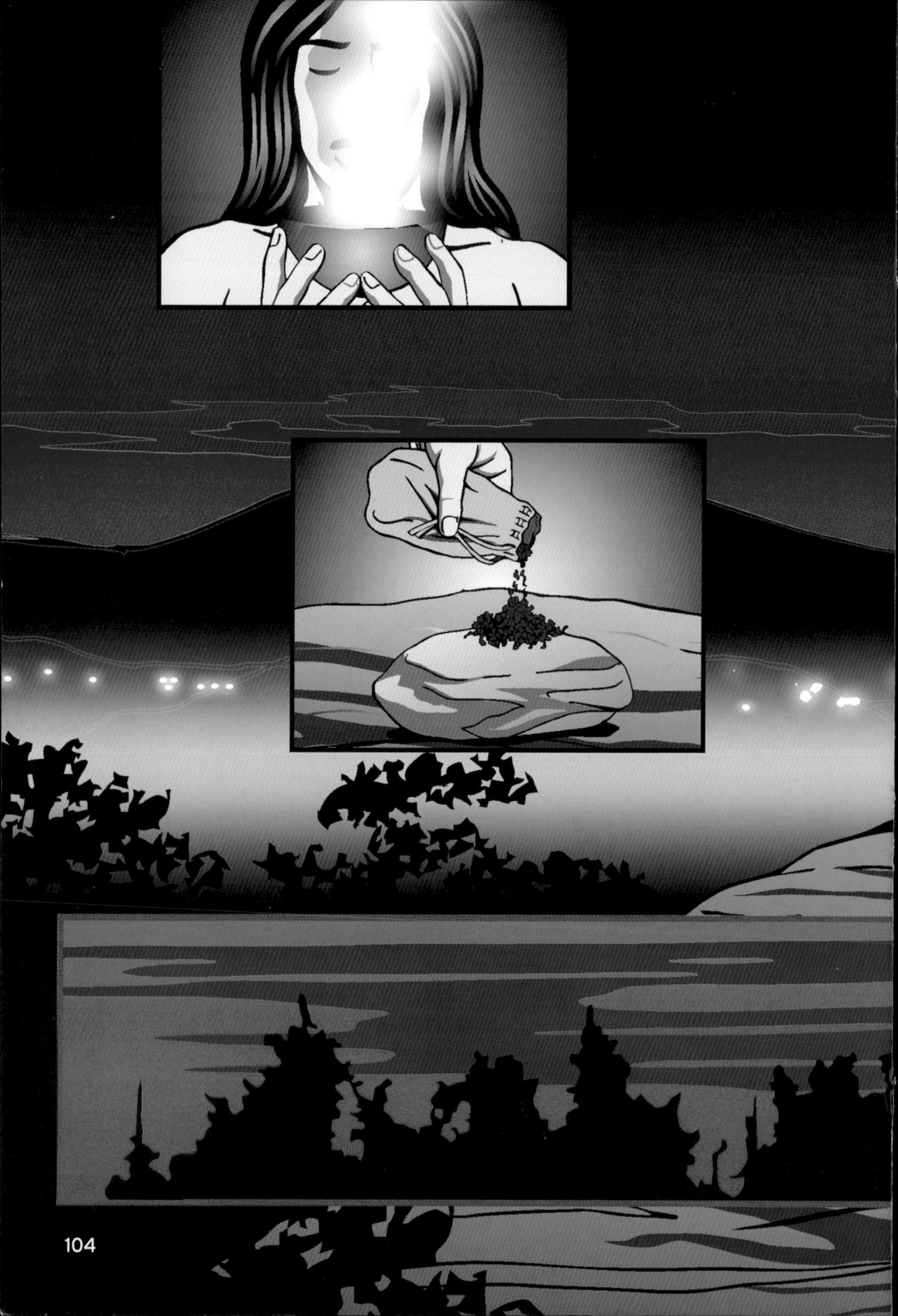

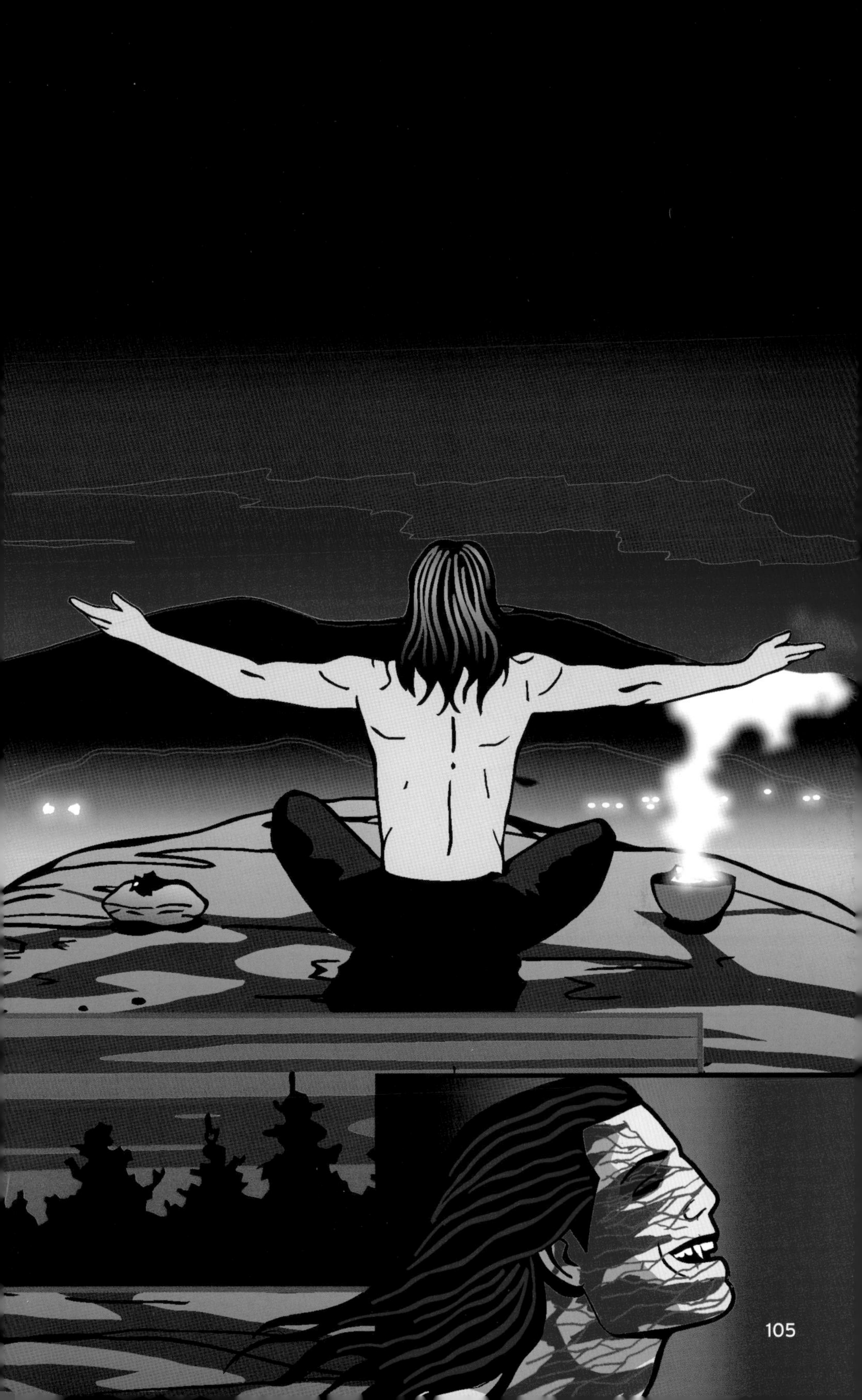

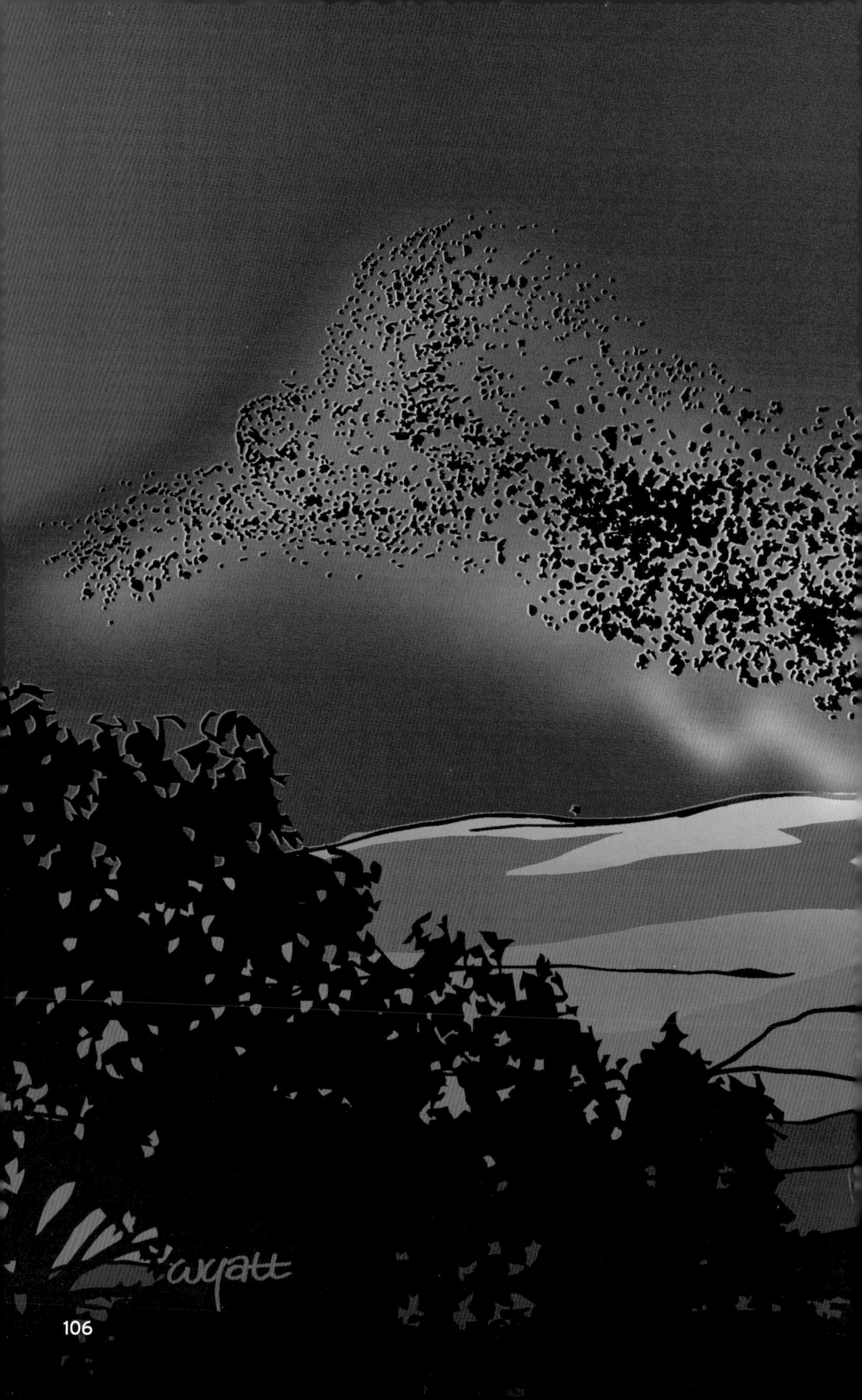
wyatt

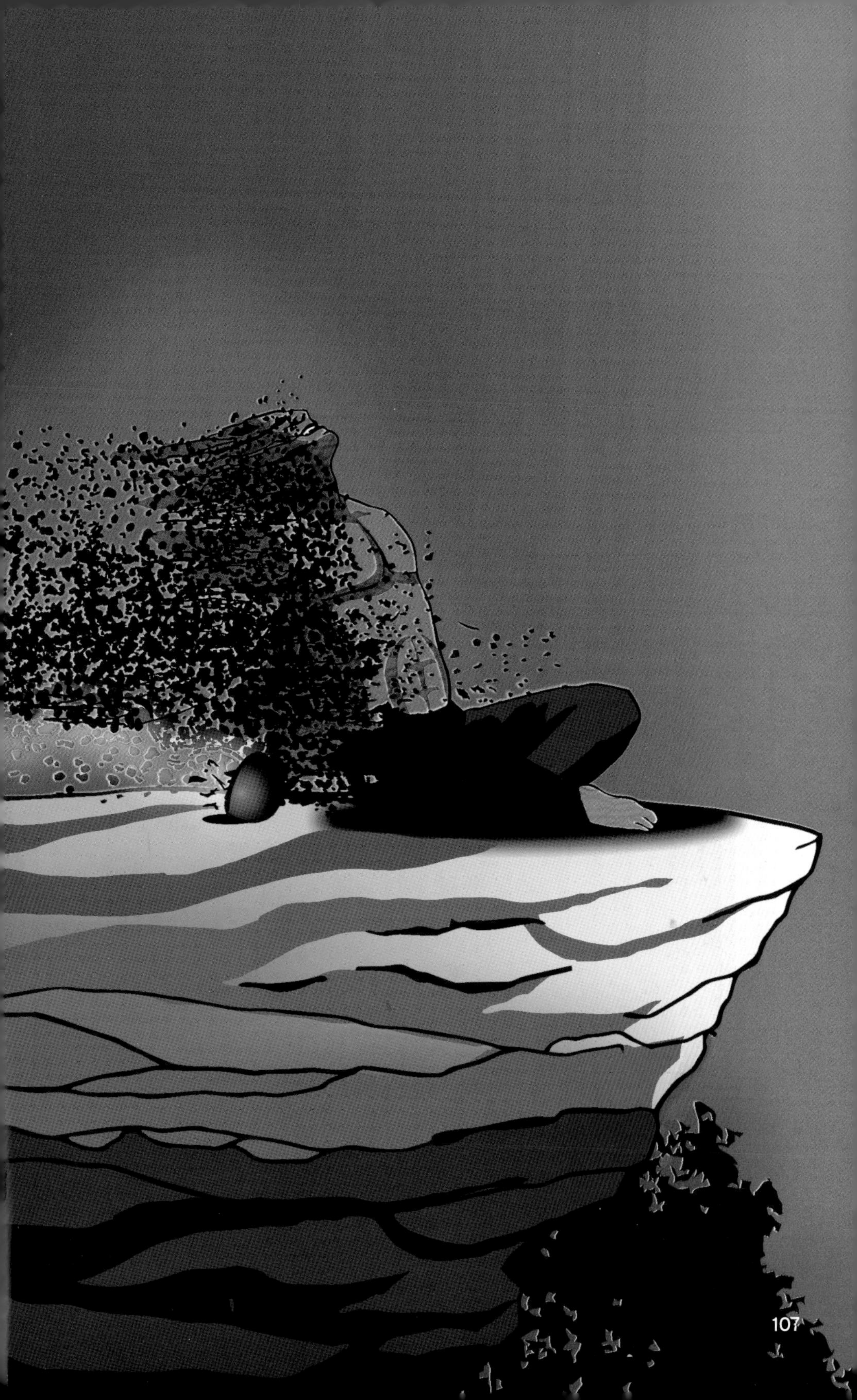

ACKNOWLEDGMENTS

As with most literary creations books are seldom born in a vacuum. Like alchemy, there are many different elements that go into the caldron to synthesize what you hold in your hands.

Therefore, there are many people I would like to thank for making it possible to write this story. *The Night Wanderer* began as a play, *A Contemporary Gothic Indian Vampire Story*, commissioned by Young People's Theatre in Toronto and originally produced by Persephone Theatre in Saskatoon.

From there it lay dormant for a long time. Then Annick Press came knocking on my door about a different project. But you can't keep a good vampire down, it seems (or a good Ojibwa teenager, for that matter).

Fast-forward a year and I find myself sitting in the mountains, at Cabin #4 of the Leighton Studios at the Banff Centre for the Arts. The grant from the Ontario Arts Council also helped foster the creative process.

As well, there are several people who provided valuable research assistance. Trish Warner helped me with various medical details. Tara Redican gave me a good boost by doing some vital early research. A special and fabulous thank you to Janine, who put as much heart and soul into this book as I did. The novel could not have been created without her patience and passion. Many thanks to Aurora Artists for believing in the project as much as I did.

The novel first appeared appeared in 2007. Fast-forward a few more years and it is once again transformed into a graphic novel. I'd like to thank Anne Taylor of the Curve Lake Cultural Centre for her assistance with visual references.

I would also like to thank Anita Knott for her assistance with several of the Ojibwa phrases. And, of course, I offer a hearty thanks to my mother, who thought the simple action of birth allowed me the opportunity to write this book. And to all the Anishinaabe/Ojibwa people in the world.

And to a lesser extent, all the vampires in the world. You know who you are.

—*Drew Hayden Taylor*

A big thank you to all those at Annick Press for their encouragement and enthusiasm.

I would also like to thank Drew Hayden Taylor for his marvelous story and Alison Kooistra for her masterful adaptation.

Lastly, I would like to thank my wife, Janet, and my children, Tyler and Madeline, for their patience, support, and love throughout all those months I spent scribbling away.

—*Michael Wyatt*